# THRILL OF THE CHASE

# THRILL OF THE CHASE

## CHRISTINA CROOKS

**FIVE STAR**

*An imprint of Thomson Gale, a part of The Thomson Corporation*

Detroit • New York • San Francisco • New Haven, Conn. • Waterville, Maine • London

# THOMSON

## GALE

™

**LIBRARY OF CONGRESS CATALOGING-IN-PUBLICATION DATA**

Crooks, Christina.
   Thrill of the chase / Christina Crooks. — 1st ed.
    p. cm.
   ISBN-13: 978-1-59414-670-1 (alk. paper)
   ISBN-10: 1-59414-670-5 (alk. paper)
   1. Women automobile racing drivers—Fiction. 2. Drag racers—Fiction. 3. Automobile mechanics—Fiction. 4. Automobile repair shops—Management—Fiction. 5. Business consultants—Fiction. 6. Man-woman relationships—Fiction. I. Title.
PS3603.R665T48 2007
813'.6—dc22
                                              2007022617

First Edition. First Printing: November 2007.

Published in 2007 in conjunction with Tekno Books.

Printed in the United States of America on permanent paper
10 9 8 7 6 5 4 3 2 1

I'd like to offer heartfelt thanks to Rob Kinnan for his constant support, and also for reading an early version of the manuscript and giving valuable technical advice. Big thanks as well to Bryan Wheeler and Troy Stephens, who answered all of my questions while showing me around one of the finest speed shops in California, Wheeler's Speed Shop in Huntington Beach.

# CHAPTER ONE

Powering up through the gears, Sarah felt all the muscles in her body tighten with readiness and excitement before the two turns. She gripped her Mustang's custom wood-lacquered shift knob with one hand, the thick steering wheel with the other. Though the late morning traffic was light, she checked her side mirrors twice and carefully scanned from left to right through her windshield, alert for any movement. There were no cars nearby. And, of course, no pedestrians. Nobody walked in Huntington Beach's industrial-zoned "automotive alley."

Jerking the steering wheel to the right then pulling it smoothly left, simultaneously heel-toeing the clutch and brake pedals with the edge of her running shoe, she felt her car's tires break free from the pavement's friction. The car slid sideways.

Maintaining the throttle pressure to keep her wheels spinning, she steered into the same direction she slid. She spotted the large, faded red letters of Big Red's Auto Performance Shop's sign out of the corner of her eye.

Right on target.

The four-wheel drift positioned her to race up the exact middle of the entrance to the shop's parking lot.

With a satisfying screech of tires, she floored the gas to gather more speed, then whipped her car into the second and final turn.

Another four-wheel drift, pressing her back into the firm, curved racing seats she'd installed. She grinned as she piloted the sideways-hurtling car with an instinctive touch, lifting off the gas pedal and feathering the brakes to bleed off her speed.

The yellow Mustang slid to a halt. It was positioned perfectly in the middle of her parking space.

"Yes!" Energized, she leapt out of the car. Another day's commute concluded.

Sarah pushed the building's tinted front door open, humming. She jogged through the shop's retail area, neither seeing nor expecting to see anyone manning the front desk. Matt was probably in the back again, complaining to the technicians. He pretended to be a gearhead, but she knew they saw through it. What he should be doing was unpacking and stocking those magazine shipments she saw lining the front wall in boxes, or cleaning the grimy glass display case. He should be sitting on that padded stool answering the ringing phone. Her dad hadn't hired him to hang out.

She shrugged. Matt didn't know a $9/16^{th}$ from a hole in the ground, but he wasn't her main problem.

Still, his absence added a new bounce to her gait. How nice that he wasn't lounging in the short hallway staring at her workout bra–flattened chest as she returned from her Friday morning routine. As she trotted into the back, a gust of motor oil–scented air cooled her forehead. She wiped at it absently.

It was perfectly acceptable for the techs to sneak a peek—surreptitiously, of course—but Matt didn't even try to be subtle. She rolled her eyes at the memory of his creepy peeping as he'd challenged her to arm-wrestle him. As if the scrawny weasel would win. Since she'd started working out she had arms of steel, powerful as any man's. Useful for lifting transmissions into place, and carrying flywheels without having to always ask assistance from the guys in the back.

"The 'ho is on the flo'," she announced, trotting past the small group of men gathered around the engine stand gazing at a shiny small-block motor.

"Don't I wish," the taller mustached blond answered. He winked at her as she passed, but his attention remained firmly fixed on the small block. The shiny chrome seemed to have them mesmerized. "Shake some ass, already. We wouldn't mind a little help."

Flipping Will off even as she began to veer toward the object of attention, at the last moment she kept moving towards her own locker area, the converted women's restroom. She was late again, but first she had to swap out her damp gym T-shirt. While she had no problem assaulting the guys with her version of ladies' perspiration, her white shirt was miraculously unstained by grease. Best to keep it that way. Remembering with chagrin the last time she'd worn a shop shirt on the weight machines— she'd left black grease smudges on three of them before the trainers threw her out—she was already beginning to pull it off as the bathroom door hushed shut.

Yanking on her jeans along with a faded shop-shirt, she spared just enough time to splash cold water onto her face, pull her disarranged hair back into a neater ponytail, and run a strawberry-flavored ChapStick over her lips before rejoining the guys. "Is this a new engine build or a refresh job?" she asked no one in particular.

"Refresh," Lee answered, fingering the pen behind his ear. He edged his small body to one side, making room for her next to the parts-covered workbench. He smiled shyly at her, the bright chrome flashing in his eyes.

She clapped him on the back, but softly so as not to frighten him. Then, looking around: "Where's Matt?"

It became very quiet.

"What? Did he forget to show up?" No, that wasn't it. As she peered at the familiar faces around her, she knew. "The weasel pissed Dad off." She said it with some awe. Her father was not easy to rile. Which was his best quality, in her opinion. Easygoing Red Mattel had a reputation in the industry for fair, laidback evenhandedness when dealing with his customers and technicians alike. It was a major element of his performance shop's survival in a city where lesser mechanic garages went belly-up after only a year or two in business.

"What did he do?" All four guys looked pointedly away from her. Lee actually blushed. "What, damn it?" Now she was really curious.

Will finally answered her. He spoke quickly, looking at the ceiling. "This morning Red was showing the new guy around storage, when—"

"What new guy?" Sarah demanded.

"Patience, patience," Will said, teasing her. "All things, ah, *come* to those who wait."

At the inside joke, the guys guffawed, then fell into embarrassed silence.

"Tell me what the hell happened with Matt or I'll start beating on you," she threatened, laying her hand on a long, lumpy camshaft. Then she watched, mystified, as all four of them broke into gales of laughter.

"*Beating.* Oh man," Will gasped, his face flushed from laughter.

"No. No way." Sarah snatched her hand away from the part. She was beginning to get the picture. "He didn't."

"He sure did. With a wad of shop rags and a pile of *American Rodder*'s Mechanic of the Month fold-outs. And guess whose picture was on top?"

"Please no," Sarah said. She knew. It was just like the little weasel to do something so gross right in her own shop. *Nearly* her own shop, she reminded herself again. "You shouldn't have snapped that stupid picture of me cleaning the transmission spill. I looked like a bimbo in a wet T-shirt contest."

"Just Craig's type. What will your Romeo have to say about all this?" Will asked, shaking his head. His eyes twinkled with humor.

She suddenly felt restless and irritable as she thought about Craig. "Probably nothing. He doesn't have a jealous bone in his body where I'm concerned."

"Guess not. Anyway, your dad and the new guy—Gordon— were so unimpressed by Matt's taste in T-shirted, smudge-faced ladies that Matt was kindly asked to accompany them up to Red's office for his last paycheck. Last I saw, Matt was trying to cling to that pull-out poster of you like it was a treasure, but Red relieved him of it before booting him out the door."

"Flattering," she said, picking up the work order and scanning the specs for the refresh job. "Well, at least we'll have someone decent to handle the front. The glass needs cleaning."

Will cleared his throat. "Didn't get the impression that's what the new guy'll be doing." When she looked at him quizzically, he plucked the work order from her fingers. "Red said to tell you to go on up when you get in. That was about an hour ago."

"Why didn't you tell me!" she growled, punching him in the arm as she passed him. She pulled the blow at the last moment. She didn't want to damage her people. And she liked Will. She liked them all. Except Matt. And now he was gone.

She nearly danced up the stairs to her dad's office.

Sitting across the desk from Red, Gordon felt the tingling in his veins that he always got with a good idea, but magnified. This one was it.

He gazed at the big man who'd just made his business instincts snap to attention. Like his name implied, Red had the requisite strawberry-blond mop of hair sitting atop a head that pushed up past Gordon's own six-foot height by at least a few inches. The man who filled his swiveling cloth chair to capacity, dwarfing it, seemed to be offering Gordon a shortcut to his dreams.

"You're offering something different from what we discussed on the phone." Gordon spoke plainly. "Why?" He interlaced his well-manicured fingers together over his pressed slacks. The business suit gave him a sense of security that boosted his confidence, though the clothes seemed desperately out of place in this shop. Even Red, the owner, wore jeans. But then again, Red had openly admitted that he had no experience in taking his shop to the next level.

Gordon did.

Red answered him with matching directness, but with a slow drawl. "You're overqualified for the tech position, which I think you know."

"I am, but the job is important." Working here was more important than he'd wanted Red to know during the phone interviews. After slaving his butt off and now going to night school to earn his advanced business degree, this was the next step. And if he played his cards right, Big Red's Auto Performance Shop would be the answer to his business dreams.

"I like your attitude, Gordon. That's why I'm offering the supervisor position, and if that goes well . . ."

Gordon leaned back in his chair, hoping to look nonchalant. "I'm listening."

"I need someone with your business acumen to run things after I leave."

"What about your daughter? I understood that this was a family company."

"It is. And she's sharp as a tack, but she's not interested in anything that doesn't have four wheels attached to it."

Gordon envisioned a tomboy in grimy overalls. From his experience in the automotive industry, chances were good she answered that phone he'd seen up front. Women—even tomboys—generally weren't natural additions to the rougher circle of mechanics who did the real work. "I understand completely, sir."

"Don't get me wrong. She knows her way around the shop better than anyone, and Lord knows I pay her enough, but all she wants to do is race." Red's expression when he looked at Gordon was mostly inscrutable, but Gordon thought he detected a certain resignation. "She's close, so close, to being what this shop needs. But close only counts in horseshoes and hand grenades, am I right?" He waved his hand as if dismissing the topic. "I believe that's her I hear pounding up the stairs as we speak."

Expecting to see an overweight tomboy in the predicted grimy overalls from the clomping sound of the footsteps, Gordon couldn't help being surprised at the sight of the slim young lady who pushed open the doors to Red's large office without so much as a polite knock. She was the same T-shirted woman as the one in the glossy photo pullout he'd first seen down in the storage room, and which was now curled into Red's trashcan. That was his daughter? No wonder Red had looked like he'd been ready to punch the guy.

But evidently Gordon had surprised her too. Her easy grin segued into a confused stare as she took in his suit. Gordon rather enjoyed the frank scrutiny. Her wide, pale lips and her pulled-back hair couldn't disguise an earthy femininity, and her clear eyes when they rose to meet his questioningly were a striking shade of emerald that he'd never seen before.

"Sarah, dear," Red said, rising. "This is our newest member of the company, Gordon Devine."

"Pleased to meet you," Sarah said, immediately crossing the floor and extending her hand to him before he could get to his feet. The scent of orange hand cleaner wafted up as she gripped his hand firmly.

Then, so quickly that he could only watch, she turned her back and strode toward Red. "Just got here. Last night's race ran late, so I slept in. Will sent me up." When she saw Red darting nervous glances at Gordon, she turned toward him again with curiosity.

Somewhat at a loss for words, and marveling at the rare sensation of being caught off guard, Gordon belatedly rose to his feet. "It is indeed a pleasure to meet Red's capable daughter. He tells me that you're a valuable asset to the shop." He watched her tilt her head up to him, her wheat-colored ponytail glinting even in the office's fluorescent light.

She was slightly older than the sixteen or seventeen he'd first assumed. Her lack of makeup and jewelry lent her an unsophisticated air. Quite unlike the women he preferred to date.

"I try," she said dryly. Her lips twitched, as if she were suppressing a grin. She nodded at his suit and raised a pale eyebrow at his leather-bound briefcase leaning against the chair. "You look too polished for this shop. Are you sure you don't mind getting dirty?"

"Sarah, dear. Be nice."

Red's mild chastising had no visible effect on the girl.

"No, Red, it's okay." Gordon gazed down at Red's spoiled little daughter—for that's certainly what she was, spoiled rotten—and spoke with precise enunciation, as if to a slow child. He smiled warmly. "We all have our uses." He made sure her eyes followed his as he looked pointedly at Red's trashcan and what lay within.

Her blush was lovely to behold. He wasn't sure until that moment that she knew exactly how her image had been utilized.

The flush of pink that suffused her cheeks had another effect on him, as well. The hint of color transformed her from being merely pretty, to being beautiful. Gordon stared, astonished. A little makeup, some high heels, she'd be a knockout. He supposed that her receptionist duties might include some work that got her "dirty," as she put it, hence the grubby clothes she had on. Not sufficiently professional. A dress code was clearly needed.

He hoped he'd embarrassed her into silence. Beginning to turn his back on her and continue his business with Red, he was stopped by her voice.

"Dad, where's that spray window cleaner you brought up here?"

"Over on the windowsill." Red spoke to her with clear fondness. Probably never saw a reason to be anything other than indulgent with her. Doubtless allowed her anything her little heart desired from the time she was old enough to ask. Gordon felt the old resentment shift and turn inside him as he compared her easy upbringing to his own lifelong struggle to raise himself up by his bootstraps. He'd had to help support his family, then pay for his own night-school education as he worked during the day. He'd gone even farther and invented a few high-performance parts for hot rods, and actually managed to sell a prototype to a big aftermarket company.

Now, finally, he was nearly ready to take his place among the automotive industry's business elite.

Gordon squelched his brief resentment. It was Red's business whether he chose to spoil his daughter. As long as she answered the phone politely and didn't drain the company coffers more than was reasonable.

He watched her cross the office with her confident, almost masculine swagger. He noticed her short unpainted nails that showed traces of old dirt still embedded beneath them. He was still wearing his polite smile as she crossed back toward him carrying the blue cleaner. "Well, Sarah, it's been nice meeting—what is this?"

The spray bottle leaked onto his fingers where she'd thrust it into his hand.

She smiled at him, a little pityingly. "It's a bit of a dirty job, but you know what they say: 'any job worth doing is worth doing well.' Please do the glass counter. It's really grungy. Welcome to my company."

Sarah sailed out, her footsteps a confident staccato on the stairs as she raced down them.

Gordon stood with the smell of ammonia wafting up, at a complete loss for words.

Red looked at him, his pitying expression a mirror of his daughter's. "Um, she's actually right about your clothes. Business casual or even jeans would probably be better."

Gordon slowly set the cleaner down onto Red's desk with what he thought was admirable self-control. "Red, I would hope that this supervisor position doesn't include taking direction from the receptionist."

Red blustered. "No, of course not. Well, I suppose I might take the occasional suggestion under consideration. But, you know, Sarah's not the receptionist. She's more of a technician. The, um, head technician." Red managed, with all his bulk, to look sheepish. "Matt was the front man who answered the phone and worked the store. When he felt like it. But now of course, he's gone." He gazed at Gordon.

"You don't expect *me* . . ."

"No, of course not! In fact, I'd like to work with you about the reorganization of the company. Business management is your area."

"You haven't told Sarah that I'll be the new supervisor, have you?" Gordon shook his head, not needing an answer. He flicked his fingers, ridding them of liquid. "Okay Red, you asked for it. First thing Monday, let's you and I have a meeting. The day after, we'll hand out the new positions. This should be interesting."

His hand was already itching to shove the ammonia bottle back into Sarah's face. It would be his pleasure to tell Daddy's little tomboy not to miss a spot.

*What will Craig think?*

Sarah watched a small crease appear in Craig's forehead. He waved a rubber dog toy at the shadows under the kitchen table. "You're kidding. Matt was caught red-handed? Huh." The crease faded, then disappeared as he shrugged. "At least he's gone now."

She could feel her mouth twist into a cynical quirk. So much for jealousy.

She peered at the man who was the longest-running crush of her entire life. He appeared to be absorbed with dancing the dog toy back and forth like a puppet. Was he at least mildly bothered? Bothered would be nice. But she had to admit that he didn't look it. He looked like he'd forgotten about it already.

Even Gordon had alluded to Matt's indiscretion with some scorn. She had to remember the source, though. Gordon seemed awfully conservative. When was the last time she'd seen anyone wear pressed pants at the shop? She couldn't remember. Dad should clue him in about the perils of wearing a business suit in a garage. Though she had to admit he'd looked okay in it. In an uptight sort of way.

He was *so* not her type. Not in a million years.

Craig, on the other hand . . .

She let a savoring gaze rest on his attractive male physique.

Craig tossed the toy across her living room, away from the table. "Your dog hates me." A growl sounded from the shadows as if in agreement.

"Ricky Racer doesn't hate you. Please don't give up. He'll

come around."

*He'll come around.* It was what she told herself every time thoughts of Craig entered her head, which was every few minutes. Sometimes she even believed it. Other times, when she was more honest with herself, she admitted she'd fallen for him precisely because he was out of reach. Since her very first crush in grade school—a completely unattainable, painfully good-looking boy who was also a gymnast-in-training for the Olympics—she'd been hit with case after case of hopeless yearning.

Craig was, by far, the longest-lasting case.

His attention had turned to their favorite subject. "So, did you notice that mid-track wobble on my second pass yesterday? It was pretty early in the evening, so you might not have gotten there yet . . ."

"I saw it," she said. "I always get there early when you're racing. All the better to practice so I can finally whup that cute little behind of yours."

"Dream on." But he gave her a slow grin, his blue eyes like summer lightening as he clearly appreciated her double compliment. Her heart did flip-flops. She couldn't remember a time when he hadn't had the power to make her thoughts jam in her head, just as they had in high school when he'd first offered up that heartbreaker grin. She supposed it had something to do with his blond-haired, blue-eyed, Greek-god good looks. And his easy attitude. And his remarkable skill behind the wheel. His passion for racing—a car-guy speed mania that he carried with infinite coolness—made everything he did look effortless.

But she knew better than to think his accomplishments actually were without effort. She could personally measure the work it took him, down to the ounces of sweat and blood, to create a fast racecar. She'd built one for herself, after all.

She also knew better than to hope her obsession with him

would ever be anything other than one-way. And yet, she couldn't help hoping. Which wasn't his fault. He treated her like a buddy, teased her like a sister, and confided too many unflattering details about himself for her to think he cared for her *that* way. Craig prided himself on being honest. He was certainly honest enough to tell her, in so many different ways, that she wasn't his type.

Not yet anyway. When she schooled him on the track, he'd look at her differently. With surprise. With startled admiration. She let her eyes drift closed, daydreaming.

*Sarah, I never knew you had it in you. I hadn't noticed* . . . His voice would catch and his demeanor would finally show a little uncertainty. The sensation of such overpowering emotion would make him humble. *Why didn't I see it before? You're my soulmate* . . . Sarah frowned in the middle of her daydream. No, Craig would never utter the word "soulmate." For that matter, neither would she. Sarah smiled contentedly, appreciating everything about him, from the way he tipped his beer to the way he stretched his muscles with the unselfconscious grace of a cat.

He extended a bare, muscular forearm and looked at his watch. "I've got a ton of computer help documentation to write by early tomorrow. Kill me now? No? Then I'd better get going." He stood, carrying one empty beer bottle, and strode to the kitchen and directly to the trash cabinet. He opened, tossed, and closed with the smooth movements of one long accustomed to a home's layout.

Picking up the black leather jacket draped over the recliner, he paused. He gazed at her with more seriousness than usual. "That thing about Matt. If it bothers you, I could make him wish he'd picked a different fold-out."

A thrilling rush of gratitude pulsed through her. She had to remind herself he meant nothing boyfriendly by his offer. It was the protectiveness of a brother for a sister.

It still made her cheeks heat and her blood pound.

"Nah, I'm good." He would never know how hard she worked to keep her voice level and her expression bored and just a little amused. Or maybe he would. He wasn't stupid. He wasn't insensitive. In fact, she couldn't think of a single flaw he had, not with his eyes on her like that.

And then she remembered.

"You better get going. You'll devastate your cheering squad at the track if you don't show up tomorrow." The tracksluts had bewitched him. She thought of them that way: *tracksluts*, all one word. They were the lacquered and scantily clad groupies who preyed on the guys who comprised most of the elite racers. As the handsome, hard-charging local champion, Craig was prime trackslut-bait. A magazine cover shot was their goal, a date with a racer their Holy Grail. They were damnably attractive women, good only for posing, pawing, and getting in the way. And corrupting racers like Craig.

Although, to be fair, he'd resisted their siren song at first. They'd noticed him years ago, of course, when he'd won his first Friday night competition. They'd looked at him with stars in their eyes, he'd told her later. He admitted he'd been easy pickings for one especially attractive trackslut, who took him home and . . . but Sarah didn't like to think about the details, even the few that Craig had provided. What was more interesting to her was what had happened afterward.

Craig hadn't known the trackslut agenda. He found out the hard way, on their second date. After listening to his attractive companion talk about herself—her modeling career, mostly—he'd reciprocated with information about himself. But she'd been disillusioned about his dull day job. She was bored by his Midwestern background. Blatantly fishing for magazine contacts and modeling jobs ("You have such a nice car. Has it ever been featured in *American Rodder?*"), she became cold when she found out he had no contacts for her to use. When he'd asked her out on another date, thinking that he'd give the desirable woman another chance—after all, he'd slept with her—she'd turned him down. Explaining with brutal candor that she preferred more of a challenge, more of a mystery than he was, she'd laughed at his astonished, hurt reaction.

The affair had affected him deeply, Sarah remembered. Stung, Craig had decided to alter all future interactions with the tracksluts. They wanted mysterious and challenging? He'd be so mysterious and challenging that even the nicest-seeming tracksluts couldn't wiggle their long fingernails underneath his armor. He'd use the tracksluts the way they wanted to use him.

They didn't seem to mind.

Trouble was, Craig didn't seem to mind either. His buddies made him into their hero for scoring so effortlessly. His own talent made him the hero of everyone else at the local track. But Sarah wished the tracksluts had never laid their claws on him. She'd had to witness his natural emotional awkwardness expand into full-on emotional avoidance.

Throw in Craig's divorced parents, whom he didn't want to emulate, and he was exactly the kind of romantic long shot she'd pine for until her heart gave out, she thought with uncharacteristic gloom.

Sensing her mood, Craig tried to cheer her up.

He acknowledged her cheerleader comment with a shrug, letting his jacket dangle from two fingers as he looked hard at her. "You going to race too? It's not the same without you there. And you're really picking up your time lately. Gonna share your secret?"

"You know all my secrets."

"Not quite all of them, Sarah."

Her heart stopped. It should be illegal for him to do that to her.

He wouldn't kick her out of bed, she knew. Sarah grimaced. He was a guy, after all. He would put his technical writing responsibilities on hold to sleep with her.

It would be fantastic.

All she had to say was "yes."

"Pass on that."

One lapse and he'd see her as just another conquest, a body interchangeable with all the others she knew he sampled.

She couldn't let that happen.

Retreating into humor, she forced a chuckle and glanced down at herself. Clean All-Star sneakers, broken-in straight-leg jeans, and a plain pale green T-shirt. No makeup, as usual. She felt the scrunchie pulling back her straight, wheat-blond hair. "I've got to wash my hair this week. Maybe next week."

"Next week works for me." He opened the front door. His lips quirked up on one side in the irresistible way he had. "Thanks for the beer and the dirty thoughts. See you tomorrow?" He waited until she nodded before closing the door.

When the door shut, Ricky Racer immediately trotted out to her from the dark corner where he'd been watching them both. She scooped him up, nuzzling the long brown dachshund. "Who's my favorite hot dog? Who is? You is!"

He yapped happily.

She held the squirming dog and nuzzled his nose.

"Craig wants a piece of me. Doesn't he? *Doesn't he?* But he can't have just a piece." Ricky yapped with orgiastic bliss. Sarah giggled, then put him down after one last nuzzle.

Through the door she heard the throaty rumble of Craig's beefed-up Mustang exiting the parking lot, and her tense muscles finally loosened. She gave a big sigh.

"He's a tough one. But when I beat him, he'll see the light. A girlfriend worthy of respect. It'll be a new concept for him. We'll be the perfectly matched couple."

Ricky just gazed back at her patiently. She knew he'd heard it all before. Many times.

"You're far more interested in a walk than listening to me go on and on about Craig, aren't you? *Aren't you?*" Ricky became the incredible bouncing hot dog at the prospect of a walk.

Sarah attached his leash and followed him outside. "But then again, you'd be more interested in a rotting dead housefly than in Craig. There's no accounting for taste."

# CHAPTER TWO

"I'd like to begin this meeting by officially introducing the new-est member of our team: Gordon Devine." Sarah felt her eyes open lazily. So it was official. She peered at her dad, who'd called them all into the unusual Tuesday-morning meeting. The last tech had been rounded up and seated. Her dad just winked down at her when he saw her watching him. He leaned against a cabinet, towering above all of them. He'd given up his chair to the new guy.

Sarah lounged in her own chair by the door, having thrust her legs up to rest her feet on the edge of a cabinet shelf. Her dad would know she was bored. Time could be spent so much more productively—and interestingly—down in the shop.

She watched Gordon give a little nod from Red's extra-large chair to the small half-circle of employees gathered in the office. At least he'd changed from his business suit into slacks and a polo shirt. Still way too starched and ironed, of course, but a step in the right direction. She'd bet good money that those tan pants would be grease-stained by noon. He was working in a *speed shop*, not a . . . She wracked her brain, trying to think of where a guy like him would work. A law firm. Or a bank. The man belonged in a tasteful, soundproofed high-rise with beige cubicles the same color as his pants, and lots of large, glass-doored conference rooms. Not like this impromptu gathering in her dad's office with too few chairs. She raised her eyes from his slacks and met his coolly amused hazel gaze.

Red continued. "Now. You all know by now that Matt has been let go. Gordon here won't be taking his place."

Sarah sat up, her feet hitting the floor. She looked at her father questioningly.

"In fact, Gordon's position is new. I've decided that we could use a supervisor—hang on, Sarah, I'll get to questions in a minute—to oversee things and help take the shop to the next level. Gordon has the background and qualifications to do this. I want all of us to cooperate with him, take his suggestions, and implement his ideas. Okay. Gordon, do you want to say a few words about yourself before we go on?" Red pinned Sarah with a warning look, and she shut her mouth.

Gordon rose smoothly. "Thank you, Red. First of all, I'd like to say thank you for welcoming me, and that I look forward to working with you all. Red has founded and built up a successful speed shop that has one of the best reputations in Southern California among automotive enthusiasts. I don't want to change that. I do want to expand its industry presence and grow its existing success in new directions. So. A little bit about me . . ." He smiled confidently, but with just the right amount of good-natured modesty. "Briefly, I grew up eating and breathing cars in a little town outside of Sacramento, California. First I worked on them, then I managed to invent a performance part and started my own company based around that for a short time before selling the interest in that company. Very shortly I will earn my advanced business degree, but in the meantime I've been looking for a company with good potential. I believe I've found it."

"What was the performance part you invented?" Sarah challenged.

Gordon turned to her with an easy smile. "It's a long-life roller lifter. Bought by Holley. You may have heard of Holley?"

Sarah sat, stunned. *Holley* had bought something from him?

That was a serious vote of confidence. Holley was a big company in the automotive aftermarket.

Gordon didn't wait for her to gather her thoughts. He summed up, then addressed everyone. "I'm sure we'll make a productive team together, and thanks again for welcoming me. Red?"

"Yeah. Good. Since Gordon has some ideas for where we should go, I think we should listen to him. Okay then . . . Sarah."

Still feeling a little bowled over by Gordon's credentials, she shook her head. "I don't have any questions, for now."

"Good. As the head tech, it's your job to give him the rundown on how things have been done, who does what, the works. Give him a tour, too. The one I tried to give him was interrupted last week."

Muffled snickers greeted this. Sarah blushed. But everyone was pushing back their chairs, meeting adjourned, so she couldn't reply. She wasn't sure what she'd say to that, anyway. "No problem," she stated, for her own sake. Everything was under control.

No, she didn't completely believe that. The techs trickled out of the office without asking any questions about this new order of business, as if everything was the same. But all kinds of new difficulties had walked in the door along with Mr. College-Educated sitting there in his pressed pants. She'd heard of so-called management experts like him coming in and then changing everything around. What had Dad been *thinking?*

Gordon's supposed background as a mechanic, likely just supervising work on upscale European cars, and that Holley sale—she grudgingly gave him full credit for *that* coup, if it were true—none of it mattered when five engines needed an overhaul in a hurry. Gordon was clearly too . . . too clean. Too lofty for real work. One clothes encounter with transmission fluid and he'd be off like a shot, updating his resume.

Dad wouldn't have hired him just to supervise. Would he? Apprehension fluttered inside her. She waited, watching Gordon speaking in low tones with her father. They were almost the same height, though Gordon didn't have Dad's horizontal bulk. He was more lean, and his brown hair far richer and thicker than Dad's graying corn-wisps. Seeing them side-by-side, she realized how old Dad was getting. He looked tired, the bags under his eyes pronounced, his face dotted with faint bruise-colored sunspots that she'd never noticed before. Old? It seemed impossible. His indomitable spirit, his encouragement and unflagging energy, had been what inspired her to be motivated and self-sufficient her whole life. It had been a powerful force to push against sometimes too—like when she'd made the decision to drop out of college and work at the shop. But mostly he supported anything she wanted to do. He'd been setting a strong example ever since Mom had died. *That* was so long ago that the warm, matronly figure in her memory might just as easily have been the babysitter.

If Dad was slowing down, then what would that mean for him? And for her? Was it the reason why he'd brought on extra managerial help?

Shaken, Sarah almost didn't notice when Red left and Gordon stood over her, waiting. She suddenly realized that he watched her, and that the office was completely empty except for the two of them.

In the stillness, she could hear the tick-tick of his expensive-looking watch. Possibly because of her observing him while he'd spoken with Dad, she was very aware of Gordon's height next to her. His broad shoulders filled out the material of his white sport-shirt to a mannequinlike perfection. He managed to exude a very professional attentiveness, enhanced by his manner of dressing.

She stared at him, disliking him for no good reason. But she kept the thought from showing on her face. She was a professional, too—just not the yuppie kind. "So I guess you won't be cleaning the glass counters anytime soon," she joked. Might as well address their earlier clash head-on. Break the ice.

"No."

She waited, but he said nothing else.

*So much for breaking the ice.* "Okay. A tour de jour, then. What have you seen so far?" She could have bit her tongue in exasperation. She knew what he'd seen—far too much in the storage room. She willfully determined not to blush as she tilted her chin up and waited for him to use the ammo she'd just handed to him.

"Not much. Why don't you show me around?" Gordon smiled at her, his hazel eyes taking on a pointed glint.

"Fine. Observe Red Mattel's office. One walnut desk. Too many file cabinets with one actually blocking the only window looking down into the main shop area. Bookcases galore sagging under the weight of publications like *Hemmings Motor News,* reference books, subscription magazines, catalogs sent by manufacturers, and one cable TV. The TV's good for watching videos of installation procedures. It helped walk me through a complicated transmission rebuild last week . . ." He wouldn't be interested in that. "Plus Dad watches the FAST channel sometimes. But hey, he's the boss."

"Why don't you show me around downstairs."

"C'mon then. This way," she said, feeling like a waitress escorting a customer to a table. She scowled. She'd start with the engine bay, walk him by a couple of works-in-progress. If she were lucky he'd smudge his shirt and run off to the dry cleaner's.

Her head pounded, and she suddenly detoured by the coffee machine to fill a Styrofoam cup, trusting that he'd follow. She heard the soft whisk of his pants behind her and gritted her teeth, pouring the industrial brew and stirring in two packets of sugar with brisk, stabbing movements. What was it about him that rubbed her so much the wrong way? He was attractive, she had to admit. Extremely so, in a just-stepped-out-of-a-clothes-catalog kind of way. Something else made her hackles rise. It was his confidence. His was *too* confident, she decided. His attitude was irritating.

Almost as irritating as her dad dropping this bombshell on her along with the rest of the guys—as if she were just another employee, not entitled to any special heads-up.

Trying not to glower as she continued around a '34 woody being transformed into a street rod—one of her father's pet projects—she paralleled the long steel workbench lining the side of the shop. She stopped a dozen feet from where Will was running the grinder, the plastic shield down and his goggles on. As he pressed a piece of metal against the spinning wheel, yellow sparks showered him. "This is the fab area. The *fabrication* area," she elaborated, not sure what he already knew. "Fabrication means—"

"Making or modifying parts. I know."

She pressed her lips together to prevent her first response from emerging. She said instead, "Moving right along . . . over here is the assembly area. Each engine has its own bench, its own area, to avoid mixing up any parts and slowing down the projects. We don't see too many import or sport compact engines here, but the few we get are kept in their own area with dedicated tools. Lee usually works on 'em. How's it going?" Sarah waved to Lee, who nodded shyly back, both of his hands occupied positioning a micrometer for precise measurement.

At the back wall of the shop, she opened a door that led to a large room filled with gray-primered cars and guys wearing dust masks. The unmistakable odor of an active bodyshop—a chalky, stale-Playdoh scent—wafted out to fill their nostrils. She moved aside to let him see past her. "This is our body and paint shop. It makes us rare among other speed shops that we can do everything under one roof. Hardly anyone else does bodywork and paint, in addition to engines and suspensions." She gave a tug and the door closed behind her, cutting off Gordon's view.

"Okay, what else . . ." Sarah looked around, taking in the whole of the brightly lit garage from the high ceiling with its exposed beams and dark gray sprinkler-system pipes down to the smooth expanse of custom rubberized flooring. Clean, busy, and well organized. The layout was standard. She wasn't going to give him the rundown on every single air tool, band saw, and hydraulic hoist. Besides the shop, what did Dad want her to show Gordon? Were they supposed to inventory the supplies? Run down the workflow? That was her job, and she did it quite well. No need to duplicate effort.

"That's about it. I'll show you where your locker is," she said, beginning to lead him toward the back of the shop where the guys kept their things. The bottoms of her canvas sneakers squeaked against the floor. She could drop him off there and be away from his condescending attitude before he turned the combination of his lock. Her dad could get Gordon situated up front. Dad was the one who'd made the mistake of hiring him.

"Not necessary. I'll be in the upstairs office."

Sarah stopped so quickly that her sneakers made a squealing sound against the floor. "You *what?*"

"Office. Upstairs." He raised one eyebrow at her. "Actually, why don't we go there now? I'd like to discuss the scope of your job responsibilities with you."

"Of my . . . ?" He had to be joking. No, she could see that even though he was amused to put her at an awkward loss for words, he was not joking. "Gordon. That is your name? I'm not sure what you think you're going to accomplish here, but one thing you're not going to do is waste any more of my time. I have work to do."

Her response was more than a little rude, but as she strode away she decided that the white-collared dude had needed the reality check. The nerve of him to . . .

"Sarah Mattel." Her name spoken with that deeply resonant voice echoed up and off the ceiling, the storage rows, and all the far corners of the shop. She froze as if she'd been caught stealing. She turned around, expecting to see a thunderous expression or barely restrained violence, something dramatic to match that voice of doom.

He was smiling politely. "Thank you for the tour. Not very thorough, but enlightening."

She was the one left watching him stride away, easy in his new environment, his matte leather loafers making not a peep against the rubberized floor. "Enlightening," she muttered as she turned around again, wishing she'd just ignored him and kept walking. He seemed to have a knack for getting under her skin in all sorts of unpleasant ways. Why had she stopped on his command, anyway? "And what the hell does he mean by 'enlightening'? And why do I care? And who says it matters?"

"And why are you talking to yourself?" Will mimicked, goosing her, laughing at her surprised shriek. "You're losin' it, babe. All that racing's shook your marbles out of order." He danced out of range of her flying fists.

When she took off after him, threatening vile punishments, she almost managed to put Gordon out of her mind. He wasn't relevant to her lifestyle. She'd been at the shop long before him, and her own *dad* owned it. There wasn't a thing he could do to her.

By the Tuesday night drags, Sarah had all but forgotten Gordon, who'd sequestered himself all day in the upstairs office with Red. She revved her engine an extra couple of times as she eased her hot-rodded Mustang into the head of the staging lanes. She was next up for her pass down the track. As always, anticipation made her pulse thrum with excitement.

Drag racing was so mind-clearing. To launch quickly, drive fast, and get there exactly as quick as the elapsed time shoe-polished on her window; that was her idea of mental therapy. Never mind the expensive shrinks other women paid to make their vacuous lives more palatable. Give her 1,320 feet of straight road and a fast car.

She glanced again at the white shoe polish declaring her time, reading the mirror-image ET number with a thrill of pride. Her car had gotten quicker in the last year, thanks to a lot of time spent working on it at the shop swapping for a bigger camshaft, and adding a less restrictive exhaust system. In the last month she'd improved on her consistency and reaction times, allowing her to move up to a more competitive bracket class. The same class Craig raced in. Her time was more consistent than the other guys she went up against on the Tuesday/Thursday rounds. Even at the more formal Friday Night Eliminations at Carlsdale she managed to hold her own more often than not.

Still, for all her improvement, Craig had her beat. She looked with some envy at him sitting in his car a few slots behind her, farther back in the crowded lanes. His dial-in was 10.50, a full second quicker than hers, and he somehow managed to run exactly on his dial-in, or just a few thousandths of a second under it, on nearly every pass. His consistency was admirable. It was desirable. In fact, sometimes she wasn't sure if she wanted him, or wanted to *be* him.

In the rearview mirror she saw bright colors and exposed flesh slinking against the hood of his blue '94 Mustang. The tracksluts surely wanted him.

Her race harness pressed against her shoulders as Sarah shrugged. Guys loved the skin-flaunting creatures. Couldn't take their eyes off 'em. Craig certainly didn't seem to have the tiniest problem with the newest batch of hood ornaments he'd acquired. His popularity with the tracksluts increased in direct proportion to his reputation as a player and a winner. She'd be lucky if he even noticed her pass down the track.

Sarah peered in her rearview mirror again. Long legs everywhere, glossily fluffed hair, lipstick and cleavage stuck in his face, painted talons tracing his fender. The women moved sinuously, then froze in strategic poses. It was as if they were metal filings, and his car intermittently magnetized.

She tore her eyes from the spectacle. She would never sink to the level of flaunting her body to get attention from a guy. Not even Craig. *Especially* not Craig.

No matter how tempting he was.

Between their changing into fresh T-shirts at the track and the familiarity of seeing each other in the near-nude every summer, Sarah and Craig both could guess to within the millimeter exactly what lay beneath their respective bits of clothing. She felt her cheeks heat at the memory of Craig whipping off his shirt in one smooth arc and flaunting his tight tummy. He never looked away when they changed, always grinning that devastating slow grin at her in her athletic bra. He was a walking, talking tease, effortlessly seductive, unashamed in his casual approach to sex.

She couldn't bring herself to match such casualness.

Trying to get her mind in the proper zone to race, she forced thoughts of Craig from her mind. She'd think of something sobering. Work. Engine rebuilds.

Gordon.

She suddenly felt her teeth grind together. That did it. Good, clean clarity, courtesy of Gordon. It had been so much fun to hand him the glass cleaner and watch that supercilious expression of his vanish. Her only victory so far. Who did he think he was to pull rank on her? He'd treated her like a lackey . . . like a *nobody*. She, Sarah Mattel, the head technician. She should be his boss.

Maybe she was his boss.

Sarah smiled as she pulled around the shallow depression of dirty water and then backed onto the thin film of moisture before spinning her rear tires in a burnout to heat them, and therefore increase her traction, barely thinking about what she did. Wouldn't it be nice if she outranked him? She'd have to ask Dad.

She resolved to also ask him what on earth had made him hire a white-collar. What use could Gordon possibly be in their shop? They were doing just fine without his kind.

It was probably just one of Dad's recent weird experiments, she guessed, like when he'd decided the shop needed Matt as a full-time phone-call fielder and receptionist—"Desk Man," as Matt had ludicrously preferred to be called. Gordon would work out no better.

Come to think of it, why *was* Dad suddenly trying so hard to make the shop more efficient, after years of doing things at his own pace? At his age he should be going to car shows on Saturdays and swap meets on Sundays instead of staying in the shop to catch up on work. He should be meeting women in cafes, or at piano bars or something, not wasting half the night poring over accounts payable.

The first yellow staging light of the Christmas tree dead ahead flashed on. She kept one eye on it as she crept forward, pulsing the brake until the second light went on to show her that she was in the proper launch position.

She held her left foot firmly on the brake and revved the engine with her right foot, bringing the rpm up to a preset point on her tachometer. Her mind became even more focused and clear as it returned fully to the action at hand. The high growl of her engine vibrated against the load as she held it steady, ready, watching the tree. The revving thrilled her to her bones. Thoughts of work couldn't stand up against the bone-quivering noise.

They tried, though. Energy shifted inside her, feeding the competitiveness in her nature that seemed most alive at the dragstrip. So Gordon thought that he could waltz in and order things to suit him, did he?

Just because he'd gone to business school and possessed more than his fair share of confidence, that didn't mean he wouldn't still be easy meat for someone of her vast experience dealing with men. Her best friends were men. She knew the species better than her own.

And that man simply didn't belong in her performance shop. His wide, chiseled mouth had looked to her as if it was all ready to shape strings of clever insults, possibly in other languages.

It was sort of sad. She almost felt sorry for him. Her father had brought him into a work environment where he clearly did not have the home-field advantage.

Poor Gordon. He was going *down*.

The tree flashed: yellow-yellow-yellow-*green*.

As soon as she saw the last yellow light, she lifted her foot off the brake, simultaneously flooring the gas. Her car leapt forward as if shot out of a cannon, the tires squealing momentarily from the power of her engine. Her opponent's time was a little slower, so he got his green light first, forcing her to chase him to the finish line. Sarah shifted, her lips pulled back in a grimace as she gained on the slower Camaro in the other lane. She needed to catch and pass the other car, but not go so fast that she ran quicker than her 11.70-second dial-in. In bracket racing that was called "breaking out," and she'd lose, even though she got to the finish line first. It was a strange rule, one that had taken her a while to get used to, but now it seemed almost natural to aim for a declared time rather than the finish line. Which wasn't to say that she didn't long for heads-up racing. One day she'd have the horsepower and the sponsors to step up to the brutally competitive, finish-line-first kind of racing. She *would.*

Around three hundred feet before the finish line, running nearly 120 mph, she caught and passed the Camaro. A split second afterward, she lifted off the gas a little to avoid running too quickly, but not so much that the Camaro could get past her. When she saw the win light in her lane she knew it was a good pass, probably very close to her dial-in. She curved off the track eagerly, hurrying only to wait for the kid in the ET shack to give her the timeslip. When he did, she stared at it, realizing that she'd nailed her dial-in right on the money. She'd run an 11.700-second pass.

*Perfect!*

Exuberant, she pulled into the pit area next to Craig's truck and his currently empty enclosed trailer. She had no trailer of her own, just access to the open one at the shop when she needed it. Craig was still ahead of her in the equipment arena.

For the moment.

She shut off her car. Instead of trailering her race vehicle the way Craig did his when he competed, she simply drove to and from the track. Riskier and harder on the car, but easier on her, as she had no need to load things up at the end of the night. Plus it was fun to drive fast on the freeways, and she could park wherever she wanted rather than being limited to the track's more distant trailers-only lot.

But if she started running the big-money brackets, or better, achieving her dream lifestyle of professional heads-up racing, then she'd definitely have to invest in her own enclosed trailer, to protect her investment. If one wanted to race with the big dogs, one had to spring for such things.

A lot would have to change if she made it to that level.

*Craig dazzled by the sight of my kicking ass and taking names. That would be a nice change. Craig bowled over by the realization that his chick-racer best buddy would make a better girlfriend. An even nicer change.*

As if summoned by her desire for his company, Craig pulled his Mustang in next to hers close enough for his passenger-side door to ding hers if someone opened it. No one would, of course. Craig allowed nobody to ride in his racecar, not even tracksluts.

He pulled off his helmet and aimed a gently chiding expression at her through his open window. He managed to look both rueful and reproachful as he scolded her. "You didn't watch my pass."

*How does he manage to stay charming while giving me a hard time for not hanging on his every move?* Sarah didn't know, but she could feel her heart responding to him as if it was an engine, and his charm a foot on an accelerator. Sarah climbed out of her car and circled around his, trying to ignore the sudden rapid tattoo of her pulse. She made her voice flippant. "Did you watch mine?"

He shrugged, grinning. "My view was blocked."

*I bet it was.*

But he hadn't watched her pass, which meant she was off the hook for not watching his. She smiled. "Never mind that." She waved her victorious timeslip in front of him like a flag. "Lookee, lookee, lookee who's not a rookie! I hit it exactly."

Craig reached one casual arm out and enclosed her wrist, immobilizing it. He didn't seem to notice her sudden indrawn breath as he examined the numbers. "Impressive. Very impressive. Your reaction time is good too."

*You have no idea.*

Sarah resisted the urge to fan herself with the paper when he released her. Her reaction-time number wasn't bad, but the achievement of hitting her dial-in should have gotten more recognition than a simple "impressive." Why hadn't it made more of an impact on him?

She found out as Craig continued, a look of disappointment darkening his light blue eyes to a compelling sapphire. "I broke out."

"Really?" Sarah fingered her timeslip, unsure of how to show her commiseration. Cuddling him to her breast and stroking his hair, her first impulse, wasn't appropriate. Unfortunately. "Bummer, dude." Poor Craig. Breaking out would be shameful, especially in front of the trackslut brigade. She tried to be supportive. "That hardly ever happens to you anymore."

"Yeah." Craig gave her timeslip another glance. He managed an encouraging smile. "But you, though. You're hittin' it. Should lower your dial-in. Want to go for beers, celebrate?"

If only he were asking her out on a date. But she knew better. And she knew he only offered out of friendship, that his heart wasn't in it at all. Even as she watched, his gaze slid past her into the distance, toward the track. He obviously remembered his own, less-successful pass. Racing meant as much to him as it did to her.

She hated to see him moping. "Nothing much to celebrate. My car's still a slug next to yours," she complained, looking at him out of the corner of her eye.

He glanced at the white shoe polish on her window that showed her slower time. His eyebrows rose and she was glad to see his usual cocky smile reappear. "Not for long at the rate you're going. And I'm gonna tell everyone I taught you everything you know." Grinning, he stepped out of his car. She didn't think it was completely an accident that when he pushed his door shut behind him he propelled his body half against hers for a moment. Of course, she was standing closer than strictly necessary. "Uh, sorry." He reached a chivalrous hand out to steady her, and she made a small noise in her throat.

"Hey Sarah." His voice was warm, his despondency over his pass gone. "Thanks. You always cheer me up. Sure you don't want a beer? I'll drive." He gestured to his Mustang, making her gasp. He'd let her ride in his racecar? Her heart beat wildly, and she couldn't catch her breath for a moment. He had to be joking. His position on passengers was firm: the racecar was for racing, period. He was superstitious about it, as if having someone else in a designated racecar would spoil its competitiveness. Was he making an exception for her? Maybe he'd meant he'd drive *her* car.

She waited too long.

Craig gazed at her thoughtfully. "Not right now, huh? Okay then." He gazed over her shoulder. Suddenly his eyes glinted with mischief. "Maybe next time."

A second later, she found out why. The tracksluts swarmed. "Oooh, Craig, you were so fast out there!" "Can I have a ride?" "No, can I?" "Can he come out to play?" This last was delivered to Sarah by an especially bold trackslut.

Sarah shrugged, wearing a bored expression that she hoped conveyed nothing of her emotions. Especially not jealousy. Taking a page from her memory of Gordon, she tried to duplicate the nuances of his condescending smile. She achieved the noncommittal tone. "Be my guest." She stalked back to her car, trying to keep her eyes off the spectacle.

Sarah could barely see Craig's blond head surrounded by the multicolored costumed girls touching him. They were positively drooling over him.

She could grab him out of their clutches, take him home, keep him, at least for a while. She could *win*. He'd choose her. All she had to do was drape herself on him and coo endearing things. All she had to do was wear painted-on clothes. All she had to do was give him the green light.

It was tempting, as always.

She grasped her timeslip more tightly and shook her head. "Be strong, be patient, and no matter what, don't look at him right now." Craig had to figure out she was worthy of a better kind of love. Didn't he know that bona-fide romance was hard to find? "Don't look, don't look . . . damn it."

He had his arm around a slender black-haired trackslut and was strolling away. She knew he knew she watched. He swaggered slightly as the pair bumped hips. Then he reached around her curvaceous form to wave to Sarah surreptitiously behind the girl's tightly miniskirted butt: *Bye-bye.*

*Damn* him. Well, at least they walked. If he'd let one of those women ride in his car, she'd blow a gasket. As it was, she only felt slightly homicidal.

She pinched her timeslip so tightly that her fingertips turned as white as the fragile paper.

A belated wave of lust washed over her at the memory of his body nudging against hers. How she wanted him. How she admired him. The attraction was his looks, of course, and his superior racing ability, and even his king-like popularity. He was a man who brought out a kind of crazy eagerness in women.

She laughed, a tight, baffled sound. She and the tracksluts actually had something in common.

Starting her car, she welcomed the familiar, centering sound of its powerful engine. Its rhythmic, throaty rumble seem to growl with frustration at the thought that repeated in her head as she steered into the staging lanes: How on earth was she supposed to win Craig's love, when all he wanted was the easy conquests?

Gordon handed off the work requisitions without a flicker of anything remotely warm in his eyes, just as he had all week. Sarah took them without comment, just as *she* had all week, setting them down on the workbench next to the carb cleaner, but a gust of wind blew the top one off the stack. It sailed past him, leaf-like, and Gordon immediately lunged to retrieve it.

She couldn't help noticing his firm butt as he bent, then came up. The light brown khakis fit him as if they were tailored for him specifically, and his taut form was showcased to its masculine ultimate in the Olympian position that he momentarily sustained. She looked away from him as he turned toward her once more, this time placing the requisition on the stack himself. He grabbed the can of carb cleaner and stabbed it down on top of the papers. Without a word, he left.

"If I didn't know any better, I'd say you had a thing for him," Will said, torquing down the head bolts of the engine they were all assembling.

"My friend, you have a screw loose." She huddled over the engine's partially disassembled four-barrel on the shop bench with a screwdriver in one hand, and began assembling the jets and metering plates to get it ready to install on the engine. "I much prefer a certain blond-haired racer."

"Of course you do. But . . . why?"

Sarah felt her eyebrows lift of their own volition. It was an odd question, coming from Will. Usually the guys limited themselves to just teasing her about having the hots for Craig. Asking tough questions wasn't their style.

And it was a tough question. If Craig's good looks and amiability didn't satisfy them for an answer, she wasn't sure what would. Why did she want Craig? Wasn't it obvious?

Sarah shrugged, flipping the bowl over to check the float level. "You know."

Lee just smiled blamelessly and went back to assembling the valvetrain on his side of the engine, but Will stopped, and then yanked the socket off his torque wrench. He set it down on the workbench with a certain precision. "No, I don't know. What is it about him, exactly, that gets you all goo-goo eyed? He's nice enough, but he's a *player*, Sarah." He said that last with the same tone he'd use to say, "The Phillips-head screwdriver goes with the *Phillips* screw."

"What's not to like?" Sarah quipped, ignoring his dig. She finished screwing the metering plate and float bowl to the carburetor body, marveling at the straightforward function of the intricate unit. Using vacuum created by the engine's pistons, the carburetor simply emitted measured squirts of gasoline. She'd just finished building the equivalent of a high-tech Windex bottle. Though much more durable, and far more useful, of course.

"Earth to Sarah? What's not to like about him? You mean aside from how he chases sluts?"

"He doesn't chase them, the sluts chase him." Everything else about Craig was relationship material. He loved racing. He was sexy, protective, fun.

He was completely out of her reach, just like all her crushes.

But he accepted her for who she was, at least. He wasn't like all the more common guys who looked uncomfortable when she talked shop. Typical men had contempt for her racing habit. Garden-variety guys didn't know quite what to make of her, a woman who not only didn't desire the ordinary suburban life, but actively avoided any trappings that smacked of it. Craig was comfortable with her appearance, her skills.

Maybe too comfortable.

Metal clinked on metal as Will rudely tapped the handle of his torque wrench against the metal cabinet near the engine and grinned when she jumped. "Did I break your train of thought? Sorry about that," he said, not sounding the least bit sorry. Sarah could only give him a ferocious scowl. She remembered Will's question. She repeated, "Craig doesn't chase sluts. They chase him."

"Sure, they force him to submit. They carry him off against his will to do unspeakable things to his helpless body. No matter how much he begs, these sexy vixens—all leggy model types with high heels and tits out to *here*—don't let go of him. Hmm." Will stopped working as a slow smile spread across his face.

Sarah rolled her eyes. "You guys are so predictable."

"Four or five horny co-eds who just won't take 'no' for an answer . . ."

"At least finish that engine while you have your walking wet dream."

"Whoa, sounds like I missed out on a good conversation," Craig said, rounding the corner. He'd slipped into the shop quietly. The flexibility of his freelance hours allowed him the freedom to race more often than she could. Sometimes he also visited the shop. She liked to think he came to see her.

Sarah leaned on one palm, her arm crooked. She wasn't about to tell him what kind of conversation he'd missed. "Hey, cutie."

He raised his eyebrows at her billowing sweat-and-grease-stained T-shirt. But he smiled. His eyes flirted. "Hey." Invisible cords of his charisma seemed to wrap around her with his voice, deep and resonant. Her knees loosened and she felt a pleasant fluttering in her belly.

The sensation made her wish, for a moment, that she didn't have oil streaks across her face. Her fingernails probably showed the dark half-moons they often collected by the end of the day too. She shrugged it off. She wasn't superficial, and she refused to care about how she looked. "So what brings you into this fine shop o' mine?"

"My favorite grease monkey, of course." His teasing threatened to turn her into a melted puddle. Fortunately he toned it down before she embarrassed herself with the incoherence that struck her when he turned on the charm. "Also, there's a new project. If you and your guys are available."

Sarah mentally counted the dozens of projects that were ahead of Craig's. "I think we might be able to work something out," she replied, keeping her voice as noncommittal as she could. She realized she still held the Phillips. Twirling it between her fingers, she smiled at Craig. "You know how busy we are. Do you need it right away? Thought so. If you stayed to help out nights, maybe we could make something happen." She heard Will's snigger, cringed inside. She hadn't meant for her words to come out sounding quite so provocative. She almost missed Craig's appreciative grin.

"I'd be happy to help you out nights anytime," Craig said, the rich timbre of his voice purposefully seductive.

Sarah could feel her cheeks heat. She would love for him to help her out nights, and every man in the room knew it.

Every man except one.

"Is there any trouble here?" Gordon appeared as if by magic, clearly holding all of his six-foot frame poised and ready for action. Across from Craig, he seemed a darker, neater version of him. Sarah was struck by the attractiveness of both. One an easygoing, unkempt blond with heavy-lidded blue eyes and a lingering smile. The other a more serious, brown-haired businessman. With a scowl. She appreciated their profiles—both intensely masculine, both strong-shouldered as they sized each other up. "Can I help you . . . sir?"

"It's just Craig," she explained.

"*Just* Craig? I am a paying customer," Craig said, mock-reproving.

"So try paying full price sometime," she retorted, but then regretted it instantly. Gordon might make a stink about their financial arrangement.

"You aren't in the habit of paying full price? Is there a special discount that you're using? Or is this something you've arranged with Red?" Gordon watched the look that passed between Craig and Sarah. "I see."

Will tried to help Sarah. "Craig's been bringing his rides to us for years."

Craig agreed. "Years and years of patronage. I don't recall seeing you here before though . . ." Then he noticed the expression on Gordon's face. He shrugged amiably. "Yeah. Well, why don't I come back later?" He tapped Sarah's hand before he left. "Call me."

Gordon looked disgusted. He glanced at his watch. "It's almost time to go. Will, would you mind closing up down here? I've got to speak to Sarah about something. Sarah, my office."

"Uh-oh," Will sing-songed after Gordon departed. "Boss-man's gonna give you a spanking."

"He's not my boss, and . . . damn it, Will, why is he messing with my system?"

"Your *work* system? Or your *reproductive* system?"

"Get your head out of the gutter."

"My *big* head, or my *bigger*—"

"Out! Out!" She snorted, then grinned as Will trotted to the maintenance closet. He would be the one sweeping and mopping tonight.

Her smile faded as she looked up at the new yellow lamp. Gordon had moved one of the bookshelves from the window so he could spy on everyone downstairs. That was one of the alterations he'd made to his half of Dad's office. She didn't think of it as Gordon's office. She wouldn't. He'd only been there a week.

She evened out the work orders, wondering what Gordon had to tell her that he could only say upstairs.

He'd kept his mouth shut about how she ran things, so far. And to be fair, he'd already suggested some clever marketing strategies to position the shop that she'd heard about from Dad. Which reminded her, she really needed to corner him

45

about his choice of Gordon.

That man just wasn't a team player. He didn't belong on her crew.

She saw a shadow cross in front of the lamp, and realized that she was simply standing there, staring up at the office.

Irritated with herself for stalling, she narrowed her eyes and headed toward the stairs.

# CHAPTER THREE

He could tell she was irritated with him by the way she raced
lightly up the stairs. Usually she stomped with a rhythmic jaunti-
ness that was easy to identify. But that was when she was visiting with her father.

She never visited with him.

Which was fine. More than fine. He neatened a stack of
papers on his large mahogany desk. It was his job to make the
shop run more smoothly and profitably than ever before. It was
his job to expand its services and build on its products. It was
not his job to be Sarah's confidant, or her buddy. She had plenty
of buddies downstairs.

From the look of things tonight, she also had a boyfriend.

He wondered why that thought made him want to pace on
his side of the office. There was no reason why her wide, happy
smile welcoming her lover should make him restless. He made
himself be still and faced the door where she'd come in.

"Craig," was his name. He'd seen a thousand Craigs in his
life, usually driving fast cars and surrounded by pretty women.
They were the men fortune smiled upon, and not just with the
inevitable endowment of Johnny Depp–like good looks. They
were the male equivalents of Sarah, in that they simply had
never encountered the harsher edges of life.

Unlike himself. He carried bona-fide scars from life's harsher
edges, and he was damned proud of each and every one of
them.

The door burst open. Sure enough, her expression held a creased, determined scowl. She hadn't even bothered to clean her face or tuck in her shirt, he observed. He was getting the *au naturel* Sarah. Not that he really minded. The dirt smudges on her cheek and forehead were strangely endearing, if one could ignore her frown. Besides, he'd been employed here long enough to know her lack of tidying up probably didn't reveal any lack of concern for what Gordon thought of her. She was messy for everyone.

Even for Craig.

He pulled out a chair for her and then circled around his side of the desk. "Sit, please," he told her.

"Would rather not," she popped back. She stood, her arms straight by her side, her hands slightly curled. Her expression smoothed a little. He watched her carefully. She hadn't relaxed, despite his little courtesy of pulling out the chair.

She was clearly glad to thwart him, however inconsequentially.

Gordon wondered how he should proceed with someone like her. Especially with what he wanted to tell her.

*Indirectly,* he decided.

"So, you're working late tonight," he began.

"Been busy."

"Mmm?" Gordon allowed the smallest amount of skepticism into his voice.

"We've finished two complete race engine builds and one freshen job in the last week. We've had handfuls of minor things come through too." He watched her pinch her lips together. Her arms came up to fold across her shirt.

*So reluctant.*

Gordon nodded encouragingly, but she said nothing else. He added, "You've done a good job."

"Yeah. But?"

He put on what he thought of as his all-business smile, but

he felt a little reluctant himself. "I can recognize a resource when I see one. This last week I've observed work flow, staffing allocations, compensation, overall organization."

"And?"

"And I've come to the conclusion that the existing positions are adequate for the time being. Your job is safe."

"How nice for me." Then, "What are you supposed to be, some kind of corporate consultant?" She shook her head in slow wonderment. "It doesn't matter. I've never been the slightest bit concerned about my job security."

"Yes. You're the boss's daughter."

He watched her bristle at his tone, then visibly relax. "You don't have any real power over me. If you're just about finished . . ."

"You're wrong. I do have some. For the amount of money that your daddy's paying you," Gordon tapped the top paper of the stack, "if you were *one millimeter* less talented as a mechanic, you would have found yourself up front squirting window cleaner and greeting walk-ins with a perky hello."

"You couldn't." Doubt fought with disbelieving laughter for dominance in her tone.

"Oh, yes. Red gave me that authority. He and I both want to build up this company to meet its potential."

Quiet greeted his statement. Did she doubt that he could do as he'd said? Gordon let his fingers play with a pen, twisting the cap around and around. He didn't want to prove himself in such a way. Heavy-handedness would be counterproductive.

"If the shop's built up any more without adding staff, my guys'll be working 'round the clock," Sarah finally said. "Why not hire another person. Someone who's hands-on," she added pointedly. "I want the best guys available to help me with my bodywork."

Her choice of words gave Gordon a totally unexpected vision

49

of Sarah's body without that boxy white T-shirt impeding the view. He suspected that what lay under it would be exceedingly distracting.

Just the thought of it had derailed his train of thought.

He cleared his throat, but she spoke first, shaking her head. "Never mind, why am I talking to you about that? I'll ask Dad like always."

"I'm quite sure. However, Red has already approved my decisions."

He was coming to enjoy her sudden alertness, like a wolf scenting danger. It made her large green eyes wide and intense, and she held herself graceful and still, as if ready to leap in any direction. There was a refreshing wildness to her.

Still, she'd been indulged for too long. That had not benefited the company. He made his voice firm. "I'm aware of the time you've spent on your own race vehicle during company hours. This will have to stop. As for hiring more people to keep up with the workload, that is not in the company budget for the moment. Therefore, I will help you."

"You'll help me with what?"

He noticed her hands had clenched and her words were clipped as if she held herself on a tight leash. So he was encroaching on her territory, was he? He pinned her with a stare meant to dominate.

"With the workload."

Something he'd said made her hands unclench and a smile return to her wide lips. Mesmerized by the new soft angles of her face and the vibrant sparkling green that the smile lent her eyes, he almost didn't realize that she was laughing at him. Another second and he connected it. "You don't believe that I can."

During his youth spent in an old RV, traveling from town to town, Gordon had learned early to be quick on his feet and good with his hands. He'd trailed his father into mechanic shops and handed him wrenches from the time he was five years old, and helped his mother with his brothers and sisters as well. Watching his dad crash out on the single couch every night until long after *The Late Show* ended or until the bent, tired man passed out from an accumulation of cheap beer, Gordon had determined not to end up the same way. Far from making him bitter or resigned, he'd let the sad environment fill him with more and more motivation until he was ready to do any kind of work, invest any number of long hours, to rise above. It had given him a lifelong admiration of people who *earned* the right to call the shots.

And a distinct lack of patience for those who didn't.

"I'm also aware that you've been offering unauthorized discounts to your boyfriend, far below jobber price. And possibly also to other, similarly favored customers?" He heard the chill invade his voice and didn't even try to moderate it. "This will stop. Good customers can have ten percent off our normal retail, but no more."

"I've always authorized my own discounts," Sarah began.

"Not anymore."

"Not . . . ? You know what," she said, throwing her hands up in exasperation. "You are too much. You're fired!"

"I don't think so."

"Well, I do."

To her suddenly turned back, as she began to exit his office, he delivered the stinger. "What are you going to do, Sarah? Tell Daddy on me?"

She froze, her shoulders as immobile as the rectangular doorframe that surrounded her. She eased back into the room, then faced him. He didn't think he'd ever seen an expression of such complete frustration. He smiled, pleased, and watched her narrow-eyed grimace dissolve into confusion.

She did have a *delightfully* mobile face.

"Look," she said, clearly striving to sound reasonable. "There are things you don't understand."

"I'd like to understand."

"Understand this, then. I'm the head technician, and I'm damned good at my job. Clients are happy with my work. So if I want to use a tiny bit of work-time to finesse my own combination, is that so bad? And if I want to offer loyal customers like Craig a small discount, is that so—"

"Yes."

"I *will* work on my car here. That's *not* going to change."

"I'm very good at implementing change for the better. But I can be reasonable. The other, unfortunately . . ."

"Craig's discount?" She stared at him with eyes like daggers. "What about it?"

He waited, silent.

She sighed finally. Walking over to her father's side of the office, her fingers trailed against Red's larger desk. She turned, leaning back against the desk and lifted both hands to rub her temples. "Why would he do this to me?"

Gordon still waited. He felt a pang of conscience as he viewed the tangles in her hair and the smudges that might or might not be tiredness beneath her eyes. She looked suddenly very young in her men's clothes, her jeans-covered bottom reclined lightly against her father's walnut desk behind her.

"Look, truce, okay?" Her voice was strained in the obvious effort to remain friendly.

"Okay. But no more special discounts," Gordon insisted.

"Craig won't keep coming back if he doesn't get his discount," she warned, her thumbs digging into her temples. "He's nearly a professional-level racer and expects VIP treatment. He's been bringing his car in for years, whenever he gets too busy with his tech writing to work on it himself. And, he's going to buy another soon. A dedicated drag car from the ground up. That's a lot of business to lose."

"He'll come back," Gordon said.

She looked at him narrowly. "I'm good—we're *all* good, down there. But that might not be enough."

Gordon suddenly understood a great many things with that comment of hers.

"Craig wants," Gordon said, thoughtful, "more than you give him. Interesting." He watched the play of emotions on her face: embarrassment, frustration, and finally, a determined thinning of her lips that stubbornly admitted nothing.

"None of my business," he said, smiling inwardly at the way she immediately shook her head, agreeing with him. "But you can talk to me about that if you want. But I see you don't want. Very well."

The silence was deafening.

He stood. He kept his distance from where she leaned against her father's desk, but he saw her go tense at his movement. "So." Gordon looked at his watch, grateful for the distraction. Her eyes were ever-changing, like chameleon paint. Pale moss in one kind of light, and a deep, knowing emerald in another. Disconcerting.

"So," he repeated. "We've covered discounts. I guess that'll do for now. Thanks for your understanding. And as a bonus, if you will," he grinned as he attempted the joke, "you'll have *me* to help you out with all those extra work orders."

"Just what I need." Her sarcasm bit gently.

He cleared his throat. "I'll see you tomorrow, then," he said.

"Up here? Down in the trenches? Or will you be up front with a perky hello?" She'd fully recovered her equilibrium, he realized with both relief and misgiving. Maybe he should have been more firm with her.

Too late now. She was walking with her usual buoyant swagger toward the office door.

"Trenches," he answered.

"Wear something appropriate, if you have anything," she tossed over her shoulder before shutting the door behind her. He smiled at the space where she'd been. He understood. It was just like someone who felt out of control to grab the last word. She felt threatened.

He was okay with that.

"Tomorrow," he murmured, looking forward to it.

Sarah turned the key in the shop's deadbolt lock, the early-morning sunshine glinting on the toothed edges of her flywheel-shaped key chain. She entered, quickly crossing the front room to punch in the alarm code.

It was too early for anyone to be there. Including her. She shivered, her hair still damp from her morning shower, and rubbed her arms as she trotted into the back. An hour or two to straighten up and organize, so that Gordon didn't give her crap for the disarray or the creatively arranged work orders—she liked to prioritize them by favorite projects—and then she'd be ready for when he showed up.

She wondered what he'd wear. He'd implied he'd done mechanic work before, but she found it impossible to imagine. *That* man wanting to soil his perfectly manicured nails? She'd like to see it. No, on second thought, she hoped he'd figure out that he belonged up where the air was rare rather than playing at being blue-collar.

She rounded a corner and halted, staring.

The light was on over one of the engine bays, soft music played from their little boom-box stereo, and the cover had been whisked off the work-in-progress, a small-block rebuild.

But her gaze had locked onto the figure curved around the engine, delving into its mysteries and tinkering. She could hear the clink and tap of a wrench against metal. He wore jeans and a tight, well-worn white T-shirt. It seemed, from where she stood staring, as if he knew exactly what he was doing.

He also looked far too attractive to be puttering around with engines. *He should be modeling underwear,* she thought, making a low sound in her throat before she could stop herself.

He heard, and straightened with a grin. Had he seen her standing there like a buffoon?

"Good morning!"

She forgot to breathe for a moment, confronted with his broad, well-defined chest and flat stomach. His form was proportioned perfectly, shirt tucked into jeans, strong legs easily balancing him over the ready-to-install parts spread about his feet like a conqueror's treasure.

*Whoa.*

"Didn't expect to see you here so early," she mumbled. She'd spotted his grimy hands. She couldn't take her eyes off his large, oil-smudged fingers and the blackened half-moons under his fingernails. As she watched, he wiped a strand of hair off his forehead, transferring a light smudge.

Heat surged through her.

She edged toward the women's restroom and her locker. "I'll, uh, join you in just a sec."

"No problem." His eyes laughed at her.

She fled.

It wasn't until she snapped a tight scrunchie around her ponytail and took more than a few deep breaths that she figured out why she was reacting so strangely. It was because he'd shocked the hell out of her. He'd morphed from a stuffy, conservative old business type into . . . into Fred with Tires. Well, maybe not quite Fred. Sarah shot a fond glance at her framed poster of the famous shirtless mechanic carrying a tire under each well-muscled arm. But close. Deliciously, powerfully close. Who would've thought that Gordon would have so much lean muscle, not to mention know his way around an engine?

"I guess I owe you an apology," she said when she emerged, approaching Gordon where he worked on the engine.

"Do you?"

She grabbed a gasket off the rack and scanned the small-block briefly. The gaskets were already installed. She put it back on the rack. "You've been here a while."

"Not long. Long enough to rearrange the work orders," he said pointedly. He put the wrench back in the toolbox. "I accept your apology, but that kind of haphazard prioritizing shouldn't occur."

"Oh, that . . ."

Gordon looked hard at her, then shrugged. "Help me with this?" he said, indicating the mat. He rolled one end and she rolled the other, until they'd both pushed it to the side. Afterward, she casually sidled over to the work orders.

After a second, she gasped. "You've put Craig's at the bottom!" She pulled it out and put it on top.

Suddenly, a warm but dirty hand covered hers. "No."

She yanked her hand away as if burned.

"Why are you so stubborn?" Gordon demanded. "Just because you're sleeping with someone doesn't mean you can—or *should*—bump him to the head of every line." He shoved the work order to the very bottom with enough vehemence that the paper crumpled. Neither of them moved to fix it.

"I'm not," she said.

"You did. I just saw you . . . oh. You're not?" Gordon looked bemused. "Well, that's none of my business."

They worked in silence for five minutes.

Finally, she couldn't stand the quiet. Sarah gritted out, "Are you sure you won't get tired of lording it over everyone here, and go back to . . . go to wherever you came from?"

"Go to hell?" Gordon laughed, coaxing a smile from her. "Close . . . Rancho Cordova, actually. It's near Sacramento," he explained at her lack of recognition. "Sorry, no. I'm almost ready to graduate night school down here and collect an MBA. I'm afraid I'm here to stay," he said, not sounding sorry at all. "Southern California is perfect for car culture. When I'm ready to market my latest creation, I'd prefer a company located here for a base of operations."

She digested that. So his goal was to start up his own company. He was quite the entrepreneur. "You've invented another performance part?" Impressed despite herself, she found her earlier impression of stuffy Gordon sliding sideways in her mind.

He continued to work steadily as he spoke. "You could say that. The one I'm finishing up now is more electronic in nature, and has to do with drag racing—a sport your father tells me you're very much involved in."

Sarah brightened. She enjoyed talking track to anyone, anytime. Even Gordon. "You could say that," she mimicked him with a smile. "When I'm racing, and I'm on a good, hard run, all of my troubles just vanish. Blown away: whoosh! People don't understand how fun it is to hammer the throttle and feel the force of a fast car pushing you back in the seat while you blast down the track. The world whips by your window and you don't care about *anything*. Except winning. It feels like flying."

She became aware of the silence, and looked up to see Gordon watching her with fascination. He shook his head. "No wonder your dad says you're obsessed with racing. You light up just talking about it."

"Yeah, well." She could feel a blush of embarrassment about gushing on about it, like some kind of bubble-headed bimbo. "Anyway. Dad wishes I'd forget all about that and go back to college. Get some employable experience. Earn my MRS degree," she joked.

"Maybe Craig can help you with that one."

She glanced over at him, but Gordon was adjusting the valve lash and didn't meet her gaze.

"Craig." She laughed wryly. She darted a glance at Gordon, gauging. She shrugged, handing him a 9/16<sup>th</sup> combination wrench. "I can't figure him out sometimes."

"Oh, we guys are easy to figure out."

"Usually, but not always," she said, feeling the long-held frustration about Craig.

Gordon looked fixedly at the fittings. "Tell me. Maybe I could offer an opinion on the matter."

Sarah began to relax. Maybe Gordon wasn't all big, bad businessman. He was willing to get his hands dirty, after all. "You guys *say* that you want someone who's fun, low-maintenance, easy to talk to. And you do. But it all gets tossed out the window for T and A and girlie girls. I understand. I just want to know what it would take for guys to pick a soulmate over a Hooters chick."

"Is Craig your soulmate?" Gordon had stopped working.

"I think so. Maybe. We have everything in common, and we have fun, and I've known him for years. But . . ." She bit her tongue, suddenly hearing herself. She was startled by the realization that she'd used the word "soulmate." "God, I sound just like those women I can't stand. Gossiping, and all the rest." She laughed, but it felt strained. She turned back to the toolbox. Where was that 5/8<sup>th</sup> wrench?

Gordon held up the wrench, but didn't walk it over to her. Instead, he waited for her to come and get it. He had that fascinated look back on his face. She saw it, and was tempted to tell him her plan. As if reading her mind, he said, "C'mon, spill."

She laughed, swiping the wrench from him. "Okay. Why not?

It's not like you won't find out anyway if you work back here with the guys for more than ten minutes. I want Craig nailed with a Cupid's arrow. I want to win the whole package, not just the hormones. His current idea of a perfect relationship is Barbie measurements paired with the word 'yes.' So here's my plan: keep on keepin' on until the boy figures out it's actually a good thing that I don't wear dresses and drape myself over his hood. I'm his equal, not an air-headed bimbo."

"No one would take you for an air-headed bimbo."

She stared at him, trying to gauge his reaction. His expression was back to being inscrutable. She shrugged. "Tell you the truth, I'm *glad* I was raised on NFL and FAST. You can imagine, a girl who'd rather go dirt-biking than to the mall. Guys were my buddies. And they gave me their perspective on things of a romantic nature. *Women can be a drag.* Don't look at me that way, you know what I'm talking about. Anxiety about imaginary health problems, cooing over bratty children, taking hours to trowel on makeup and fluff their poofy hairdos and shop for curtains. I mean, who wants to spend time with a woman whose brain is full of flower arranging?" she finished triumphantly.

"You don't like flowers?"

"I have no *problem* with flowers," she began, disappointed that he'd missed the point.

"You just don't understand them." Gordon laid a forearm across the engine's shiny valve covers.

"What's to understand?"

He smiled, tapping the shiny chrome. "A demonstration is in order. Stay here," he commanded, then walked out of the shop.

Sarah stared after him, baffled. A demonstration of what?

She found out when he returned with a small white star jasmine on a green stem.

"Observe. This is a star jasmine." He held the flower out. It was one of those small weed-like flowers that dotted the hedge next to the parking spaces.

"I can see it."

He smiled, completely unfazed by her tone. He seemed amused. "Relax, already. I promise not to bore you for too long. This is a much-needed lesson in flower-appreciation."

"Actually, I guess I don't like flowers."

"Why not?" He twirled the flower, holding his arm straight out.

"They die. They're yanked off the plant, then someone gives the poor things as a gift, then they wilt and begin to stink. Bad gift."

He asked, "Does this smell bad?" He lifted the flower to her nose. It smelled wonderful.

"Not yet," she said.

"Flowers are a token of affection. Cut flowers give up their scent, their beauty, their lives, to please you. That's the meaning of the gift. The giver wishes to please you."

"And then they die."

"Have you ever considered working in a mortuary?" he asked. "How morbid you are. From the top: flowers are a token of affection, they smell good, and they indicate that the giver wants to give you pleasure." He twisted the star jasmine between his thumb and forefinger, lifting it to her. She couldn't take her eyes off his mechanic's fingers rolling the small, smooth green flower stem. Callused fingers, smudged from the morning's work. She hadn't noticed his calluses yesterday. Now the delicate flower imprisoned between them was all she could see. The scent of faint gasoline and star jasmine wafted toward her like the finest perfume. It was making her lightheaded. She'd always loved the smell of gasoline.

White petals spun hypnotically. As if in a trance, she reached out to take the flower. "Yes . . ." She held it to her nose, smelled it. Jasmine petroleum. She could feel the heat from his body where he stood not quite an arm's length away. She couldn't look at him.

Was *this* what flowers were supposed to do?

She would never bad-mouth flowers again.

And Gordon . . . reluctant, she let her gaze rise from the flower, over his T-shirt and up to his face.

"Lesson over," he told her. His penetrating look was making her knees feel wobbly and uncertain.

Gathering strength from somewhere, she managed to put on a smile and hold out the flower to him. She shrugged. "It'll still die, especially in here."

His eyes narrowed, and he immediately plucked the flower from her and stalked to the workbench, where he filled a spare oil cap with a small amount of water. He tossed the flower into the middle of it, where it lay as if bathing.

"I'm sorry, was that my job?" She grinned at him, then rifled through the toolbox as if searching for something.

"I'm going to offer you some free advice," he said after a moment. "Guys *are* attracted to femininity. Dresses, makeup, jewelry. A little bit of vulnerability, a fair amount of feminine poise. All those things you disparage. You say you want to figure out this Craig guy? Well, try being yourself and see what he does."

"I'm always myself. I'm not feminine. I'm definitely not 'womanly.' " She almost laughed at the image of herself as womanly. Sarah the fertility figure.

"How do you know? Have you ever *tried?*" His voice was compelling. "I think you are. A little bit, at least."

The way he was looking at her certainly made her *feel* sort of womanly. It was disconcerting. She gulped, taking a step back from him. "I'm not about to turn into some brainless Barbie doll in high heels."

"Ah yes, your Mattel name. Were you teased because of it?

You don't need to worry. You'd be the Grimy Mechanic Barbie Doll. Complete with a utility belt full of tiny tools."

She couldn't help laughing. There might be a small amount of truth in his words. She liked guy things, but she wasn't a guy. Maybe it wouldn't hurt her to try—at some point in the future, when it was convenient—to locate her inner woman.

Wherever she was.

But then she heard the telltale swell of voices from outside. The guys had arrived.

She grabbed a wrench, not knowing or caring which one it was, and dove on the engine. The unsettled feeling receded with the familiar smell of grease and oil. She exchanged the wrench for a more useful screwdriver, carefully not looking at Gordon.

"What's this?" Will said.

She stiffened, knowing what he'd found.

"A flower? How'd this get in here?"

She turned, grabbing the oil cap that Will tilted right and left to slosh the flower around. "That's mine. I, uh, saw it on the floor and rescued it." She plucked out the flower, tossed the oil cap, and glared at Gordon to compel him to silence.

"*You* did?" Will looked at her as if she were a stranger. "No shit."

"None whatsoever." Sarah made her voice tough and businesslike. "You guys obviously know Gordon. He'll be slumming it back here to help us catch up. He knows his stuff."

Will sized up Gordon, then smiled, offering his hand. "If Sarah says you know your stuff, you must know it. Glad to have the help."

Sarah ignored their discussion about the current project. She felt strange, holding the flower in one hand and a screwdriver in the other. "Back in a bit," she said to no one in particular, walking toward the stairs.

She returned to drop the screwdriver into the toolbox. Gordon glanced at her with eyes full of laughter, and she clenched her hand around the flower. Jasmine-scent puffed up.

She nearly ran toward the stairs.

# CHAPTER FOUR

"You want me to fire him?"

"No! Just . . . how about you keep him up here?"

Red's expression grew fierce as he looked at his daughter. "Has he done anything to make you feel uncomfortable?"

Sarah squirmed inside. She knew that the discomfort Gordon made her feel wasn't his fault. And she wasn't going to lie and say it was. "No," she said. And then, reluctantly, "He actually does know his stuff." *Especially about flowers.*

Red stared at her, confused. "Well, what's the problem then?"

"The problem is that you handed over control of the shop to a stranger without even consulting me. Why?" She folded her arms across her chest as she remembered to be mad at him for his role in events.

"I wasn't sure you'd take an interest."

"Of course I'm interested. I've only waited this long to bring it up because this last week has been a big one at Carlsdale. I'm improving, consistency-wise, but my time is still too slow. Anyway." She looked at him sheepishly. "I'm interested."

"In racing. But Sarah, my dear, I want to take the shop to the next level. Gordon can help me with my plan." He spoke quickly, cutting off her rebuttal. "Trust me that I know what's best."

"For me, or for the shop?"

"Both?" He looked at her with his most earnest, aim-to-please expression, an open appeal that he rarely used on her.

She hesitated.

"So. That's that. Now, what's this problem with Gordon about?"

"Nothing. Never mind." Sarah was vexed with herself. What could she expect Dad to do? The shop was inundated with more work orders than they could keep up with. Gordon was qualified to help. End of story.

It was just that she was having a hard time concentrating where Gordon was concerned. And she still felt a little light-headed. The scent of jasmine seemed to be stuck inside her nostrils.

She felt the stem poking the soft flesh of her palm. The flower had to go. She threw it into Dad's trash before she could think about it. She gazed at it nestled between the crumpled sheets of paper, and felt a twinge of sadness. The little wilting piece of nature looked so out of place.

"Are you all right, Sarah? You look strange."

Sarah pondered, then put the back of her hand to her forehead. Was it a little bit warm?

Then, horrified, she snapped her hand back down. She was being a hypochondriac. First flowers, then imaginary health woes. Pretty soon she'd be slobbering over children, lecturing about Feng Shui and wearing floral dresses to her weekly manicure!

She had to get out of there. She'd worked enough for one day. "I've got to go racing. Have to clear my head."

Instead of his usual easy nod and a "have fun," her dad frowned.

"I'm feeling fine," she insisted.

"No, it's not that. It's still early, you know. Maybe you should put in a full day."

Sarah stared at him, aghast. Was this her *dad* who was suddenly watching the company clock?

65

"I got here really early today," she said, the excuse sounding weak in her own ears. But why was she even having to *make* excuses? What was going on?

Her dad's voice was slow and heavy, as if he'd been thinking seriously. "The thing is, you should go back to college."

She shook her head. "C'mon, don't start that again. *You* didn't go to college."

He just looked at her, saying nothing.

She edged toward the door. "I'll catch up when I get back."

He looked away, then down at his desk.

She stopped. "It's never been a problem *before*," she said, exasperated.

"Just . . . consider college. You were doing so well in your classes—"

"I was unbelievably *bored* in my classes," she said, laughing. "And you needed someone trustworthy and skilled. Here I am."

"All I'm suggesting is that you consider it. You've been a godsend in the back . . . when you're here. But maybe college should be explored too." He fiddled with the monogrammed pen she'd given him for his birthday.

"Why the fixation about college? We buried that subject months ago."

"It's nothing," he said abruptly. But then he smiled with extra sweetness. "Look, dear . . . go racing. Have fun."

"Are you sure?" But Sarah was already imagining the landscape streaming by her window at a hundred mph. She wanted it. She *needed* it.

She backed out of the office before he could change his mind and raced down the stairs to retrieve her keys, waving cheerily to the guys. "I'm off!"

"Like a rocket," Will agreed.

Gordon said nothing at all.

The stands were casting long shadows over the track by the time Craig found her. She saw him brush aside two tracksluts as he hurried over to where she was trying to interpret the staging guy's latest hand signals.

She'd never seen that particular staging guy before today. He had to be a brand-new track official. Unfortunately he crooked his forearms as if he were doing biceps-curls, then turned around and gave an upside-down squatting "stop" signal. It looked more like a weird new dance routine than directions for a burnout.

Craig blocked both her view of the staging guy and of the setting sun. "I just came from the shop. Got a minute?" He didn't sound as easygoing as usual.

She gave him a grin. She, on the other hand, felt relaxed and magnanimous, which she knew were by-products of numerous well-executed passes. "Hi there. Just one more." It was good to hear his familiar voice and see his light blond hair falling over his forehead as he leaned into her open driver's side window. She had a sudden urge to take off her driving gloves and smooth those shiny locks back from his face.

His voice developed an edge. "Now, please? It's important. Your dad seems to think I'm no longer entitled to my discount. He said something about a new company policy?"

Sarah eased her car forward in the lanes slowly enough that Craig could walk next to her, then shifted into neutral again. "It's Gordon," she said. "He must've said something to Dad. Damn." Her racing high began to dissipate. Gordon's influence over Dad startled her. So Gordon had decided to meddle with her domain? How stupid of him.

But Craig still seemed unsettled. "Who is that new guy to be setting your shop's policy? Is this a permanent situation? I've started looking into the possibility of going somewhere else. I have to budget."

Sarah stared at him. *Somewhere else?* She didn't see nearly enough of Craig as it was. The other shops would be delighted to offer him good-guy deals, discounts on parts, and all the other VIP treatment needed to capitalize on his local-celebrity status. Craig brought in not only his own work, but the word-of-mouth spillover jobs of fans and competitors, too. For him to take his business elsewhere was unthinkable. "But aren't you happy with the work we do for you?"

"You know I've got to take my racing seriously. Especially now. I'm not rich. To break in to the big leagues, I need those discounts."

"You need the best people working on your car!" Indignant, she revved her engine. "We've got the biggest stock of speed parts, we're convenient, we're thorough, we have the best technicians . . ." *And I work there!*

His expression softened as he looked at her. "You do have all that. And you are the best. I'd rather go to you than anywhere else. But, can we talk about this privately? C'mon, jump out of the lanes. I've got to get this figured out one way or another." He had to shout the last part over the sound of the competitor's burnout a few feet away.

She smelled the burning rubber and the pungent odor of special race gasoline. If she leapt out of line when he crooked his finger he'd never respect her.

She compromised. "Meet you in the pits right after I take this pass."

His usual amiable expression faltered into surprise. He was surprised she didn't jump to do his bidding? "Sarah, I'm serious. I've got a racecar that needs attention because . . . oh, forget it. Take care." He strolled away from her.

"Aw, don't be that way," she called after him, flippant, but aching inside that he'd given up so easily.

She watched him walking around the stands, toward the pits, and then she shifted her attention to the track official. She managed to decipher his looping hand gestures to mean that he wanted her to pull forward and halt while a water-box guy dumped sufficient water to moisten the burnout box. Sarah drove up, then waited.

She hated it when Craig played these kinds of power games. On the other hand, of course, she fully understood it. It was a guy thing. Gruff and posturing and uncommunicative, all in the name of winning. She'd seen it first-hand at the track, at the shop, everywhere. Hell, she even did it herself sometimes.

Craig might still be waiting for her in the pits after her pass. Or he might have departed, underscoring his displeasure. Either way, she hadn't capitulated to his demands. Likewise, he hadn't begged; instead he'd stalked away. So when they met again it would be as equals.

They were well matched in so many ways.

When would he figure out that she could be so much more than a grease-monkey buddy? If only he'd look at her, just once, with a soft, slightly dazzled smile, the kind that would tell her she was everything he needed, discounts be damned, tracksluts tossed. Then she'd know that he wanted her for the right reasons.

*What* on earth was that track official trying to tell her? The young man gave up on his combination of hand and finger gestures and instead shouted over the surrounding engines. "Sir, please pull forward and perform your burnout." He repeated the gestures when she didn't immediately move.

*Sir?*

She stared at him in shock. She knew that her hair was pulled back in a simple bun, and her makeup-free face was doubtless grimed with soot. Her oversized white T-shirt worn over a sports bra did nothing to advertise the fact she had boobs. But still . . .

*sir?* She hadn't even put her helmet back on yet!

All of Craig's casual "grease monkey" comments flooded her mind. For the first time, she wondered if she had a problem on her hands.

Was it so easy for Craig to forget she was a girl? Did all guys see her so completely as one of them that she could actually pass for one? Did Gordon see her that way too? For some reason she found herself thinking of the flower incident. Hadn't he said something about her being womanly? If he could only see her now . . .

Her face burned with embarrassment.

She shoved on her helmet and followed the track official's instructions. She pulled her car through the water box, made sure her rear tires were sufficiently wet, and then nailed the gas to spin the tires to make them hot and sticky. She performed the burnout without much concentration until she realized the engine was spinning too fast. She was so rattled that she'd forgotten to engage her two-step rev limiter *and* she was in first gear when she should have been in second. Rookie maneuver. She hunched lower down in her car than she strictly needed to be, and waited for the Christmas tree to flash.

She'd make a special effort to increase her time by a few split seconds, she decided. Leave the negative thoughts behind her in the starting-line's track dust. She had to get back on her game.

*Yellow-yellow-yellow-green!*

She stood on the gas at the last yellow as she simultaneously released the brake. Too much throttle. Her Mustang shivered as it leapt forward with a tire-squeal that continued for too many split seconds. Sarah felt the beginnings of the usual speed-exhilaration and clarity, but something was wrong. Her car trembled . . . she passed half-track still picking up speed, but it just wasn't accelerating as hard as it normally did. That was a sign that something was failing. A popped head gasket? Were the spark plugs going away?

In the next second she heard a muted *pop*, and streamers of smoke suddenly leaked from under her hood, blown past by her speed, which was already slowing. She lifted her foot off the accelerator, knowing she'd broken something.

She swore at the top of her voice. Nobody would hear her over the revving-down of her engine, and even if they did, they'd understand. Smoke during a burnout was good; smoke during a pass was very, very bad.

She limped her car past the timeslip booth, not bothering to take the little piece of paper. The smoke poured out more thickly now, and without the speed to help diffuse it, the car was a main object of attention as she passed the stands trying to get to her pit-spot. There were few people left in the stands this late. Every one of them rubbernecked as she slowly drove past.

Then the wounded Mustang guttered and died. She steered it to the side, and immediately got out, her helmet still on. She spotted the person she was looking for. "Craig!" she shouted.

He turned so slowly that she knew he was aware of what had happened. She'd sent up too large of a smoke signal for him not to know. Far enough away that she could only see the outline of his body in front of his own Mustang's open door, he waved to her. She waved back violently, but he didn't move to approach her.

Instead, as she watched with her mouth falling open in shock, he climbed into his car. He started it.

He drove in the opposite direction.

At a loss, she looked around. She hadn't planned very well, she admitted to herself. She hadn't even considered how she'd get home if her car broke and Craig wasn't around.

Cursing herself, Craig, and her car with equal flair, she yanked her helmet off and fumbled in her backseat backpack for her cell phone. She dialed she shop's number to ask her dad for a ride.

"Big Red's Auto Performance Shop," the voice answered. It wasn't her dad.

"Gordon," she growled. "Please put my dad on the line."

"Sorry. Red's left for an evening engagement."

"What time is it?" She rubbed away an indentation the helmet had left in her forehead and smoothed sticky strands of hair off her skin. The sun had set and the few cars crossing the parking lots and pits to leave the track had their headlights on.

"Seven thirty," he said, brusque. He obviously would rather be doing anything but talking to her.

"Fine, well . . . see you tomorrow then," she said, and hung up. "Crap." But all was not lost. She still had that AAA roadside assistance card her dad had given her. A few minutes of digging through credit cards finally turned up the white-and-red plastic card with the emergency number embossed on it. She called.

"Triple-A Roadside, how can we help you?"

"I need a tow."

"Card number?"

Sarah gave it.

The dispatcher asked, "Where are you located?"

"At the Carlsdale track," Sarah responded.

"Were you racing?"

Sarah looked at her Mustang with its shoe polish white dial-in and her drag slicks. She bumped her helmet against her thigh. *Uh-oh.* "Sort of?"

The dispatcher's voice turned saccharine-sweet. "I'm sorry, but we can't offer a free local tow on race vehicles. Additionally, the Carlsdale location is outside of our coverage area. Would you like a referral to a local towing company?"

"No, thanks," Sarah said, hanging up, then dialed a number. She was going to kill Craig. He could have given her a ride, but he'd abandoned her. Stupid, macho, arrogant . . .

"Big Red's Auto Performance Shop," Gordon answered.

"Gordon, did Dad say where he was going?"

"A farewell business dinner for an old friend."

If Gordon's voice were any cooler, she'd have frostbite on her ears. She thought for a moment.

"If there's nothing else you need, I have some work to catch up on."

"No. I mean yes. Gordon? Is the trailer being used by anyone right now?"

"The trailer. No, I'm looking at it right now. Why? You sound like you're on a cell phone."

"Yeah. I sort of broke down. At the track. I need a tow."

Silence.

Then, "You need a tow."

"I need a tow to the shop." Sarah paused, hoping that Gordon wouldn't hang up on her. If she'd really left him so much work that he was still there finishing up, then she supposed she couldn't blame him if he *did* hang up on her. She crossed her fingers. "Please?"

"You are, by far, the most irresponsible, selfish . . ."

He cut himself off. Sarah heard the ratcheting sound of a socket wrench being twisted violently. Then a sigh.

"I suppose somebody has to rescue you. Where's your knight in shining armor? What's his name? Craig."

"That's none of your business," she began.

"*Au contraire.* If I'm filling in for your boyfriend I'd like to know why."

"He's already gone," she said, hating the forlorn tone that had crept into her voice. She would not tell Gordon that Craig had turned his back on her. That was just too embarrassing.

"I'll be there in thirty minutes. Stay by your car."

"Okay. Thank you," she said, but the dial tone told her he'd already hung up. "Nice," she mumbled, hitting her cell phone's off button.

He was considerate to come to get her. She only hoped that he knew how to work a trailer and that Dad hadn't swiped the '72 Chevy shop pickup. He probably had, preferring to drive the customized truck to his newer Suburban. So Gordon had better be driving something powerful enough to tow. What kind of car would he drive? A day earlier she would have guessed a Camry, or a Maxima, or a two-wheel-drive SUV. Beige colored. Now, though . . . maybe a six-cylinder Grand Am, or sporty four-door Mazda. Maybe even a small truck.

Thirty minutes later, she heard the low rumble of a powerful engine even through the closed glass of her driver-side window. Sarah looked over her shoulder into the headlights of the car driving toward her. He pulled beyond and ahead of her car, the trailer behind him.

Gordon drove a *Mustang?*

And not just a mid-nineties GT like hers and Craig's. The smooth, throaty rumble of the engine warned of serious speed. The no-nonsense bodylines of the Mustang were those of an SVT Cobra. The priciest, fastest Mustang ever sold. And it had a trailer hitch.

Gordon positioned both car and trailer expertly, then hopped out and helped her load her broken vehicle onto the trailer without a word. He wore the same jeans and T-shirt he had on that morning, but Sarah noticed his hands were clean as he tightened down the straps. He must've soaped the grease and dirt off himself before he left.

"Get in," he told her. Without waiting to see if she did, he slid behind his steering wheel and started his car.

Sarah opened the passenger-side door and sat in the enclosing stock leather seat. "Thanks for the lift." She ran her hands

over the leather edge of the bucket seat wonderingly. "Is it yours?"

"I park behind the shop," he said, explaining why she hadn't yet seen it. He shifted into low gear for the small incline away from the track. "There's more shade in the back."

"How fast is it?"

"Fast enough."

"You haven't tested it? You don't want to find out?"

"It's fast enough. Not everyone needs a timeslip."

Sarah watched his hands move over the steering wheel. "You've raced before," she said.

"Yes."

She waited a full minute. "Okay, where have you raced?"

"Nosy, aren't you?"

"I prefer 'inquisitive.' "

"Nosy. I raced in Sacramento. That's how I tested my speed parts—on my friends' cars, and my own. My old car, that is. This one's brand new." His eyes narrowed and his mouth turned up with more satisfaction than happiness.

"Dad pays pretty well."

"Not your dad. You're the only one at that company who arguably makes more than you're worth."

Stung, she digested the insult. He was giving her a much-needed ride. "I see. So you cashed in on this invention of yours. Did you give up racing entirely, at that point?"

Gordon glanced at her, his eyes speculative. "I've given up nothing. Racing's always been just an off-hours hobby for me." He looked straight ahead. "Unlike some people, who use racing to avoid real work." The line of his jaw was tightly controlled.

Sarah decided she didn't need the ride that bad. "Couldn't hack it, huh?"

He wasn't fazed. "Believe what you like. Me, I'm going to own those tracks that you drive on, run the magazines that cover the races, and direct a company that produces, among other things, aftermarket parts."

"Ambitious, aren't you."

"I prefer 'enterprising.' " He grinned finally. "It's been a struggle, but things are starting to come together."

"Really?" she asked, intrigued despite herself. "What kinds of things?"

But for some reason he suddenly became very busy with taking the freeway exit and peering at the street signs, and didn't answer her.

A few minutes later, he backed her car into the shop's garage and they unloaded it. "Tomorrow, you'll repair *this*," he patted the fender of her car, "very early in the morning to get it out of the way." He leveled a stare on her until she nodded.

"Agreed." It didn't bother her to act humble for a change. "Thanks so much for the ride."

"Oh, I'm not finished with you yet," Gordon said.

"You're not?" Now why did her pulse race to hear him say that? She shifted from one foot to another, suddenly conscious of her dust-streaked face and her clothes, dirty from racing. She probably smelled like tire smoke, exhaust, and sweat. She knew her forehead sported a slowly fading horizontal mark where the helmet rested. And her hair felt as if half of it had pulled free from her loose bun. She tossed her head, trying to get the unruly locks to hang behind her ears and shoulders where they belonged.

He tracked her movements, and the corners of his mouth quirked up as if he could read her mind and was amused by her thoughts. "Were you planning on hitchhiking home from the shop? I don't think Red would approve of my letting you do that."

"A ride home. Of course. I'd forgotten." She felt her face heat, and was glad for the grime that hid it. She sighed and added, reluctant, "I owe you."

He said nothing, but opened the passenger-side door for her, as if she were a date. "Shall we?"

She was unnerved to find that she felt like his date. She wished, very much, that she didn't.

Ten minutes later, when Gordon pulled up in front of her garage below her apartment, she still felt oddly self-conscious. Attuned to his every small movement, she was aware of when he steered, shifted, and adjusted his rearview mirror.

Now he set his parking brake with an authoritative pull, the deep throaty rumble of the engine still making the seats vibrate.

She owed him, she remembered with relief. That had to be why she'd felt so strange ever since he'd shown up at Carlsdale to give her a tow. Time to pay up.

"I owe you a beer or three," she said airily, opening the passenger-side door. "C'mon up?"

He didn't move or shut off his car.

She tensed, but kept moving and talking, hoping to bull through the awkwardness by sheer strength of will. "Good cold beer? Yum?"

He turned the ignition key. He spoke into the comparative silence, looking straight ahead. "Beer. Why am I not surprised that you're offering beer." He palmed his keys. "Okay. A cold one would go down pretty well right now."

"Great." He was coming. She'd pour some beer down him, end her indebtedness, and start feeling normal again.

She led him upstairs. "Sorry for the mess," she said as she opened her front door. "Ricky Racer likes to chew. And he drags around anything that's not nailed down. Please don't worry about him. He'll probably run and hide."

Excited yapping drowned out her last few words, and a long brown form wiggled around her legs toward Gordon. Its tail-wagging was so enthusiastic that the dog's back end grooved left then down then right in a bizarre dance.

Gordon stooped to the form and patted. "He's cute." He reached out and enclosed the dog in his hands.

"No," Sarah said, alarmed. "He's suspicious of strangers, he might . . . oh. Well, I guess it's okay." She watched as Gordon held Ricky Racer against his chest and scratched behind the dog's delicate ears. Ricky didn't snap, or growl as he always did with Craig. He didn't even wriggle as he sometimes did with her. Instead, he went as limp as a relaxed cat and all but purred.

Sarah just stared. Then, shaking her head, she tossed her keys on the breakfast counter. "Some watchdog you are," she scolded as she passed the pair. Ricky ignored her, eyes closed in bliss.

Gordon moved his hand to caress the dog's back. His voice was pitched so that she'd hear it from where she opened the refrigerator door. "He isn't usually like this, I take it?"

"No. Craig has the teeth-marks to prove it."

Gordon muttered something about Craig and teeth-marks that she didn't catch. The harsh white light inside the refrigerator picked out the dirt and grease on her jeans, she noticed, looking down. The jeans had become more brown than blue. When she brushed at the spots, she saw matching streaks on her hands and forearms. She grabbed two bottles of beer and shut the door on the bright light.

"I should go hose off," she said, twisting off the cap off one and holding it out to him. "And change clothes," she added, plucking at her T-shirt. It was white just that morning, but was now a light brownish-gray shade and clung to her in sweaty sections. Drag racing was a dirty activity. She idly wondered if she smelled very strongly of oil and rubber. And if he minded.

Gordon set the dog down gently, then looked at his watch. "Well. I should be going anyway. Though I hadn't planned on bringing this with me." He sipped from his beer while he hooked his keys out of his pocket.

"No, no, no," she protested, understanding. "I'll only be a few minutes. Sit."

Hearing the command, Ricky Racer sat.

Over him, she told a still-standing Gordon, "I take the quickest shower in town. Back out in five. Seriously, come here and sit down."

Hearing "come" and "down," Ricky Racer galloped over to her and then lowered his long body onto his belly. He peered up, hoping for a treat.

Gordon cocked an eyebrow at her. A smile played about his mouth. She felt the two sets of eyes on her: hazel and brown.

"You're not very obedient," she informed the owner of the hazel eyes.

"And you now have less than four minutes." Gordon watched her with clear amusement, then strolled to her recliner and sat with easy grace. He set his beer down on the adjacent coffee table without looking away from her, and she had to tear her gaze from the pointed glint in his eyes.

She showered triple-speed, soap lather flying into her hair and shampoo getting slapped everywhere the soap didn't. Skip the shave, since she'd already done it that morning. She'd never shaved yet without a regret for that very first time she'd begun the ridiculous process of defoliating her legs and armpits. If she'd never started, she wouldn't have had to continue every day just to keep the stupid stubble away. Another dumb feminine cultural tradition, striving to be smooth as babies. Her legs were starting to feel pokey. She grouched to herself even as she decided to quickly run the razor over her legs again. There was time, so long as she really hammered the throttle getting dressed.

Flying out of the bathroom as she toweled herself dry, she yanked on fresh underwear, jeans, and a T-shirt without needing to look. They were all the same size, all sporting automotive aftermarket logos and race sanctioning body logos. The only difference was T-shirt color. She owned a couple of special-occasion greens and blues.

She took off the white and put on a blue shirt. She paused to look in the mirror. The blue darkened her green eyes. Not bad. She felt refreshed and clean. *Degreased,* she thought with some satisfaction.

But . . . sort of plain. She *could* put on something more than strawberry-flavored ChapStick for a change, she thought, looking at the familiar and unexciting expanse of her pale lips and face. Something pretty, if she had anything. She looked in her medicine cabinet with a frown. No makeup beyond a stick of concealer for pesky and fortunately rare pimple breakouts. Aspirin, toothbrush and toothpaste, Pepto-Bismol . . . she picked up the three-sided pink bottle. It was nearly full. She'd only drunk some of it that one time after Craig had convinced her to try a drink called Liquid Valium on top of three shots of tequila. The guys had egged her on, and she couldn't be a *wimp* . . . but the next morning her stomach had felt like one of Ricky Racer's oldest chew toys.

Scooping out a finger-full of pink stuff, she held it next to her lips. It was a nice shade of rose. She had nothing else.

Moments later she smacked her lips together. The chalky mint smell made her nostrils flare, but the thick liquid goo spread with oily ease over her lips.

She smiled widely in the mirror, testing the look. Her skin seemed more luminous, her green eyes more sparkling, her water-dark lashes wetly spiky. Her damp hair was parted in the middle and draped pleasingly over her shoulders. Her lips . . .

Her wide smile froze. Small pink gooey stringers connected her top lip to her bottom. She tasted the stringers. Pepperminty.

What was she *doing?*

She licked her lips, ridding them of the colored medicine.

There. Now her face was back to its original appearance.

Plain.

Too much like a guy.

*I'm being ridiculous.*

But the track official had called her "sir."

Maybe something about her appearance could be changed in a small way. Very small. Microscopic. She'd buy some lipstick, but nothing else. Maybe that would do it. Guys never wore lipstick.

She emerged from her bedroom still pondering. She made a beeline for her full beer and joined Gordon where he waited, settling in carefully to his right on her extra-large overstuffed dark blue beanbag. She wiped surreptitiously around her lips, hoping no trace of the pink goo remained.

But she noticed with relief that Gordon didn't seem to be examining her closely. In fact, he was looking down at his watch. "You did it. Impressive. I didn't think that even you would be able to—hey, what's wrong?"

She felt the weight of his gaze fall on her, and had trouble meeting it. "Um . . ." She peeled nervously at her beer label, then took a quick sip before replying. "Actually, I have a question for you. A request, actually. Feel free to say no." She peered up at him from her seated position on the firm and rounded edge of the bag.

He'd extended the recliner's footrest, and his legs were folded one over the other with purely masculine ease. His big, six-foot frame didn't look soft, though. He appeared as confident and in control of his surroundings as if he were in his own living room, and ready for anything.

His hazel eyes became more intense. He toggled the recliner's lever, and his feet hit the floor with a soft thump. He swiveled the chair until he fully faced her, then bent forward until his elbows rested on his knees. "Yes?"

The single word was deceptively soft. It invited her to "spill," once again, and she felt a sudden strong urge to do exactly that.

But first she took a larger swig from her bottle. Should she leave herself open like that? "No, never mind."

Maybe it wasn't even a real problem. It'd sound ridiculous. If she told him her concerns, asked him what she wanted to ask, he might never take her seriously again. He might laugh.

She forced a chuckle. "It's stupid. Forget it."

"Oh no you don't. Tell me what's on your mind."

To her alarm, he rose from the chair and closed the distance between them in one step. He plucked her half-empty beer bottle from her grasp, and set it down next to his on the firm carpet next to the beanbag. He knelt, settling onto his heels. He tilted his head in an almost canine manner. She felt naked with all that intensity aimed at her. She suppressed a shiver.

Gordon was close enough to her that she could smell the scent of the shop still clinging to him: orange hand cleaner, residual engine grease, and clean sweat. She met his gaze in fascination. His eyes had darkened to a shrouded and mysterious color, not quite green and not quite brown. Sarah felt her breath catch in her throat.

He seemed to sense her reaction. She saw him tense. He pinned her with a piercing stare that zinged through her like an electrical bolt. Her mind was spinning, and it owed nothing to the half-bottle of Newcastle. She could drink with the pros, could handle far more than that.

But as her mouth touched the brown glass, she tasted peppermint. She licked her lips. The chalky residue made her decide.

She took a deep breath. "Okay, here goes. You've got experience in this area, and a fresh perspective, and no one'll believe you if you tell them I asked you this. Give me your advice. Can

I have a different . . . what would be the best way to . . . tell me how to become more, just *slightly* more . . . well, girlie."

# CHAPTER FIVE

"Tell you how to *what?*"

At Gordon's look of surprise, she felt the blood rush to her face. Yes, he was rocking back onto his hands, clearly dizzy with astonishment. "I said slightly. No big deal." Sarah felt more flustered than she could ever remember feeling before. She should *not* have said anything. "Never mind."

His silence became more unsettling with each passing moment.

He'd been so understanding in the shop when he'd talked about flowers. But that didn't necessarily mean that he was willing to offer more advice. She'd been stupid. "I've been stupid. Breaking my car must've bumped my brain offline." She exhaled heavily, marveling at her misjudgment. Usually she read guys better.

Gordon finally spoke. "Ah. This would be for Craig." His surprise vanished. "Of course. You spoke of this at the shop. With a slightly different emphasis."

Her face burned but she pushed on. "I just figured that since you had some strong opinions on 'dresses, makeup and jewelry,' you might not mind passing on some pearls of wisdom. Not that I need them. But the more tools in the toolbox, the better. So how about some tips and tricks. Like the flower thing."

"The flower thing."

"Yes, the flower thing. Remember?" Was he making fun of her? She charged ahead, the sensation of recklessness making her speech bold and louder than normal. Her face felt as if it were about to melt off. "I didn't know about the flowers. I'm willing to admit that I could stand to learn a thing or two about other, similar subjects." She gave a self-deprecating shrug. "You could even say that my feminine intuition is underdeveloped. Which is usually just fine with me. But I'm not up to speed on how to . . ."

"Be girlie."

"Exactly," she said with a growl, remembering the incompetent, pimply track official who'd totally missed the fact she was a girl. If Gordon laughed at her request, she'd smother him with her beanbag. She'd sic Ricky Racer on him. Come to think of it, where *was* Ricky Racer? Sarah glanced around, but he'd vacated the living room for the moment.

To her great relief, Gordon didn't laugh. "Okay. But I'm just wondering. Why don't you ask Craig about this? He's your *soulmate.*"

"Maybe. We're sort of . . ." She wasn't sure what it was called, when you'd spent so much time aching and longing for a man that it was as much a habit as breathing. When he was perfect for you in every way, but didn't realize it. Winning Craig, like winning races, had become so much a part of her that she rarely thought about it objectively. It just *was*. "I want to surprise him," she said instead. It wasn't strictly Gordon's business. Just like it wasn't any business of his that she'd been mistaken for a man back at the track. That was need-to-know only.

"So you want to impress him with your new and improved ability to wear dresses and makeup?"

Gordon *was* making fun of her, she realized with a sinking feeling. She didn't feel like smothering him with the beanbag. A chill sense of disappointment joined the embarrassment, leaving her suddenly drained of energy and slightly sick to her stomach.

She stood, wishing that the beanbag didn't make her movements so awkward, and that her knees didn't brush against him where he still sat in front of her. "Done with your beer? Good," she plucked up his empty bottle and stared pointedly at her clock. What kind of guy was this that she'd confided in? She was damned if she knew. Or cared. All she knew was that she shouldn't have uttered a word about any of it.

"Sarah."

She heard his voice rising from the floor, so she knew that he'd stood up. His tone was so full of laughter that she felt her lips twitch despite herself. "Uh-huh?" She tossed their two bottles into the trash and avoided looking at his face. Why couldn't he take the hint and leave her to stew in humiliation?

"Don't change."

Now she faced him and his dreaded grin. She tapped one hip with the too-short nail of her right index finger as she gazed at him, considering how best to suggest that he leave. Gordon stared back, his eyes sparkling so brightly that it looked like he was about to break into laughter. It wasn't a cruel expression. More friendly than anything. Even a little bit endearing.

She relented. "I'd hoped that you'd toss me a little advice." She shook her head, smiling back at him. He looked positively sure of himself. Worldly. Too bad he wouldn't give her a couple pointers.

"I did give advice: *Don't change.* You don't need makeup and dresses. If you need to act like something you're not to get this—Craig's—attention, then he's not the right guy."

"I know *that.* But truthfully, Craig's perspective on women is shared by most guys." Like the track guy. She remembered her reflection in the bathroom mirror. Not bad, but plain as a primer-gray paint job. Sufficiently non-girlie to be mistaken for male at twenty feet. "Craig once said we're a lot alike, he and I. What if it's true?"

"A relationship isn't a car," Gordon said bluntly. "You can't swap out the engine—your personality—and expect it to work like before."

"No, but I can tinker with it till it works better. Update the body here and there. You know, until things are sportier. It's still the same car."

Gordon stopped shaking his head. "You're obsessed with this guy, you know that? It's not healthy."

Sarah made a rude sound. "Who's obsessed? I'm mildly curious to see if a little change—very little customizing—might be good for the soul." She liked Gordon's honest replies. She felt her blood zinging through her veins as she spoke with him. Conversation with him was exhilarating, almost as much as racing. "So," she said, pinning him with her most direct look. "One more beer, in exchange for one tip from Mr. Flower Enthusiast? Fear not, I don't expect you to transform me into a sex kitten."

"You? A sex kitten?" Gordon scoffed. He looked at her hair. "More like a rained-on alley cat." But he smiled, and his hazel eyes snapped and flashed.

"So I'm a challenging case." She spread her arms out, and her blue T-shirt billowed gently over her well-worn jeans. She felt the heavier weight of her wet hair and the cool dampness on her shoulders.

"This is crazy."

"But so much fun," she replied. "C'mon, one little tip?"

"Do you always get what you ask for?"

"No, never."

"Liar. You're as spoiled as they come."

"I'm going to take back the beer offer. You can go thirsty."

"I don't want another beer." He slowly walked toward her. He folded his arms on the breakfast counter. She rested her forearms on her side of the counter. Gordon's appraising presence so close to her made butterflies beat against her chest.

She smiled politely, waiting. Gordon was a cool one. But he

was almost as much fun as Craig once he loosened up. And every bit as good looking. In fact, if he kept those charismatic eyes on her for much longer, she'd start thinking things. Like, what would happen if she eased around the counter oh-so-slowly and just kissed him? How nice would it be to feel those strong, capable arms enclosed around her, and his lips moving on hers? How much nicer to strip off their clothes and move together more intimately?

But those were inappropriate thoughts. She shook her head, turned her smile away from him so that he wouldn't sense the direction of her dirty little mind. Maybe Will had had a point about her being attracted to Gordon. But then again, who said that a girl couldn't recognize male beauty without falling into a swoon? Guys certainly did that with the girls. All the time. And Gordon had barrels of beauty. He had that animal walk, and all those nice muscles, and his features were roughly attractive without being delicate.

"C'mon. Tell me one thing that women do, or have, that really gets your attention in a good way."

"A sure-fire way to get this Craig to take notice, huh?" Gordon's eyes took on an almost-wicked glint. "I can think of a few ideas."

"In a *wholesome* way," she insisted, flicking his forearm with a finger. What a hypocrite she was. "And like I said, it's just another tool in the box. Maybe I'll never use it."

He looked down at her finger, then back up into her face. "Well, how about getting a manicure. Grow your nails long and paint them. That's girlie."

"Can't. Long nails would break off the first time I tried to use a wrench in a tight space. They could do with some filing and cleaning, though, couldn't they?" She held her right hand up, palm out, to view her nails. Residual grease smudges remained in thin slivers underneath the short and—now that she noticed them—uneven tips. She made a mental note to give them a good scrubbing and do something about their bandsaw-like edges. "So girlie talons won't do. Next?"

"Jewelry? You don't seem to wear any."

"Never got my ears, or anything else for that matter, pierced. Rings and necklaces could get caught in machinery. I do have a watch that Craig gave me for my birthday. Does a watch count?"

"No. He should have given you something non-utilitarian. Doesn't he know anything?" Gordon snorted. "And he has a problem with you not being girlie?" He shook his head. "Whatever. How about the big guns. Dresses. Do you even own one? You must have played dress-up in mommy's clothes at some point."

He clearly expected a quick "no" answer to the dress question, and Sarah could tell that her lengthening silence aroused his curiosity. She spoke softly. "I do own a dress. A long, silky black dress, with matching sandals. It's pretty. And very dusty." She shrugged unrepentantly and plastered a smile on her face. "As for mommy's other dresses, they went wherever the dresses of good mommies go when they die. I never missed not playing dress-up. I'm glad Dad raised me like a boy. Boys always have more fun." She maintained her steady gaze with an effort, even managing to widen her smile. "I love wearing jeans and a T-shirt."

Gordon nodded a few extra times before speaking. "I'm afraid this is out of my league," he said with a rueful smile. "You're a dedicated tomboy. Quite hopeless."

"Hopeless. I see." Trying to hide how his words disappointed her, she began to turn away. "Well, you earned a beer anyway. For the effort."

"Hey," he said, touching her hand to stop her. "I was kidding. You're far from hopeless, you know."

"How kind of you to say so." She hoped that her raising one

eyebrow conveyed a graceful disdain for his opinion. And covered her primal reaction to his gentle touch. She could get used to that calming, honeyed tone of his.

She suddenly felt an impish urge to shake him up. She flicked his arm again, but this time more slowly. "So. Exactly how far from hopeless am I?" she breathed, mock-coy. Her eyes locked with his, and all mocking disappeared.

"That's a start," he said after a moment. His eyes almost seemed to glow. "Very flirtatious and direct. Powerful, yet feminine." This time he was the one to turn away, toward one corner of the living room. She felt a keen disappointment at the absence of his gaze, and wondered at it.

She wondered even more when she heard his next words.

"Sarah, you could consider getting some sexier panties."

She flushed. How the *hell* did he know what kind of underwear she had on? Was her panty-line showing? The plain white hip-hugger briefs that she favored had the advantage of not creeping, which she appreciated when leaping into and out of her high-sided Recaro racing seats, not to mention all the bending and twisting that she did at the shop. She felt the sides of her beltline. Maybe the elastic had snapped. But how could he see? She frowned, easing away from the counter to check her fly.

A low growl made her snap her head up. It came from the corner of her living room. The mystery of where Ricky Racer had gone was solved. He'd been relocating her clean laundry, piece by piece, from her bedroom. She remembered dumping the clothes, still warm from the dryer, onto her bed that morning and grabbing from the pile what she'd needed.

Now that same pile was in the living room, and her little dog sat on top of it while gnawing on one edge of her admittedly unsexy underwear's elastic waistband. He growled a warning at Gordon, who approached with the stealthy stalk of a large muscular tiger.

Gordon stopped and addressed the dog. "Ricky Racer, I'm dismayed at your change in attitude." Gordon sank with controlled grace into a sitting position on the carpet. He took off one shoe and offered it in exchange for the chewed underwear.

Sarah was impressed by the sacrifice. It looked like a quality tennis shoe, only slightly stained from the shop, and Gordon held it out to the dog without hesitation. "You might not get that back in the same condition," she warned.

"Anything to prevent that underwear of yours from looking any worse."

"Ha-ha." She watched, intrigued, as Gordon smoothly executed the transaction. One new-looking tennis shoe for one soggy, slightly ripped, and rather baggy and unattractive pair of undershorts. Ricky Racer snapped up the shoe and then promptly ran over to the opposite corner with it, relinquishing the pile of clothes.

"Please let me throw these away," Gordon said, pinching the elastic between two fingers. "Please?"

Sarah grinned, giving a regal gesture with her hand to indicate her permission to pass through to dump them into the kitchen trash.

The trouble was, Gordon had to squeeze between her on one side and the oven on the other to look for the trash. He didn't know where it was, and approached her where she stood next to the sink instead. She started to scoot over, but he didn't wait for her to move. She only had time to turn sideways, which allowed her hips to brush against his thigh as he passed. She sucked in her breath. What was it about him that kept getting to her in so many ways? Trusting ways, then bad ways, then whatever this way was—well, she knew what way this was— when he wasn't even *looking* at her? It was as if he traveled within a kind of aura that made her arm hairs rise in a tingling response every time he got anywhere near. If he'd just look at her with a smirk, or a wink, or generally act like a typical, predictably lecherous male, then she would know how to act. Or react, as the case was.

She kept her gulp inaudible and her thoughts to herself . . . although she did notice that he didn't look at her as he passed by going the *other* way, either. Even when it meant he had to hunt without assistance, opening two more cabinets before locating the one containing her trashcan.

Was she affecting him the same way?

Abruptly, letting her movements outdistance her confusion, she went to her dog.

So did Gordon. She was aware of each movement he took as he knelt by her. She immediately felt the tingles.

He had to have heard her sudden sharp intake of breath, but he didn't look at her.

Instead, he offered Ricky Racer one of the many small, discarded chew-toys that dotted that side of the room. As he held out the knotted strip of rawhide he spoke matter-of-factly. "Ricky, I need that shoe more than you do. How about a trade, huh?" He wiggled the rawhide, and the dog obligingly stopped ravaging the shoe and took the piece of rawhide from Gordon's hand with dainty precision. With his other hand, Gordon reclaimed his shoe.

Sarah spoke up. "If it's damaged, I'll pay for it."

"Oh, Ricky was just helping me break it in." Gordon grinned at her, and her tingles multiplied. She smoothed her hands over her arms reflexively.

As Gordon tugged his shoe back on, she stared at him, thoughtful. "You know, I have to say . . . you're not the kind of guy I expected." How could it be possible that she was starting to feel the same kind of attraction for him that she did for Craig?

He didn't pretend ignorance. He returned her gaze with a

small smile playing about his lips. "Yes. And you . . ." he scooped up her hand with the same smooth ease that he'd scooped up his shoe. Her heart thudded against her chest, and she couldn't help gasping in reaction, though she managed to do it quietly. He chafed her fingers slowly, once, then tightened his grip before letting go. The impression of warmth remained with her.

His smile became speculative. She was afraid that he'd seen in her face a reflection of the inner turmoil that had erupted at his touch. "And you aren't the completely spoiled tomboy I'd first thought. I was wrong. In fact, you are a very attractive, intriguingly multi-faceted woman. Though still a tomboy, of course."

Gordon's reminding her, the way so few people did, that she was a woman made her *feel* womanly, sitting next to him on the carpet. Or maybe it was just her becoming more and more aware of him as a man. His well-worn jeans from the shop encased strong-looking legs, one of which was mere inches from her own jeans-encased thigh. She imagined she could feel his heat radiating across the small space, meeting with hers and making a field of invisible electricity that hummed dangerously between them.

Neither of them moved. She felt a sudden longing for that zap, painful though it might be, as a relief from the growing tingles that assaulted her. Their close proximity and the continuing silence were working her over. Did he feel it?

She dared to look up, directly into his eyes, and forgot to breathe. Yep, he felt it.

Maybe it was simply her too-long-repressed sexual need, and him being so attractively *there* . . . but she suddenly couldn't quite recall what Craig's face looked like. Craig, who had abandoned her earlier that very night. And this delicious swirl of desire was like the sweetest leash pulling her closer. All thoughts disappeared under the wave of yearning that surged through her as she felt his sweet breath close to her lips. Gordon was going to kiss her!

She leaned into it.

It took her a moment to realize that the quick, rhythmic pounding she heard wasn't her heart. Somebody was racing up her stairs.

She could only think of one person who would drop in on her at night without calling first.

Sarah's eyes were still locked with Gordon's so she could tell he read everything she was feeling in an instant: disorientation, realization, guilt.

She was pretty sure it was the guilt that caused that bleak coolness to cover his face. Intimacy disappeared, replaced by a more familiar look: the "professional" mask.

The loud pounding on her door, though half-anticipated, made her jump. Gordon's suddenly wry gaze took in that reaction, too.

He rose gracefully to his feet, then merely stood waiting for her to finish smoothing her T-shirt and answer the door. With a fierce effort, Sarah regained a semblance of calm.

She strolled to her door as if she were in no hurry whatsoever, schooling her warm face not to betray her agitation. She opened the door in the middle of the next series of urgent raps.

"Hello, Craig."

# CHAPTER SIX

Craig pushed inside without an invitation.

His voice vibrated with relief. "Where *were* you? I looked everywhere—the track, the shop, I drove down about fifty different surface streets to see if you'd tried to limp the car home. I called your cell but it was turned off. I called Red, but he didn't pick up. So, where'd you go?" He folded his arms across his chest for a second, but then unfolded them right away to jiggle his keys impatiently. His agitation made her feel a dark wash of guilt and regret for worrying him.

"I've been here." She was glad that her voice came out calm. She waited for him to notice Gordon standing near the wall. He didn't.

The tension inside her stretched tighter. "Have you been looking for me this whole time?"

He gripped his keys so tightly she saw his knuckles whiten. "Sarah, what *else* would I be doing? Why didn't you stay put? Didn't you see me wave to you after your car died?"

She felt worse and worse. "I thought you were waving goodbye."

"I waved to let you know I saw what happened. I went to get my trailer. But when I got back to the track, you were gone, your car was gone . . ." He exhaled heavily. "Sarah, why didn't you wait for me?"

She simply stared at Craig. He hadn't abandoned her after all. And he was worried about her. "I got another ride," she said in a near whisper.

"You got another . . . oh." Craig noticed Gordon. "You? *You* gave her a ride?"

"I find it difficult to believe, myself."

"And yet," Craig said, stalking closer to him, his nostrils flaring, "you're still here. Wrangled yourself an invitation for your good deed, huh? Maybe looking for a little off-the-clock action?" His normally resonant tone dropped to a low, scratchy growl, all the more ominous for its comparative quiet.

Sarah watched, astonished, as Craig's body language radiated menace. He held his strong, tall frame poised tightly, bunched muscles clearly defined. The expression on his face made her heart lurch oddly. She'd never seen him act like that before. There was going to be a brawl in her apartment. And she wasn't sure who she wanted to win.

Gordon smiled coldly and showed the palms of his hands, a graceful acquiescence that admitted no weakness. "Clearly I shouldn't have bothered. Sarah." He brushed past her almost too quickly for her to feel the tingles. "See you in the morning. Early. Before the sun comes up. You have to get your car fixed and out of the way as quickly as possible."

She tried to think clearly with both men glaring at her. "And am I supposed to hitchhike?"

Watching Gordon make the connection that she didn't have a ride to work, she saw him grasp the wrist of his left arm with his right hand and twist slowly, back and forth. The muscles of his forearm stood out in ropes, but his face remained inscrutable.

"I've invested enough time in your personal transportation issues. Have your boyfriend give you a lift."

With that, he stalked out her front door. Craig marched to it and shut the door firmly, turning the lock with enough force to make the deadbolt echo in her apartment.

"Are you all right?"

Sarah nodded, looking at a spot of blank wall to gather her thoughts, not trusting her voice. She sensed Craig standing near her, the tension in him still communicating itself by his body heat and abrupt movements. She looked at him only when he touched her arm. "He didn't . . . ? He didn't hurt you, did he? If he did . . ." His eyes darkened to blue steel even as she shook her head again.

She smiled at him, beginning to enjoy his concern. His—dare she hope it?—jealousy. "Was he walking with a limp, grimacing in pain? Then he didn't hurt me."

"No, he was walking normally—like he had a stick up his butt."

Sarah grinned at Craig. Gordon didn't walk that way, but she could see how Craig'd have that impression. The dignified businessman had a stiff bearing. When he wasn't working on an engine. Or tipping beers with her. Or leaning in, almost kissing her. Sarah gulped, the remembered tingles reverberating once more through her body.

Craig extended a finger, tilted her head up to him. Her body jumped to his touch in a different, but equally elemental way. He was shaking his head at her, his lips curved into a one-sided smile that struck her as disturbingly knowledgeable. About women in general. About her in specific.

"Next time, you don't worry me like that. Promise me."

Sarah pursed her lips, making a mockery of pondering, even as her heart revved like an engine.

Craig's thumb brushed over her lips, just grazing them.

Her wide eyes locked with his.

"Well, ah . . ." Craig backed up a step, then another, suddenly looking everywhere but at her. His knowledgeable expression had vanished, replaced by a disconcerted frown that was as foreign to her as his earlier menace. "Sorry. I think there's something . . . weird in the air tonight."

"Weird is right." If the adrenaline kept surging in her, she'd soon get the shakes.

"How about I go." Craig was smiling again, a rueful one this time. "Before we do something we'll regret."

She waited until she heard his car roar to life before she said aloud, "You wouldn't regret it. But I would." Collapsing into her beanbag, she picked up a convenient *American Rodder* back issue and fanned herself with it.

Gordon knew that he should have expected Craig to accompany her into the shop that morning. Gordon himself had been the one to suggest her boyfriend give her a ride. It wasn't unreasonable to presume Craig would linger to view Sarah's broken car, even help her fix it, considering how eager he'd been to find her yesterday.

He caught himself twisting his socket wrench too fiercely. The bolt he was tightening made a gruesome squeal against the stamped steel of the engine's valve cover. He had to stop himself, back it off, and remind himself yet again that what Sarah did or didn't do wasn't his concern, so long as it didn't affect her work.

Even if she did look especially luminous with her long, water-darkened hair framing a naturally attractive face still innocent of makeup. And even though her fit, feminine figure couldn't be hidden by such masculine accoutrements as jeans and a white automotive T-shirt. She glowed with health and energy, even at six in the morning. Her bouncing walk carried her directly to him, Craig trailing a half-step behind with no expression on his face.

Gordon mastered himself enough to put on a professional smile for both of them, but he felt it slip when Sarah spoke, nodding toward the car. "You've finished that install already?

Man, don't you sleep?"

"Had a long night," he replied shortly. He slammed the hood of the car, a late-model Camaro.

"Sorry," Sarah said, looking stricken. "I forgot . . . I didn't mean to tie up so much of your evening last night."

"You didn't." He brushed hair off his forehead with the back of his hand. He looked down at her. Her face was all contrition. Sighing, he explained. "I had to stay up studying for tonight's final exams. After the first five mugs of coffee, sleep was not an option." It would be so much easier if he could despise her. If she would simply remain a self-centered brat long enough for him to affix the label, it would help his equanimity.

But if he were honest, he was only angry with himself.

"Why don't you have Craig help get your car off the trailer," he suggested. "We've got to get it out of the way before the others arrive."

"*Craig* is glad to help Sarah anytime." With one deliberate yet perfectly casual move, Craig insinuated himself half into Gordon's immediate space. He continued, smiling his challenge, "They go way back, Sarah and Craig do." Craig lingered just long enough to put a strain on Gordon's self-control, then sauntered off toward the trailer.

Sarah bit her lower lip and shrugged as she looked at Gordon. "Thanks for the ride last night."

Following Craig to the trailer, Sarah seemed deep in thought. *Well, that makes two of us.*

Gordon slid behind the wheel of the Camaro and turned the ignition key, barely noticing the smooth, throaty purr of the repaired engine. As he steered the car from the engine bay and around to the pickup area, he castigated himself again.

The boss's daughter. Of all the women in Southern California, he had to develop an infatuation for the boss's daughter.

And as if that weren't bad enough, she, of course, had a boyfriend.

And if *that* weren't bad enough, she'd had the gall to request tutoring on how to be girlie.

He barked a laugh. Unbelievable.

Yet strangely erotic.

He drove slowly, smoothly, all the while raining mental kicks and punches down on himself. He'd been foolish and impulsive last night. Not by rescuing her—that was something any decent man would do—but by visiting her apartment afterward. He shouldn't have done that. But the invigorating tête-à-tête of their conversation and her shocking request for advice had taken him by surprise. That had to be why he'd acted so irrationally.

He remembered that he'd actually had to restrain himself from helping himself to her lips. Just a few moments more and he would have. And that would have been just the beginning.

She had no idea how seductive she was. Her innocence was one of her charms.

Well, one thing was certain. He had no right to be thinking about her that way. More importantly, it wasn't in his best interests. He was being groomed to take over the shop from her own father, for God's sake . . . something that he was painfully aware Sarah didn't yet know. She wasn't interested enough in the future of the shop to know.

She'd rather race.

Gordon, on the other hand, would rather be in charge. Of everything. Not just this first shop, or even of a big corner of the industry, but all the things yet undiscovered that he could control. The long, hard climb from poverty and obscurity had taken too many years of his life for him not to finish what he'd started. Success was the end game, and prospering to a truly obscene degree with a jewel of a trophy wife by his side, was the prize. To hell with anyone who didn't fit into his plans.

He smiled. Thoughts of success always cheered him.

His next invention, the Devine Nitrous Plate, or DNP, would cement it. The speed part was brilliant in its simplicity, and simple in its manufacture. He'd always believed that the best ideas were the most straightforward ones, concepts that made others wonder why they hadn't thought of them first. It was that. His nitrous system was adjustable and electronically controlled for each power level. The electronics he'd invented would revolutionize racing.

Aside from the centering stability of this shop as his core business, he was going to make a bundle on DNP, and the other inventions to follow. He'd already confirmed the prototype's performance on his own car, and tested it up to the five setting of the ten total settings. Now he had to install it on a professional drag race vehicle, one that got a lot of hard use, ideally one piloted by a driver who made a habit of winning publicly. It was a sound marketing strategy. He could raise awareness of DNP and sell thousands in a matter of months.

All he needed to do was find a winner who would allow the part onto his engine. So far, no luck. It was a catch-22. The confirmed winners used only confirmed parts, and the parts were confirmed when the winners won.

Which meant that Gordon might have to take a chance on an unknown. Someone who was still fine-tuning an engine combination. Someone who'd risk DNP on his car, hoping for a winning edge.

As he walked back into the shop from the pick-up area, Gordon heard Sarah's raised voice.

"When were you going to tell me? After you'd left?"

"I thought you might be happy for me." Craig's soft words were clear, even at a distance. The man had a good voice, Gordon had to admit. Casual, convincing, with only a hint of reproach. Gordon didn't like that such a voice belonged to Craig.

They pushed her car, Sarah on the driver's side with one arm stuck through the open window, pushing and steering, and Craig on the other side of the car, also pushing. They spoke across the two front seats, so involved with their argument that they barely glanced up to see where they were going.

"Happy for you." Sarah thrust her weight forward, giving the car a shove. "When you sneak off to compete where the pros are made, and I'm stuck with a broken car and Carlsdale's piddly little Friday night eliminations?"

"I was afraid of this." Craig gave his side an even bigger shove. "First of all, it's not my fault your car broke. Second of all, here I am telling you, so I'm not 'sneaking' anywhere. Besides, you have to admit I'm faster, I've been doing this longer, and I'm ready for a heads-up series. You're not. Not yet."

"The hell I'm not."

But even from where he watched, unnoticed, Gordon could hear that there was more hurt than anger in her voice, and he knew she'd taken a blow with his words. Annoyance stirred in him. Craig didn't have to be such an ass. Gordon strode forward to tell him so, but suddenly he heard Craig yell.

"Brakes! Brakes!"

So involved were they in their exchange, they'd shoved the car into a fast roll toward the engine bay and the yellow Mustang was gaining speed . . . heading straight at a wall. Yelping with sudden realization, Sarah yanked the door open and jumped in, jamming her foot down on the brake pedal. The car skidded on the polished concrete floor, overshot the engine bay, sledded sideways, then slowed. Craig also hauled back on the car, and it came to a stop inches from the storage shelves lining the back wall.

Clearly shaken, Sarah nonetheless leapt back out and began pushing the car in reverse, to position it over the hoist. Craig silently helped.

As if her thoughts had never left the subject, she asked, "You really think I'm not ready for heads-up?"

Craig pushed his blond hair off his forehead with one arm. His expression revealed his discomfort with the topic. "Well, maybe you are. You know I think you're one of the best local bracket racers." He tried catching her eye with a contrite smile, but Gordon was glad to see that Sarah was having none of it.

Craig's smile faded to a pensive expression. Gordon watched him examine Sarah for a moment. Then, suddenly, Craig snapped his fingers. "I have an idea." Craig walked around the hood of her car.

Gordon began to casually move toward them both. It was time to begin work on Sarah's broken engine, get her Mustang out of the way.

Craig edged against Sarah, shoulder to shoulder, encircling her with one comradely arm. "You're going to like this idea." He paused for dramatic effect. Gordon rolled his eyes. "Will you be on my pit crew?"

"Your pit crew." Sarah repeated each word with singular lack of emphasis. She remained very still.

"Yeah." Gordon could hear the excitement in Craig's voice. "It's perfect. That way you can come too. I have two guys already, but that's the bare minimum for a crew. Things have happened so quickly since I found out about this race series— that's got to be why I didn't think of this before. Besides, you're better with tools than anyone."

"That didn't keep you from jumping ship here when your discount disappeared."

Craig waved his free hand. "I was irked, I'll admit. But I got over it. I realized I'm going to need the very best tuning to win, and that means this shop. That means you."

"It's nice to be appreciated," Sarah admitted, her voice softening. Gordon felt like growling when Craig immediately capitalized on it, giving her shoulder a squeeze as if to underscore how much he appreciated her.

"With you on my team, I can't lose. This race series is such a killer opportunity for someone like me. And now you'll be there, watching and rooting. You're not allowed to root for Jesse Stanton, or Skip Greeley," he joked, naming two well-known front-runners in the sport.

"You're actually going to race against those guys," Sarah said with some awe. "What I would give to do that. I'd probably have to dress like a trackslut just to get their attention."

Craig snorted laughter. "You, a trackslut? In an alternate dimension maybe."

Sarah's face went expressionless, which Gordon could see as he circled the pair by way of the supply shelves. He pulled one plastic container off a higher shelf, slid the identical one next to it into its place, then filled the gap with the original container. He was waiting until he was sure he could trust himself to not throw Craig all the way across the engine repair area, preferably to land on polished concrete. Head first.

"Look, Sarah. You're the best at what you do, and I could really use your help. Besides, you're dead in the water car-wise anyhow."

Gordon shook his head unbelievingly. *Dig yourself a little deeper, pal.*

"When's the first race?" Sarah asked with deceptive softness.

"Two weeks, but I've got to leave in a week to tow out there. It's a four-day drive to the first race at the St. Louis track. That's not much time to work on my car, is it?"

"And you say there are three races?"

"Yeah. The NMRC Mustang series. It's an up-and-coming

104

sanctioning body with great publicity—the perfect way to get noticed by sponsors—and these three events are back-to-back weekends in St. Louis, Kentucky, and Columbus. But, listen, this is the unbelievably great part: The NMRC World Finals in Columbus is the first time in the entire history of grassroots racing that they'll have live TV coverage on FAST! Do you know how big of a deal it is to have live instead of tape-delayed coverage? It's a fantastic opportunity. With only three races, an unknown can sweep the points and have a shot at the championship and the media at the World Finals. There are big cash prizes, too. Sarah, say you'll come."

Sarah looked at him sideways. "Okay. I'll be there."

"My odds of winning just went up." Craig looked happy. He hugged her, one-armed. "I know I'm lucky to have you on my team. Thank you."

Sarah smiled. "No, Craig." Her resolve communicated itself in nearly palpable waves. "What I mean is that I'll be racing there too."

# CHAPTER SEVEN

The resoundingly loud crash of the dropped container made Gordon swear even as he picked it up with narrow-eyed determination not to reveal any more of his surprise. The box had slipped through his fingers as soon as he'd heard Sarah's declaration of war.

That's what it was, he knew: a statement of her intention to beat Craig despite her broken car. To take him on rather than cheering him on.

It was just like her.

Out of the corner of his eye, Gordon could see that they'd stopped talking to stare at him.

He rested one palm against the container as thoughts spun through his mind. Sarah wasn't ready for a major drag race event by any stretch of the imagination. She was a bracket racer, not a heads-up racer.

Did Craig mean so much to Sarah that she was willing to enter a national competition to win him?

There was more between them than he'd thought.

Decided, he turned and walked directly toward them.

Craig had already lost interest in Gordon's accident. He seemed almost panicked as he spoke to Sarah. "Sarah, you don't understand what's involved."

"It's not complicated."

"Yes it is." Craig stood in front of her. "What you're talking about doing is impossible." He glanced at Gordon's approach, but seemed to look through him. Exhaling heavily, Craig looked back at Sarah as if he'd change her mind by sheer willpower. "For many reasons. Biggest one is, you could hurt yourself if your car's not ready. It's nowhere near ready."

Sarah lowered her voice to a confidential whisper that Gordon had to strain to hear, even though he was almost upon them. "Better find somewhere else to tune your ride, my friend. My guys will be too busy this week working on mine."

Gordon cleared his throat.

Craig ignored him. He was still focused on Sarah, his eyebrows raised with incredulity. "You have less than a week. You're completely insane."

"Guess so."

"At least my car's a contender. Yours . . ."

"Yes? What about mine?"

Gordon noticed that an odd smile had appeared on Craig's face. His eyes had ignited with a competitive light. Sarah's, he saw with trepidation, had also.

"Well, I don't want to say anything demoralizing . . ."

"Demoralize away."

Neither one of them paid the slightest attention to him.

"And shatter your cute little pretensions? What kind of friend would that make me?"

*The bodily injured kind,* Gordon thought. *First a right punch to the face, then an uppercut to the stomach . . .*

"You really don't think I can do it."

Craig turned serious. "I think you'll give it your best shot." He looked at his watch. "Whoa. I'd better get going. Got a tech-writing job to finish—the last one, if I can land a deep-pocket sponsor—and of course, now I've got to find another shop to squeeze me in this week. Since you're all booked up."

"That's right."

"That's right, she is," Gordon echoed. "In fact, I need to

speak with her about scheduling."

"Hey, look. It's Gordon. Didn't see you standing there." Craig grinned in a way that made Gordon's hands clench. "Sarah? I still hope you change your mind, but if not . . . good luck."

"To you, too." Gordon watched Sarah watching Craig saunter away.

She turned to Gordon. "You won't *believe* what he just told me," she began, before getting a good look at Gordon's face. He decided that it must look fairly forbidding. She actually flinched. "Uh, are you okay?"

"Peachy." Gordon made an effort to smooth his expression. He picked up a clipboard, glanced at the top sheet of paper without reading it, put it back down. "Do I understand correctly that you intend to enter this car in a national competition? Next week?"

"Oh, you heard." She cocked her head at him. "Yeah. What about it?"

"You can't do it."

Only her flared nostrils betrayed her as she spoke. "I'm getting tired of hearing that." She placed her palm on her car's hood as if protecting it. "So why do you think I can't do it?" He watched her watching him across the yellow hood of her car. He stilled his fingers from twisting the cap on the clipboard's pen.

He nodded to where her palm lay against the hood. "The engine, for one thing. You'd need to repair whatever's broken, upgrade, optimize, then test and tune before your car has the remotest chance of being competitive even at the lowest rung of heads-up racing. That's *heads-up* racing—direct, wheel-to-wheel competition, unlike what you're used to. And neither the prize money nor the exposure is at the lower rungs. So you'd have to ratchet up your own performance. You'd need to run nine-second ETs. I don't think you can do that in a week."

"I do." She smiled at him, her chin up at its most stubborn angle. "I'm gonna build it into a Renegade car, which means I don't have to change a lot. But I do need to add nitrous. Lots of it."

Gordon stared into her glittering eyes and at her wide, mobile lips. He wasn't quite sure if he wanted to strangle her or kiss her.

Her confidence was inspiring, even admirable. He had something more important he had to keep in mind, however, and as much as it pained him to wipe that determined, happy, excited look off her face . . . "Sarah, you can't. Not by yourself. And I'm very sorry, but this shop isn't at your disposal for such extensive personal use. It would take you all day, every day, and most of the night too, with help from others to even have a shot at being prepared, and that's just not going to happen."

She went very still. "Playing the supervisor card. I see."

"Look, I said I'd help you this morning. And every morning, before business hours," he added recklessly. "All week, if that's what it takes to repair your car."

"*Repair.* But you won't help me race. Did you know," she said with ferocious intensity, "this is my *dream?* My chance to do what I've been doing for fun, but professionally, with live TV coverage?"

Gordon tried to lighten the mood. "I thought your dream was to be more girlie."

He saw immediately that that was the wrong thing to say. She froze, her eyes wide and betrayed. Visibly reaching for her dignity, she put on a tight smile. "Clearly an impossible dream." She rooted in her large red Craftsman toolbox for a wrench. "Thanks for your offer to help. I've got it handled."

"Sarah, I'm serious about helping. I'm quite willing. And the others will arrive in—" Gordon checked his watch. "In a little more than an hour, and this has to be out of the way, as I'm sure you understand."

"I hear you. I've got it handled."

Gordon shuffled from one foot to another, feeling oddly uncomfortable. "Would you like me to get some more lights, or lift you down some boxes of transmission fluid, or anything?"

"Nope. I've got it—"

"Handled. Right." Gordon stood there for another minute as Sarah went blithely about her business, popping the hood and setting lights and draping fender protectors. When his discomfort at being so thoroughly ignored reached an unbearable level, Gordon retreated upstairs. He would check for phone messages.

As if anyone would have called in the last twelve hours.

But as it turned out, someone had.

Red had come down with a case of food poisoning at his business colleague's farewell dinner the night before and decided to take a few days off. He put Gordon in control of the shop for the interim—a gesture that Gordon knew Sarah wouldn't appreciate—with the admonition to "keep an eye on my little girl."

Gordon listened to the message, then lowered his forehead into his hands.


Over the next days, Sarah threw herself at the task of building her vehicle into a respectable racecar. On the first morning she barely accomplished removing the engine and getting it onto a stand for analysis before the guys arrived to work and she had to stop. She endured the requisite teasing over her broken car with a smile, knowing that busted cars happened to even the best racers—and she intended to be better than the best.

The guys, who'd initially ragged her, gradually took an interest in her quest. Avoiding their other jobs in favor of discussing strategy for hers, they spent time on the wrong side of the hanging plastic divider that separated her Mustang from the shop's larger work area. Will and Lee, especially, held hour-long debates over whether to install a supercharger or a turbocharger onto her car, even when supposedly working on the shop's work orders.

If her father had been around to enforce the rules, she knew they wouldn't have dared so much or been so blatant, but as it was, by the third day the entire work force had radically extended their lunch hour to help build her car. The larger work area remained silent and all but unoccupied.

From where he was stuck up in the office performing accounting and other management duties in Red's absence, Gordon must have noticed the extended silences. Sarah figured he was humoring her, the way her dad often did when she pursued a race goal. She didn't have time to wonder about it, though, and didn't see him open the upstairs office door, or hear his quiet approach the third day, until he stood next to the half-circle of men surrounding her Mustang.

When she did notice, she jumped, startling Will into silence.

With hands fisted by his sides, Gordon spoke in a low, flat monotone that carried all the more menace for its softness. "She doesn't have time for a supercharger or turbocharger. Or a nitrous kit. Quite frankly, I don't have time to pick up the slack on all the neglected jobs over *there*," he said, nodding toward the pile of work orders. He stared over the heads of everyone present. "Please get back to work."

Sarah felt her face darken with embarrassment for her friends. And irritation. Her hands went to her hips automatically before she realized that her fingers were still coated with oil and transmission fluid and she'd just wiped some of it on her white T-shirt, Craig's recent gift. The shirt showed his new car and his signature, as if he were already famous.

She'd immediately decided to use it for a work-shirt. Remembering, she wiped her hands across the shirt deliberately, taking destructive pleasure in ruining the pristine whiteness.

How *dare* Gordon dismiss her guys like that and order her around as if she were a short-order cook? If her dad were back, *he'd* let her work in peace. He'd understand and respect this huge goal of hers. She protested. "Gordon, I'm down to my last three days. Give me a break."

"A break. You mean a longer break than two and a half hours with free labor commandeered from the work-flow system you set up?" As he stalked toward her, she had to physically stiffen her spine and tighten all her muscles to keep herself from backing away. She noticed that all the other guys except for Will and Lee had already vanished, melted out of the circle of contention that suddenly boiled around her car.

"You want more breaks, but I spent a full, unpleasant hour on the phone this morning apologizing to one of your father's more loyal, not to mention wealthy, customers because his street rod won't be ready in time for the Street Rod Nationals. Only one project of many gathering dust around here, I might add. It's clear that instead of performing the job I've designated for you, you're taking advantage of your father's absence to work on your car during business hours."

The way he was looking at her, she could have been something scraped off his shoe. "Now wait a minute," she began.

But Gordon cut her off. "I've waited three days to see if this situation resolved on its own. I'd hoped you'd finally realize that you're attempting the impossible. But enough's enough. Now I'm going to assess the damage this delay's caused." With a raised eyebrow, his expression managed to condemn both Will and Lee, who stood by Sarah, as well. She watched him dismiss her from his mind as he turned his back. Anger zinged through her.

She controlled it, speaking to the two guys. "Lee, Will, would you mind excusing us for a sec?" Her voice vibrated with a tension that made Gordon stop, then turn around slowly.

"Uh, sure." Will shouldered Lee in the direction of the other techs, where Gordon had been headed until a moment ago.

Now he walked back to her with a poorly concealed scowl. "Something else?"

With his pressed slacks and his buttoned-up blue shirt, he was obviously not dressed to help out the techs. Even so, his tapered waist and broad shoulders, his narrow hips, his predatory stance made him as masculine as any jeans-and-leather-clad guy, and she could have wished he didn't look quite so aesthetically appealing. If only he looked prissy. But he didn't. He was as handsome as a *GQ* heartthrob, and he commanded people as ruthlessly as a gang leader. Despite her irritation with him—or perhaps fueled by it—her blood surged hotly in her veins.

It was impossible to remain cool and indifferent. It didn't help that he was right, either. About some things.

She looked into his determined hazel eyes and steeled herself against her own inexplicable reaction to him. He was the one obstacle standing between her and her chance to make it in real racing, *and* to show Craig how badly he'd underestimated her. She *knew* she could win. All she needed was her car finished in three days.

She couldn't let Gordon get in her way.

She glanced around to make sure that they were alone, or as alone as one could get in the shop's work area. She could hear rock music—the techs on the other side of the heavy plastic divider had switched on the CD player. Tools clicked against metal, indicated that they'd picked up where they'd left off on the street rod rebuild.

She smiled grimly and stepped close enough to Gordon that he blinked in confusion. She had to crane her neck a bit to meet his gaze, but she did it with some effort. Simultaneously she poked him right in the middle of his broad, dress-shirt-covered chest with one finger to emphasize her words. Since she was looking into his eyes at the same time, she clearly saw the look of surprise that he couldn't hide. "You're out of line," she declared.

"Excuse me?"

"I never said I wouldn't work on my car during business hours. Or that I wouldn't get the guys to help me out."

He bristled. "I told you *not* to."

Sarah smiled grimly at the way Gordon visibly struggled to hold onto his temper. What she would say next might push him over the edge. "Gordon, I don't take orders from you."

Sure enough, new color appeared high in his cheeks, and his hazel eyes snapped and flashed. She could feel the ire radiating off him in waves, standing as close as she was. His lips thinned as he gritted out: "Yes. You do. By your father's direction, you do."

"He's not here. And even if he were, he doesn't care what I do. He doesn't get disturbed when I work on personal projects, or even when I leave to go racing."

"Are you sure about that?" Gordon's voice remained quiet, but dark shadows skidded across his eyes, as if he knew something she didn't.

It made Sarah pause for a moment, remembering the way her dad had reacted the last time she took off to go racing. He'd objected at first. Hadn't he?

Then she shook off the uncertainty. Yes, he'd objected at first, but he'd come around. Like he always did. And always would.

Gordon was a bad influence on him, she decided.

"I know more about what goes on at my shop than you do," she retorted. "You think you can come along, sweet-talk him into handing you the wheel around here, change whatever you want and micromanage the rest? Well, you can't, and you won't.

I'm the head tech. I've been the one getting things done here all year."

"Have you really? Then what would you call that backlog of work orders?" His quiet voice was cool and determined.

"I'd call it typical," she admitted. "But it's typical for lots of speed shops, especially the ones with a reputation for quality. We're always flooded with work."

"Has it ever occurred to you that we could be far more 'flooded with work' if only it didn't take weeks or months to complete each order? Did you know that this place barely breaks even, but it's capable of seven-figure profit?"

Taken aback by his impassioned tone, Sarah almost missed his possessive "we." He really was invested in the shop's success, she marveled. "What's it to you?" she asked, honestly curious. "You're a hired hand like everyone else. You aren't making a commission. Are you?" She waited until he shook his head, terse. "Then what's the difference to you whether we complete two, or ten work orders each week?"

He looked at her coolly. "I find it important to deliver a day's work for a day's pay."

"Oh-ho, and you think I don't. My methodology offends your work ethic. Is that what this is all about?" She tried to needle him, but was disappointed to see that his handsome face didn't so much as twitch. He was granite. A classic granite statue plunked between her and her goals.

Her physical attraction to him was inhibiting her more quick-witted jabs and retorts, she realized with consternation. As she cast about for something sufficiently withering to say, he beat her to it.

"You don't have a work ethic. I wonder if you even have a rudimentary sense of honor."

*Ouch.* His insult had the effect of a slap to her psyche. Desperately trying to maintain her dignity, she pressed her lips together tightly. Her body vibrated with the force of keeping her normally slow-to-boil temper under control as his words resonated in her mind. *"No work ethic . . . a rudimentary sense of honor."* He actually had the nerve to attack her *honor,* of all things. If he only knew.

She carried more honor and integrity around in her little finger than anyone else she knew. Just last month at the track in a local heads-up race, her third round opponent came over to ask for help. He'd broken a valvespring and didn't have a spare, and asked Sarah if by chance she had an extra. She did, and loaned it to him along with the valvespring tool to help him change it. He got his car fixed. Then he proceeded to beat her in the race. But in that case losing didn't matter. She had helped a fellow racer, just as she would hope to be helped herself if the shoe were on the other foot. In the racing world, that was the ultimate in honor.

And as if that weren't enough, as a woman she was a shining paragon of honor and nobility compared to others. Listening to the stories the shop guys spilled, she was an angel compared to the dishonorable wives who robbed their buddies during divorce; the flaky women indiscreetly yakking away all sorts of secrets about their boyfriends to anyone who'd listen; the deceitful women showing one side of themselves early in relationships and then morphing into Susie Wondershrew once things got serious.

She had honor. Gordon was an idiot.

But as her thoughts swirled in self-righteous circles inside her mind, she recognized that there might be a slight element of truth to what he'd said.

Very slight. It wasn't that she didn't have barrels full of honor. But maybe her hours off racing weren't perfectly compatible with an ideal work ethic, technically speaking. Even with racing as her real and true calling, she supposed her dad did have the right to a little more reliability.

She reluctantly nodded her head, a regal concession. Hoping she looked to him like a granite statue too, and fully as unmoved and expressionless as him—and maybe just a little bit tougher—she tonelessly said, "I can catch up the work orders."

Just as he began to nod and turn away, she added, "*And* I can finish prepping my car."

With admirable control, he merely paused, then raised an eyebrow. "Exactly how do you intend to accomplish this miracle? And who will take care of the work orders when you traipse off to the races?" His eyes flashed, but she couldn't tell if it was with irritation or honest curiosity.

She felt suddenly tired. There was so much work ahead of her, especially if she had to put in time with the shop work too. She also had to take care of Ricky Racer. The complicated scope of her next few days loomed ahead of her, daunting. And Gordon just stood there in his pressed slacks, clipboard in hand like the world's most overdressed and hard-to-please gym trainer.

She wiped her hands absently on her already-greasy T-shirt. The images of Craig's car and signature were nearly buried under the gunk. She decided to ignore Gordon's question about who'd handle what in the shop while she was away. There were too many other things to worry about. "Gordon, if you're not going to help me, would you mind letting me get back to work?"

"You have the most infuriating tunnel vision." Sarah saw him looking at Craig's old T-shirt. Gordon began twisting his clipboard's pen cap again with his fingers. "You know you can't possibly work on both. It's impossible, unless you plan to sleep here."

"Got a pillow?"

"Going to sleep in the back seat of your car?"

"Have a better place in mind?"

His eyes flamed. If she wasn't mistaken, he was thinking the same thing she was. She sucked in her breath, surreptitiously she hoped, and tried to think of something to say to bring the subject back onto safer ground. "I'm not going to let you sabotage my chance to compete," she told him. "It's very important to me."

He nodded and gave his pen cap a final twist. "Very well. This time. Don't expect assistance from employees during business hours. And see that you do address the work orders. You may also work on your own, personal projects. On your own time, of course. Agreed?"

She hated feeling like she had to have his permission to do what she already planned to do. Reminding herself that he was being as accommodating as he knew how to be, she swallowed a couple dozen different rude retorts, and the sensation was like choking. She nodded diplomatically instead. "Agreed."

"Good luck, then," he said. *You'll need it,* she heard. She restrained herself from giving his perfect granite butt a swift kick as he walked away. *I'm irritated because I'm overwhelmed,* she told herself. Had nothing to do with Mister Managerial making her feel like a beggar in her own domain.

But to race professionally, on camera, for money . . . the electrifying possibility surged over her, demanding her focus. Just the thought of such a thing fired her up like nothing else. It would be *heaven* to do what she loved for a living.

She grabbed a wrench. It was lunchtime, and therefore her personal time. Time to work. " *'Sticky smoke, speed dope, making me high,'* " she began singing her favorite rock song. She removed the fuel injection subassembly. " *'Ripping down the quarter mile, making you cry!'* " She worked on her car with an equally fast tempo that soon had her sweating, swearing, and busting her knuckles . . . and vowing she wouldn't miss the window of racing opportunity that loomed dead ahead.

# CHAPTER EIGHT

"I'm getting too old for this," Red said. He sat hunched over a stack of papers on his desk with his fingers massaging his temples.

Surprised at the confession, Gordon stared at the man across the large office. Now that he thought about it, Red actually hadn't been quite the same since he'd returned that morning from his days away from the shop. The food poisoning seemed to have leached away some of his vitality, but he looked more haggard than could be explained by a bout with bacteria. Gordon carefully laid his pen on his own desk.

"Oh, you don't need to look like that," Red said, correctly interpreting Gordon's glance. "I'm healthy enough. Won't be keeling over anytime soon."

"Of course not." Gordon stopped, unsure of how to proceed.

"What do you think about Sarah?" Red asked, the sudden change of subject startling but not completely unrelated, Gordon knew.

*I think she's the one who's making you feel like keeling over.* Then again, she might be the one to keel over first. The grueling, round-the-clock schedule she'd been keeping in the last few days would have made most men he knew collapse, but somehow Sarah managed to slowly prep her racecar and stay on top of each day's work orders. If her workmanship on her own car was half as good as the results she generated with the work orders, she might actually be the one to beat.

He smiled, remembering their exchange of the other day. The unspoken tension between them hummed whenever they were even in the same room. Did she feel it? She had to. How much stronger might it be if they acknowledged it? He'd seen her makeshift pallet near the storage area, pulled up next to Ricky Racer's dog crate. He knew Sarah slept in the shop when exhaustion caught up with her. How many times in the past two days had he been tempted to return to the shop at midnight with that pillow she'd so casually requested?

He'd noticed growing bruise-colored circles beneath her eyes. The night hours spent prepping for the first race were taking their toll. Her determination made him want to abandon his own duty to pitch in and help her, the way he knew Will and Lee did during the day when they thought he wasn't paying attention.

Her single-minded intensity astounded him, impressed him . . . and infuriated him, because it was at least partly for *Craig*.

None of which was appropriate for Gordon to share with Red. He appreciated the man's candor, but couldn't bring himself to match such forthrightness; not about his daughter.

"What do I think about your giving her the next three weeks off from the shop to race, plus this afternoon to test her car at the track, you mean?" Gordon asked, keeping the topic limited to strictly business.

He wasn't sure how much the older man guessed of his thoughts, but knew it was more than he'd wished by Red's keen gaze and long, slow pause before answering.

"Yeah. She was so glad when I gave it to her without a fuss. When she left today to test and tune, she actually kissed me." Red tapped his cheek fondly, his eyes distant. "She's happy. Anyone can see she's in her element. Makes it that much harder, what I'll do to her."

"She's made her choice," Gordon said, hearing the harshness in his own voice. He spoke as much to convince himself as Red. "She's taking three weeks off this time. What'll it be next time? Nobody forced her to put the shop a distant second to her racing hobby. She doesn't want the responsibility of business ownership."

"Just the same, it'll be hard."

"She's worked here a long time?" Gordon asked, gently probing.

"After she dropped out of college, oh, almost two years ago now," Red assented. He grinned suddenly. "She's a bit of a tomboy, isn't she? Irresponsible and wild and stubborn. Not like her mother was at all. I should have put my foot down long ago. Racing is dangerous. The shop is, too, of course, but it's not exactly an extreme sport, working here. Happy mucking around in the grease, she was, holding her own with the mechanics in the back. Maybe I could have guided her better." Red shook his head, his eyes looking inward. "It'll be hard," he repeated.

"Are you sure you want to do this? If I buy you out next month, and you retire, I won't need—I won't *want*—a partner." Gordon spoke the warning gently, but he meant every word. Even with his attraction to the girl, even though she wasn't bad as a mechanic, he wouldn't dream of gifting Sarah with partnership. It wasn't in his plan.

Gordon crushed an odd feeling of guilt. He knew Red was making the right decision.

Red indicated the piles of paperwork on his desk. "I'm just tired of wading through this stuff. Records, correspondence, reports, meetings. You've taken most of it off my hands already. Why not the rest? It's time. I," Red declared, "would rather enter 'Honey' in every custom and classic truck show in the state. Not become more nearsighted than I already am."

"You've certainly earned it," Gordon said roughly. He'd personally seen the man work on weekends and manage his employees as cunningly as he managed himself, all with an easy grin like the one he was wearing now. If he played as hard as he worked, he would be a show champion within a year. "Sarah won't be happy with your decision, of course," Gordon pressed.

Red tilted his large head and a rare scowl crossed his face, making him look for a moment like a fierce Irish warrior. "Being unreliable has consequences. In this case it means she won't get the top-dog position. You will."

"When will you tell her?"

"You don't want to buy me out right now, huh? So much for golf this afternoon." Red sighed plaintively. "Well. I figure she's got her mind full of racing right now—last-minute tuning, the trip out next week, the competitions—so I'm going to wait till she gets back. I wouldn't want to wreck my little girl's concentration."

Was that pride Gordon heard in Red's voice? Protectiveness? Regret? Probably all three. A man who'd allow his daughter to pick her best friends from among mechanics—and look like one of them—would of course have his priorities skewed. *None of my business,* Gordon tried to tell himself. *None—of—my—business.*

"Mind if I drop by Carlsdale this afternoon and pay her a visit?" he heard himself ask. At Red's quick look, he hastened to add, "I won't say anything about your decision. I respect that it's your place to tell her. She leaves in the morning, and I have some last-minute productivity questions." He cleared his throat, as surprised by his own impulsiveness as by his trumped-up excuse for it.

Red nodded once, then gave Gordon's perfectly clear desk a wry glance, grinning at him. "You seem to be better at this than me. Damn college boy. Go on, have fun."

"Thank you, Red." Gordon pushed out his chair to stand. An unexpected surge of affection for Red flowed through him. "Don't strain your eyes over that pile of paperwork, now. Elderly short-timers shouldn't take unnecessary risks with their health."

Red roared and flung his pencil at him, but Gordon dodged, escaping the shared office with a mounting sense of anticipation.

It was an impulse that brought him out to Carlsdale. Gordon frowned, examining the strange sensation. An odd, almost light-headed feeling. He decided he didn't deal well with impulses. The thirty-minute drive down the interstate to Carlsdale's exit ramp was enough time to begin to regret making the trip. It wasn't strictly necessary. Spontaneity was for those who didn't have such large goals and such a well-detailed map of how to reach them.

He must feel more guilty about the Sarah situation than he'd thought, Gordon realized as he took the turnoff. But that wasn't necessarily a bad thing. He was simply exhibiting perfectly healthy, normal signs of conscience by this courtesy trip down to say goodbye to the girl. Never mind those images that plagued him, memory-snapshots of wide lips, a lithe figure unsuccessfully hidden by T-shirts, and most of all, her stubborn, brilliant green eyes.

Gordon's shifting hand reached across to the passenger seat to the small cardboard box containing his latest invention, as if the small rectangle was a steadying anchor to his mind's unrest. He was multitasking, after all. He patted the box, letting his hand remain on top of it. This little trip wasn't completely unproductive. His prototype was as ready as it would ever be to test on his Mustang. Once he determined that it installed as easily and performed as well in the field as he predicted it would, he could begin the manufacturing and marketing phases.

Plan of action determined, Gordon felt better. He paid the

bored attendant at the booth, then negotiated the curved, narrow road leading to the parking lot and pits.

As the only local dragstrip, it wasn't very impressive—small, with minimally maintained pavement, skeleton-crew personnel, and bleachers so old that the metal had long since faded to a brown rust color and the wooden seats to an aged gray—but at least it was near the ocean where the high atmospheric pressure aided speed and tuning. It was one of the few things the track had going for it.

As the only place to race within three hours, it was popular despite its worn surfaces.

Distant cheering greeted his ears when he stepped out of his car. Someone had just made a good pass, he surmised. Maybe even Sarah.

He decided to temporarily hold off on his own work and head directly toward the staging lanes. He'd take a peek at the race action, find Sarah and politely wish her luck, then get down to the business of putting the prototype—he already thought of it as DNP, or Devine Nitrous Plate—on his car for a few passes of his own.

He turned his head, looking to the right and left as he approached. Where was she? Shielding his eyes from the glare of the sun, Gordon scanned the pits, the bleachers, the staging lanes. Ah, there she was, just steering into the lanes again, her yellow Mustang dingy with test-hours of track dust.

Walking closer, he realized that he never would have recognized her without her car. In profile, her helmet shielded her face and hair from scrutiny, and her strong, capable fingers twirling the steering wheel didn't reveal so much as a speck of jeweled rings or nail polish to even identify her gender. She could have been any young guy awaiting his shot at the 1320.

She saw him a moment after he spotted her. A reflection of the sun flashed on the front of her visor for a moment, then she pushed her arm through her rolled-down window to wave vigorously. "Hey! Over here!"

Gordon noticed that at the sound of the female voice, many guys turned their heads to look in the direction of the staging lanes, and some ahead of Sarah craned their necks looking back. The world of racing was still mostly a man's world, Gordon observed wryly.

"Congratulations on getting your car running again," he began.

"Thank you. Look at this!" she crowed, waving a rectangular piece of paper like a miniature pom-pom. "Just look. And this one, too. And this one."

They were her timeslips. Remembering the distant sound of cheering when Gordon first arrived, he hazarded a guess. "You're doing pretty well, aren't you?" He read the numbers on the timeslips. "*Very* well." He was impressed. Not even his own car was that fast, and he'd paid big bucks for a Cobra. Of course, he hadn't installed DNP yet, either.

The sight of him at the track seemed to register with her for the first time. "Gordon, what on earth are you doing down here? During *work hours?*"

Her question made him smile. "Even workaholic manager-types need a break every now and then. Plus I have a new part to test." He watched as she removed her helmet, shaking out her wheat-colored hair. She gave a satisfied sigh, the fabric of her T-shirt tightening gratifyingly across her chest as she smoothed strands of hair off her face. It was a beautiful image . . . until she scratched furiously at her scalp.

She noticed his look. "These things make you itch," she explained, setting her helmet on the seat next to her. "Especially when you have long hair."

"I hadn't considered that," Gordon replied. He took in her sweat-streaked face, her eyes and lips totally devoid of cosmetic artifice. The look was attractive, refreshing. It made her appear very young, and highlighted the lively spark in her green eyes. "You're a very natural person, aren't you?"

He could tell that she knew to what he referred. Her reply was short. "Out here there's not time to be anything else."

Had he offended her? He made an effort to keep his next words pertinent to racing: "I didn't mean that in a negative way. You look capable—like a pro behind the wheel. I almost didn't recognize you. At first," he said sincerely, hoping to erase her earlier impression that he thought looks mattered on the track, "I couldn't even tell whether you were a guy or girl sitting there. Just a competitive racer to be taken seriously."

Now why would that kind of compliment make her blanch and squint her eyes? She was over her "how to be girlie" phase. But just as clearly, his words hadn't helped. And he'd come all the way down here to ease his conscience. This would never do. Her formerly wide, expressive lips were expressionless.

"You'll do great next week in Columbus." Gordon looked at her hopefully. Her lips uncompressed a little.

"St. Louis is first. I think I will too."

No false modesty with her, Gordon noted. He supposed she needed none. She had her did-it-herself car, years of racing experience, and even the edge—he knew it was an edge, whether she was aware of it or not—of being an attractive woman competing on a man's playing field. Sitting in the driver's seat with a helmet on, her gender would be indeterminate, but whenever she stepped out, it would be impossible to hide. She would be an object of attention whether her car won or not.

*Hmmm.*

She jumped in her seat as a horn blared from directly behind Sarah's car. Gordon immediately saw why. There was an expanding open space in the lanes in front of her car. She needed to move up.

He backed away from her car, observing that embarrassment had brought lots of color to Sarah's cheeks, almost enough to be taken for makeup. "I'll see you after," he told her, but she'd touched her foot to the throttle at the same time, making her car leap forward a trifle too fast for the staging lanes. He stared after her, annoyed until he remembered his idea.

If her pass was as impressive as her timeslip claimed, he could seriously consider the brand-new marketing opportunity that had just entered his field of vision.

He made his way to the stands and settled onto the bench to watch Sarah and her car with great intensity.

Sarah went through the routine of staging automatically, her disgruntled thoughts preventing the highest levels of concentration. Even as she feathered the brake to enter the first of the two staging beams, his words repeated themselves, rekindling and confirming her concern.

*"I couldn't even tell whether you were a guy or girl sitting there."*

She felt her teeth bare in a grimace.

But this was a drag strip, for God's sake. She wasn't *supposed* to sport the badges of femininity here.

His comment still bothered her.

As she sat there with the top pre-stage bulb lit on the Christmas tree, her opponent inched forward and lit the top bulb in his lane. Grateful for her helmet concealing her features, she spoke fiercely and aloud. "Concentrate, you stupid, pit-poppy wannabe conceited little trackslut." She couldn't think of anything lower to call herself.

Why should she *care* if she was mistaken for a guy? Why should it bother her so much more this time, with Gordon doing the mistaking? She had to *refuse* to care. She'd spoken the truth when she'd told Gordon that there was no time for vanity at the track. Not if one wanted to win.

And she wanted nothing more than to win.

The knowledge that he was watching her car made her hands slippery on the wheel. With a grip that made her forearm muscles stand out in slender ropes, she squeezed the wheel, trying with the effort to squeeze all thoughts of Gordon from her mind.

Her opponent finally went "all the way in" and staged, and Sarah let up on her brakes just enough to allow her car to creep forward to light the stage beam, signaling that both cars were ready to go.

Less than a second later the Christmas tree flashed green, and in the split second before that she'd already released her brake and pressed down hard with her right foot. Her reaction time felt dead-on, her car solid and smooth as it leapt forward . . . but her mind played traitor. He was watching. What did he see?

Did he *like* what he saw?

It wasn't a long interruption of her focus, but it was sufficient to throw her off. Her legs and arms, physiological machinery, stuttered, costing her precious tenths of seconds as her car swerved slightly.

But then the finish line cones flashed past and it was over.

Cursing herself until she ran out of breath, she turned off the track to collect her timeslip. She looked at it glumly. Then raised her eyebrows. It wasn't as bad as she'd thought. In fact . . . she reached for the old slips to compare . . . it was only off by a tenth, and her reaction time was her best yet.

That was something. But still she cursed herself, because there simply wasn't room for that kind of discrepancy next week. Her reaction time *shouldn't* have improved, and her pass *should* have remained smooth and utterly predictable.

Maybe Gordon hadn't noticed the swerve.

"Oh, you're pathetic," she muttered at the part of her brain that had originated the thought.

Anyway, he surely would have noticed. He noticed everything.

Where was he? She yanked off her helmet when it impeded her view. She didn't like the idea of him gloating where she couldn't see him. She wondered when he'd get around to trying to talk her out of leaving in the morning, "for her own good," or "for the good of the shop." Why else would he *really* have come down to Carlsdale? She peered at the bleachers as she drove, searching for his tall figure.

He wouldn't have left already, would he? She craned her neck.

A man stepped directly in front of her car, and she stomped on her brakes.

Gordon's hands slapped against her hood.

With jerky movements that spoke of agitation, he opened the passenger door and climbed in.

"Sorry about that," she muttered, feeling herself blush again. Now he could give her a hard time for nearly flattening him, too. She drove forward, her gaze fixed to the poorly maintained stretch of road connecting the track to the pit area where she'd parked Dad's Suburban and the trailer she'd used for the first time to tow to the track. She felt the weight of Gordon's stare, heard him clear his throat.

*Here it comes.*

"Sarah, I did come down here for one other reason. It's—"

"I know, I know. Don't go to the national races. Did Dad send you down? Let me save you the time. My mind's made up." She gave him a determined grin that she hoped expressed boatloads of confidence. Her grin faded as she watched him shake his head.

"Uh, no. Red didn't send me to change your mind. Though perhaps he should have." Then, as if he'd given the subject a lot of thought, he said, "I have no further doubt of your ability. Of course, you might want to keep an eye on that mid-track wobble."

She grimaced. She'd *known* he'd notice her tiny swerve. Nit-picky little man. Well, not so little. He took up a lot of car space with those long, powerful legs and his broad shoulders. He looked rather wedged-in, actually.

He continued with a dignity that curbed her scrutiny. "At any rate, I've had something of a last-minute idea that could help both of us."

She glanced at him in surprise, noting the way he'd focused all of that high-powered intensity of his directly on her again. She suppressed a shiver. He really needed to stop doing that.

"I'm open to ideas," she said slowly. She steered into position behind the shop's flatbed trailer, shutting off her engine in the same movement. She turned to him, hoping that the sudden silence coupled with her own stare—one she hoped was one-tenth as intense as his—would have as disconcerting an effect on him.

She saw a muscle jump on his jaw, but that was it. "Remember when I told you that I had a new part to test here? My new DNP component will give you the edge you need."

"The edge I need."

"You've been working so hard to prove yourself to Craig. Here's your chance."

Her mind whirled and darted, making connections. She wanted to correct Gordon's misapprehension about her racing for Craig. The truth was that she wanted to prove herself to herself *and* Craig. Winning would mean that being a tomboy could carry big rewards instead of just being a comfort zone. She shrugged and kept silent, concentrating on Gordon's offer. He was willing to give her his newly invented part . . . was he serious? He seemed serious.

She thought, then shook her head. "Thanks, but I drive out

there first thing tomorrow morning. I don't have time to install and test a new part."

"You do have time, if I help."

"So," she said, thinking it through aloud. "You came down here to test a new part, but when you saw my numbers you decided to give this part to me instead, for the big race. I get it. Basic marketing. I bet you have racing decals all ready to go, too? Big flashy ones." She chuckled, feeling a little disappointed. Of course it was ridiculous to expect Gordon to be visiting her and helping her for personal reasons.

"Yes. I've already prepared the standard marketing tools as part of my business plan. I do have professional stickers for DNP. They're reasonably attractive."

Sarah shrugged, already decided. "I don't care what they look like," she declared. "If your DNP can pick up my car's ET to make me competitive with the top drivers, then I'll cover every square inch of my car with your decals, even if they're magenta and shaped like spiders." She gave him a grin. "Well, shall we begin? The sunshine only lasts all day." She flipped the toggle, popping her hood like punctuation, then jumped out to fetch her toolbox from her dad's Suburban.

Out of the corner of her eye she watched his struggle to get out of her car. His look of concern as he pried his body from the narrow racing seat made her grin widely. Her seat didn't seem to want to let him go.

She couldn't blame it. Gordon's perfect backside looked pretty wonderful when he strode away to fetch his DNP component. She caught herself staring. *Bad girl.* She had Craig. Partly. She would fully, soon. There was no percentage in ogling Gordon.

None at all.

# CHAPTER NINE

Gordon felt inordinately pleased at Sarah's awed expression when she pulled off her helmet again. She'd just completed her third pass with DNP, and it could only be described as a roaring success: steady, fast, and utterly indistinguishable from her first two passes after the part was installed. She handed him her third timeslip as carefully as if it were a precious document.

"It's incredible," she told him. "I don't think I need to keep testing."

Gordon compared the timeslips. Her time was respectable. It would be sufficient. "It's getting dark. We'd better get you loaded up and on your way. I'm sure you have some last-minute packing to do."

"Not really." Her voice was richly satisfied, and he could tell she still savored her last pass. "Most of my stuff is packed into the Suburban already. I'll be leaving real early in the morning."

He nodded, walking beside her car as she steered it back to the truck and trailer. She was cutting it close for such a long drive, especially one in which she towed a car behind her. Speeding wouldn't be a good idea.

With him directing and her careful positioning, they loaded her Mustang onto the flatbed trailer. Sarah tightened the wheel straps. She didn't look at him. "You set the nitrous controller at five. What would happen if I dialed it higher?"

"Don't." Gordon gave her a stern look that went completely unnoticed, since she contemplated her car rather than him. Still perched up on the trailer, she traced the outline of the large door-decal he'd given her. The red oval actually looked tasteful and objectively attractive, he knew, with the DNP lettering in white and a gradient spray-pattern that illustrated the power-adding injection of nitrous. It matched the other four stickers placed on the hood, the other door, and a miniature version on the rear window. "Sarah. The plate is set at five out of a possible ten, where it's safe. It'll help both speed and consistency, as you've seen. But until that prototype's higher settings are fully tested—and by that I mean in my own simulations at the shop as well as far more extensively here at the track—then you simply cannot risk dialing it higher."

"Everything's a risk."

Gordon wanted to shake her. He breathed slowly and controlled his exasperation. Stronger persuasion was clearly called for. "Do you know what happens to a body in a car fire? The first thing that usually happens is that you are thrust into immediate shock by the force of the explosion and the heat of the flames. Because you can't see to control the car, it often hits the wall, hard. Many drivers are knocked unconscious and burn to death. Even if you're still conscious, you're rattled from hitting the wall at more than a hundred mph, and by the time you bring the car to a stop, you're totally engulfed in flames. Your fire suit will give you between fifteen and thirty seconds of protection from serious burns, but you'll feel the heat, which means most people panic and can't remember how to unhook the safety harnesses. At that point, the fire is breaching the Nomex in the fire suit, and you start to burn as you struggle to free yourself of not only the belts, but also crawl over the roll-cage and out of the car. This is the point where the oxygen is completely gone from inside the car, and you pass out and burn to death. Nobody really knows what that feels like, but the scientists say the skull protects your brain, so that's the last thing to die, meaning that you might feel agonizing pain the entire time you're burning to death."

Her eyes rounded for a moment, and he saw her throat work as she swallowed. Then she clearly shrugged off the images. She was skeptical and blasé once more. "What are the chances of that happening."

"*Whatever you do* . . . don't turn it up past five. That's an order."

"Order? What do you think this is, the military?"

"Promise me, or it comes off."

"Okay, okay. I promise I won't do anything to get turned into a crispy critter." Her arm snaked into her open window and her fingers returned to the knob on the dash, tapping it, and he could tell she itched to twist it further. Perhaps just to annoy him.

"I'm serious, Sarah. It's still a prototype. The specs are an unknown past five. Exceeding them could have catastrophic consequences."

He was relieved when she withdrew her arm and hopped down from the trailer. "So, Sarah . . ." His voice trailed off as he realized that he sounded too hearty. He sounded like a grandfather about to ask about her school day.

The wide, happy smile that she gave him had him blinking in confusion.

Not sure what to say, he simply looked at her. Sincerity, determination, and if he wasn't mistaken, a growing fondness was being offered up to him if he correctly interpreted those bright green eyes. He liked the way she smiled so easily and without the slightest artifice directly into his eyes. He felt himself smiling back tentatively.

Then she lifted her toolbox off the trailer and carried it with only the smallest amount of visible strain toward the back of the big Suburban. When she fished for her keys in her pocket, balancing the toolbox on her hip, he leapt forward to lift the toolbox out of her arms.

"Thank you," she said. She sounded more amused than pleased. For a moment he was tempted to drop the toolbox on the ground. Why should his chivalry *amuse* her?

He had to admire the attractively well-developed lean muscles of her arms as she rearranged heavy objects in the back, though. She really was a tomboy. He exhaled silently, regretting the disappointment she'd feel about Red's choice. When Sarah returned to find that her father had sold his company to Gordon, she would probably feel very betrayed. By both of them.

He already regretted the loss of her easy, fond smile.

She folded open the double doors to the huge truck and indicated that he should place the toolbox within.

He wasn't sure, at first, whether it would fit.

The back was stuffed. Four spare tires, boxes of replacement parts, auxiliary-powered lamps, extra oil and transmission fluid, a heavy-duty jack and jackstands, and then there was the luggage. He counted two battered black rectangles shoved crookedly into the back corner, handles turned out for easy access, three identical forest-green backpacks bulging with their contents, and a tall cardboard wardrobe balanced between a tire iron and what he assumed at first was a generous collection of fluffy blankets.

It was filled, stacked to the roof. Aside from the narrow corridor of blankets, and the slot where he saw the toolbox belonged, the entire back of the enormous truck had been used.

As Gordon stuffed the toolbox into the slot, something caught his eye. He looked more closely at the pile of blankets. An expanse of soft ivory sheepskin—with a glint of gold lettering— looked familiar, as if he'd seen it recently somewhere else. Then he knew where he'd seen it. Recognition made him frown.

"Sarah, that's a dog bed."

He felt the rough cotton of her shirt graze against him as she shrugged. "I can't leave Ricky Racer with Dad for three whole weeks. Even if he *liked* Ricky, which he doesn't—he has a prejudice against so-called 'kick-dogs'—Ricky would have . . . well, he'd have separation anxiety. He cries." She stared, clearly daring Gordon to call her sentimental.

Gordon wasn't about to. He was touched by her soft concern for her dog. It was sweet. Though she was capable, tough, and in most ways just like one of the guys down to wearing dirty jeans and T-shirts, hearing her talk as if she were a *woman* for a change struck him forcibly. It was as if an otherwise macho guy suddenly launched into comparing the attributes of mauve versus periwinkle kitchen paint. Surreal. But sweet.

She scowled, tracking the direction of his thoughts. "The dog comes with me. I like having him around."

Gordon felt a surge of completely unreasonable jealousy for the dog. "And you don't think the motels will object to your having him around?"

She frowned, averting her face so that he couldn't hear all of her words.

But he'd heard enough. "Sarah . . ."

"It's not like I *need* a motel. And the guys do it all the time. Craig's sleeping in *his* truck . . . actually, he has a small motor-home . . . but the serious racers do stay out by the track. They rough it, have barbecues, bench race. It's fun. Like camping. Craig said he'd save me a spot next to him."

"And does Craig know that you're bringing a dog?" He gestured to the pile of blankets and sheepskin impatiently. "Sarah, there's hardly enough room for you to stretch out back there, much less to make room for a pet."

Which is, of course, when he had the unpleasant thought. Maybe Craig was saving her a spot *right* next to him. In his motor-home. In his bed.

His body went cool as he glanced into the truck, confirming. There wasn't enough room to sleep comfortably. She would either be hellishly cramped as she "roughed it" in a vehicle never meant for overnight stays, or else she'd be cozied up in Craig's arms. It wasn't an unreasonable assumption.

He felt his pulse begin a slow pounding. Craig had, no doubt, a large and exceptionally ergonomic towing vehicle. His motorhome probably boasted a kitchen and television, bathroom and bedroom . . . with plenty of room to sleep two. No wonder she didn't seem worried about her narrow sleeping arrangements.

*Not your concern.*

With more effort than it should have taken, he wrenched his mind away from the images. He would not get involved in Sarah's love life. He wasn't objective anymore. His pulse beat in his ears and his body responded independently of any objections from his brain when he stood next to her naturally relaxed, warm, and fit young body. Her oversized T-shirt did nothing to help his peace of mind, concealing just enough to make him want to yank it off and confirm the curves that revealed themselves in subtle suggestion when she moved. And her jeans. They were a special torture when she bent and twisted over her arranging. Shapely calves, firm thighs, a spectacular butt. She was close enough to touch, if he wanted. He looked away.

He glanced at her once more, desperately seeking ugly bulges, stringy hair. Didn't she at least have bad breath?

Gordon swallowed, tightening the reins on himself. There was no denying it. She was attractive to him. Her dark blond hair fell in natural waves, and even though it wasn't brushed to a shine, the tousled look worked for her. Her figure clearly possessed all the curves it needed and revealed no hint of the ugly bulges he sought. Still close enough to her to feel her shirt's cotton sleeve brush tantalizingly against his arm, he enjoyed sharing airspace with her. Her breath, sweet and inviting. And her face . . . she suddenly looked up at him, her eyes locking on his with surprise tinged only the slightest bit by fear. He understood her fear, finding that he shared it. It was most unsettling to feel the tension vibrating between them, knowing that they both felt it, and that it couldn't—it *wouldn't*—be acknowledged.

That would be irresponsible in the extreme.

Her green eyes were dark with the absence of sunshine, mesmerizing him. Her lips parted, showing just a trace of moisture and a hint of her even, white teeth.

Irresponsible, and irresistible.

He took a step closer to her, reaching toward her, wanting to bury his hand in all of that golden hair and pull her lips against his.

Clearly panicked, she leapt back. A flash of green as her eyes widened, and Gordon was knocked sideways as if punched.

He stumbled against the heavy left-side double door, grasping at the juncture between it and the truck to keep from falling down. She had a hell of a left hook. Shaking his head to clear it, he moved his jaw to make sure it wasn't broken.

"I'm sorry! I'm sorry! I'm sorry!" she wailed. "The door, I don't know how it got away from me, I swear I didn't do that on purpose!"

He felt her hands ministering to his face, stroking his jaw. Her earnest eyes on his told him that she spoke the truth. That, and the now-closed door. Gordon leaned against the other, glad for the support and her touch.

He rubbed his jaw, feeling his fingers brush against hers. She snatched her hand back with a moan. Of contrition?

He deliberately made his voice cool and professional. "That's one way to conclude a business meeting."

"Business meeting." She looked at him for a long time. "Product placement?"

She'd managed to transform his efforts at dignity into something ridiculous. It made him snappish. "Why else? There's no other reason for me to be here." He looked at his watch.

Unfortunately, when he looked back up, Sarah was smiling. "No other reason? Let me see . . ." She narrowed her eyes at him, and he couldn't help reacting to such a wicked, knowing look. Or being disturbed by it. "You, Gordon Devine, are here because I'm very good, and you know it. You've seen it. But you haven't seen everything. Would you like to see everything?"

At her playful, almost seductive tone, his body betrayed him. Gordon cursed himself silently. He'd forgotten that she liked to tease and didn't easily back down. Her sudden stubbornness paired with her continuing proximity was having exactly the effect on him that she intended. Her playful voice was an utterly intoxicating blend of straightforward and suggestive.

How on earth was she so very, very good at being seductive while managing to be straightforward at the same time? It wasn't an approach he knew quite how to handle.

He made an effort to extricate himself. "It's late. You're tired. I'll just . . ."

She placed her palm against his chest to restrain him.

He could have easily broken away. He could have withered her with a condescending barb and forced her retreat.

Curiosity and desire overrode his better judgment. He did neither.

She tilted her face up to his. He wondered if the healthy flush of color on her cheeks was courtesy of the track. She certainly radiated enough glow to account for a day of exhilarating racing. And heat. It was as if she were a heated engine, well-tuned, ready for action.

The energy transmitted through her palm to his chest.

He had to get away from her.

He couldn't make himself move. "Sarah . . ."

When she stepped to close the distance between them, the spike in full-body heat hit him like a shock. Her hand—the one he was so aware of touching his chest—inched downward. He knew the exact moment when his control left him. It was when her lips curved up knowingly as her fingers teased the juncture where his shirt disappeared into his jeans.

Without another thought, he crushed her against him and let his hands move down her back, over her butt, and up again to bury themselves finally in the glorious silky mess of her hair. As he abandoned his rein on himself, he groaned. His mouth plundering hers the way he'd dreamed of exhilarated him even as the sensual shock reverberated throughout his body.

And she wasn't stopping him. As he moved against her she writhed, making little helpless wanting noises that communicated directly to his nervous system. Her kiss met and matched his, her tongue play as urgent and hungry. When he ran his hands under her loose T-shirt, over her smooth skin, he found the barrier of her tight bra and shoved it up. His mouth muffled her cries as he thumbed and played with her breasts, but the sound made him weak enough in the knees that he again had to grasp for the solid support of the truck's remaining open door.

The blankets were soft and inviting behind him.

As soon as the thought occurred he'd acted on it, pulling her inside with him. Aware of nothing but her body, her mouth, her teasing touch, he didn't even shut the door behind them. The narrow corridor of blankets pressed their bodies together, maddening him, making his movements frustrated and rough.

At her gasp when their mouths separated, he became aware that she felt his desire. But far from recoiling, she tentatively moved against him in a rhythm that had him reaching for her jeans.

His questing fingers found the button fly, but as she moved

back to accommodate his maneuvering, her body pushed against a cardboard box. Two drag slicks stacked unevenly on top of it trembled, and an eight-pound bag of dog food near the roof began to slide down toward her.

A crinkly noise was the only warning Gordon had. It was just enough of an alert for him to shield Sarah by rolling on top of her. The thud of the dog food impacted his skull right where the door had, and Gordon winced. The bag split open. Dog kibble skittered over them both like hard marbles.

"Thank you," Sarah said.

Gordon shook his already bruised head. Her soft words were *thank you?* He was pressed against her so hard she had to be hurting, yet she was thanking him.

*What am I* doing?

He rolled off her, feeling the crunch of dog food beneath his body. "I'm sorry," he said. He smoothed his hair off his damp forehead, taking deep breaths. He'd been just minutes away from making love to her. A very few minutes. Gordon felt chagrin making his face heat. It was unacceptable, what he was doing. Even unforgivable, considering the welcome home for her that he'd arranged with her father. "This is . . . not professional. This is impossible."

*Don't look at her, don't see her bare skin or her parted lips or her . . .*

Gordon skittered away from her like one of the kibbles and slid back out of the still-open doorway. He felt a return of sanity as he stood up, as if the upright posture helped him to remember his responsibilities.

Gordon couldn't help it; he looked back at her. She emerged behind him, and fortunately she'd pulled her shirt back down. It rode up as she slid out of the back, and he jerked his gaze away from the way her jeans hugged the curves his hands had so recently explored.

"I'm sorry," he repeated, watching the way her eyebrows rose at hearing his stiffly controlled tone. "You should go. I . . . Here," he amended, thinking of a way to cushion the awkward parting. He fished out his wallet, extracted the small pen within it, and wrote on the back of a business card. "My cell number," he explained. "Call me if you have any questions about DNP. Or anything. I'm here for you." Gordon almost choked on the words. He felt so low. "Let me know how it goes. Um . . ." He cleared his throat. "Do you have everything you need?"

He was tempted to flee at the look she gave him, but he held his ground for a moment more, even holding out his hand. She finally took it with a calm professionalism that had him admiring her again, nearly as much as he wanted her.

Swallowing, Gordon squeezed her hand, and released. "Good luck, Sarah."

"Thanks. Bye-bye."

He heard the words and their delivery, but he'd already turned his back. He strode toward his car as fast as he could without breaking into a trot. *Distance.* Soon she'd be more than halfway across the country. An adequate distance.

When Sarah returned, he probably wouldn't have to see her again. She'd quit in protest when she discovered he now owned the place and her Dad had retired without leaving any part of the company to her.

He hadn't done anything with her to feel guilty about. Almost, but almost didn't count. What was it that Red had said about close? "Close only counts in horseshoes and hand-grenades."

Thinking of Red, and their plan, and *his* plan—his long-cherished, much reviewed road map to financial success—Gordon steeled his resolve. He climbed into his Cobra and thought about money. About success. He thought about taking his place among the CEOs and millionaires of the world until he began to feel almost back to normal.

Gritting his teeth as he remembered Sarah's warm and willing heat, feeling his body still aching with frustration, he knew that "close" was all they'd ever have.

★ ★ ★ ★ ★

# PART TWO

★ ★ ★ ★ ★

# CHAPTER TEN

Sarah's heart thumped madly as she gripped the steering wheel. She eased her car out of the staging lanes and toward the starting line for the final round, feeling another thrill of amazement go through her.

She'd planned on getting this far, had worked her butt off for it, but it was almost a miracle to have progressed all the way through the eliminations to the quarterfinals and semifinals, where'd she'd managed to knock some drag race heroes out of the running. Those were guys she'd read about in magazines and seen on TV for years. She'd beaten them.

*That* had made the TV cameras finally sit up and take notice, she thought with no little satisfaction. Such attention was tough to get and jealously coveted. She'd seen how the racers worked in the pits, wearing greasy T-shirts and jeans, until a sighting of a camera crew sent them dashing into their trailers to clean up and put on their pressed crew uniforms. It was vital to present a good image for any sponsors, and a big deal to land a taped interview, since it was the very best coverage, aside from live, that a racer could hope to get for himself and his sponsors.

After ignoring her for a nobody and circling the defending champion and the class's other heavy hitters like star-crazed paparazzi, the camera crews were finally aiming their equipment at her as she lined up.

The print media, the other racers and the fans had finally noticed her too. It was unprecedented for a girl racer to rocket up from obscurity into the final round. The money round. The one that decided who won and who finished runner-up.

It was the climax to a national-level heads-up race.

*And here I am, doing a burnout with my heart in my throat.*

She'd performed burnouts so many times before that it was second nature, but she imposed a supreme level of concentration on this one. Making sure she knew precisely when the rear tires had rolled through the water and were wet enough to start the burnout, she engaged the line lock to immobilize the front brakes and let the rear tires spin freely. Then she floored the throttle to get the tires smoking.

If she won, she'd claim the event win. The victory was close enough to taste. She'd get money, of course, but also a healthy dose of respect, the media publicity, and maybe even the attention of a big sponsor to fund a racing career.

Forcing the distracting fantasy from her mind, she inched up to the starting line and lit the pre-stage bulb. Meticulously going through the routine she'd practiced a thousand times getting ready for such an important moment, Sarah cleared the engine, engaged the line lock again, and slowly rolled the car forward into the stage beam. She waited for her opponent to fully stage, watching his own stage lights on the tree. As soon as both stage bulbs were lit, all three floodlamp-bright yellow bulbs beneath them would light up simultaneously, and then, four-tenths of a second, later the green would flash. The instant she saw the yellow begin to light, she'd launch.

And Craig would witness it.

Craig had dropped out in the third round. In the staging lanes before this final round, he'd hugged her for luck. She was pretty sure she'd spotted a worried look in his eyes. That, and admiration. The admiration made her mood even more buoyant.

His look when she'd first arrived at the track ready to go with her yellow Mustang had been simple amazement.

She wanted more of the admiration.

*Watch this, hon!*

On the other side of the tree, the stage bulb came on. She punched her right foot to the floor and her Mustang's engine roared at 5,000 rpm on the rev limiter as if screaming with frustration for her to let go of the transbrake button. At the first hint of flash of the yellow light, she did, and her car launched so hard that her entire body was slammed back in the seat.

Her howling engine and her fierce concentration combined to mask everything except the track in front of her. Thousands of yelling fans in the stands blurred by her window. The amplified rapid-fire chatter of the announcer faded to white noise. Even the roar of the beefed-up Mustang careening down the lane next to hers barely registered. She felt the usual speed-hit of adrenaline, flooding the level already in her bloodstream from the previous day's qualifying and that morning's elimination matches. The rush surged through her body and gave her vision a familiar sharp clarity. Glancing in her left-side mirror, Sarah could see her opponent, and knew that she was well enough ahead to win. She smiled as she crossed the finish line.

She had won.

For another split second she savored the incomparable exhilaration of her just-completed pass, enjoying the closed-loop memory of g-force and speed and victory.

Then she braked. With the reduction of speed and noise, reality returned. She flipped up the visor of her helmet and turned off the track, on her way to the ET shack.

The first thing she saw was Will and Lee running toward her in the distance. It seemed odd, for a moment, to see them outside of the shop.

She collected her timeslip, and felt a confirming sort of satisfaction when she saw her numbers. She'd nailed it. Not only had she won, but she'd run the quickest pass of the weekend for any car in her class. As she sat staring at the timeslip, lost in a pleasant daze, the guy she'd just beaten drove by and honked, waving in congratulations. The next sound she heard was Will and Lee pounding on her roof and shouting.

"You did it! Woo-hoo!"

She grinned, pleased with herself and grateful again that her two friends had agreed to fly out and pit for her. Every professional racer needed a pit crew. Trusting them with her fledgling racing career just as she'd trusted them at her shop had paid off. Her eyes nearly closed in cat-eyed pleasure thinking of Gordon stuck back in the shop, wearing his Fred-with-Tires style T-shirt as he worked with the remaining staff to keep up with the work orders. Her father had intervened to give the best two tech guys the time off to join her. She wasn't sure how he'd gotten Gordon to agree to that. However he'd done it was of minimal interest to her, though, at the moment.

The shop was important, but it faded to insignificance next to this. She wasn't a wannabe; she was a real racer now. Winning made her status legitimate. For a moment she actually choked up, though she made herself breathe deeply and blink only a normal number of times to avoid revealing her surge of emotion.

*This* was what she was meant to do with her life.

Heads-up racing had addicted her instantly, the additional stimulation of roaring crowds, admiring attention, and out-for-blood opponents in the next lane rousing her to a fever pitch, and all that was *before* the launch. And the win.

Just thinking about it made tingles run up and down her arms. The victory was validating, arousing, and scary, all at the same time. The combination of emotions felt similar to another sensation. She didn't want to think about who'd caused the sensation, or when. Why did she keep thinking of *him?*

As if reading her mind, Will said, "Gordon's missing out on your moment of glory."

"Yes, he's missing out, isn't he?" She shrugged as if it didn't matter, but it did. Not that he wasn't there—she was sure Gordon would never dream of spending his tightly guarded time or resources just to come watch her race—but that he hadn't even been interested enough in her to stick around when she'd all but flung herself at him.

*Correction,* she reminded herself with grim honesty. She *had* flung herself at him that evening. She'd shamelessly, eagerly crawled over him like a trackslut. She'd taken leave of her senses.

Crushing embarrassment, a mere ghost of the agonized shame she'd felt after he'd left the track that day, coursed throughout her body. The memory was still enough to bring an uncomfortable warmth to her face and a grimace to her expression.

Will noticed her grinding her teeth, she knew, but wisely said nothing. She tried to shake the feeling off. So Gordon wasn't interested in her physically. So her feminine wiles still needed some fine-tuning. No surprise there.

His rejection wasn't the end of the world.

Lee tapped her windshield, giving her a welcome distraction. "Hey. It's FAST. They're headed this way." His soft voice brought her back to the present.

She brightened. With racing, at least, she was becoming one hell of an adept, even a celebrity. "Think they noticed me?" Others certainly had. As she cruised at walking speed off the return road and navigated carefully through the throng toward the pit area, she heard soft slaps as strangers patted her doors and trunk lid. A few other, braver souls even thrust their arms between Will and Lee to shake her hand. It was heady stuff. And now the FAST channel.

"Sarah, they look pretty excited," Lee replied. It was all the warning she had before the television crew arrived, immediately setting up lighting and clearing a small space around her car.

"Ms. Mattel! Right there is good. Stop right there. That's it. Just a brief interview. You don't mind, do you?" Without waiting for her reply, the man directed the camera angle, readied the mic and even positioned one young female assistant just out of camera range, holding what looked like an oversized aluminum fan that caught the last rays of hot afternoon sunshine as the woman lifted it carefully to help illuminate Sarah and her car.

"She needs hair and makeup, Mr. Genthe," the aluminum-holder told the director, looking at Sarah with a woman-to-woman smile. Sarah started to smile back.

The man made chopping motions with his arms. "No she doesn't. We're doing a zero-to-hero piece. She's a racer, not a model. If they have to look twice to figure out she's female, all the better. We want rubbernecks. Double takes. Adds intrigue." Then he looked at Sarah's face. "Well, maybe some lipstick. And something to bring out her eyes. Go on, look in the grab bag. Take off the helmet but leave it visible. That's it. No, leave some dirt-smudges on her cheeks. Hmm. I see what you mean. On second thought, don't."

Sarah felt as if she were being attacked by small birds as skillful hands rapidly touched her face, tugged at her hair, patted her eyelids and painted her mouth. She looked desperately for Will and Lee, finally spotting where they'd been whisked off to the side.

"Come here," she commanded them, startling the woman who brushed her eyelashes. She felt the makeup brush miss and skid across her forehead. The woman's mouth shaped into a moue of concentration as she dabbed at the mistake with a moist towelette.

Sarah ignored her. "You guys," she whispered when they bent down to hear her. "Distract them so I can wipe this junk off."

"Let them do their thing. Smile pretty and say nice things.

Television's good publicity, and it pleases the sponsors. Or sponsor, singular, in our case," Will advised.

"I know, but . . ." With the mention of a sponsor, Sarah was again reminded of Gordon. How he'd love it if she sang the praises of his DNP on national TV. Not that she cared what he loved or hated, of course. But she knew it was a race-winner's proper protocol to mention sponsors, to give them publicity, which made them back the money they invested. She should publicly thank Gordon. "You're right. But . . ." She wiped the back of her hand over her mouth, showed the resulting swab of color to Will. "Guys don't get primped like this. What if people don't take me seriously? Hey, do you mind?" Sarah reared back from the woman's massaging color into her cheeks. "I don't usually wear makeup," she explained. "You're doing a great job, though," Sarah called after her guiltily when the woman stalked away.

"*Is* she doing a great job?" Sarah asked Will and Lee, briefly regretting that she'd yanked out her rearview mirror to eliminate its half-pound of weight. "I feel like the whore of Babylon with this gunk slathered on."

"Best looking whore I ever saw," Will assured her with a grin.

She rubbed at her cheeks and then looked at her hands. Bright pink. "Wonderful." The publicity wouldn't hurt—didn't they say that even bad publicity was good? It might even help her land a deep-pocket sponsor—a big corporate one with lots of money to bestow upon her career. Maybe more than one sponsor. It could happen. And then Gordon could eat his heart out when she didn't need DNP anymore.

Suddenly she felt generous. She'd be happy to thank him. If she didn't faint from nerves first. She couldn't remember being the object of so much scrutinizing attention. So many people. The camera lens looked huge, ready to capture every single one of her flaws and gaffes. What if she said something stupid?

"Sarah!"

"Craig?" She wiped more vigorously at the makeup. If Craig saw her looking like this, he'd never let her live it down. He'd take one look at her clown makeup and forget all about the important thing, her victory. She'd waited *years* for him to see her as a winner, as an equal. Not as a trackslut.

She scrubbed with a sense of panic.

Craig pushed past the circle of people and cameras and halted. "Wow. You look . . ."

She lowered her hands and turned to him with assumed casualness. "Ridiculous. Yeah. This stuff must have plaster of Paris mixed in." She swiped at her cheek with the palm of her hand.

"No, don't." Craig caught her hand in his. "Wow, Sarah. You look phenomenal. Almost as phenomenal as you drive," he allowed, an odd smile momentarily lifting both corners of his mouth. "Congratulations. Looks like you won yourself the right kind of attention." He eyed the camera crew still adjusting their equipment. His gaze returned immediately to her, as if he couldn't quite believe what he saw. "I haven't seen you in makeup before. Did they do that?"

"Yeah." Sarah gazed back at him, feeling strangely shy. Craig never looked at her the way he was looking at her. "It's not bad?"

Craig's eyes darkened, and she knew he spoke the truth. He leaned in closer to her. "No, it's not bad. It's really, really not bad. Don't wipe it off."

Sarah felt her head buzzing. Too much was happening at once. To have won the race and have Craig admire her too . . . it was exhilarating to the point of being almost painful. Add in the cameras, and she knew she neared system overload.

She swallowed, took several breaths. "I'll have to take it off when I race. The stuff might melt or something, get in my eyes."

She had no idea if it was waterproof or not, but she couldn't take chances with her budding racing career.

Craig nodded, thoughtful. "Yeah. When you race." His smile slipped slightly. He didn't like the idea of her taking off her makeup? Was she so unsightly to him underneath it? She searched his handsome, familiar face, so close to hers.

Was he jealous of her also having a racing career?

"Fella, either kiss her or don't, but would you mind getting out of the way?" The director stared pointedly.

"I'll get out of the way. For now," Craig answered with a grin. He winked at Sarah.

"Craig," she hissed, feeling suddenly panicked. There were cameras turned on her, ready to roll. She felt grateful that Craig stood between them and her at that moment. "I don't know about this."

Craig nodded, his eyebrows knitted together briefly in commiseration. "It'll be fine. I've studied racer interviews. They're pretty straightforward." He touched her hand, his skin a welcome coolness. "Hey. I have an idea."

As he straightened, he exposed Sarah's face to the glare of the reflected light. He rounded her car, opened the passenger door and got in.

"What are you doing?"

"Helping."

"How?" she whispered, squinting at the additional bright camera lights that suddenly flooded her car, illuminating the interior as if it were a convertible under direct sunlight. "Oh, wow, that's bright. I don't think I can . . . I think I might throw up."

"Don't worry," Craig whispered. "Just follow my lead."

He draped a comforting arm over her shoulders.

". . . and in a story of zero-to-hero we have Sarah Mattel and her winning '94 Mustang GT. She ran with a 347 stroker small-block Ford with nitrous, and the secret component reportedly is her prototype nitrous system, something we haven't seen before. Along for the ride is—from the looks of things—a *close* companion in the passenger seat. Sarah, introduce us to your co-pilot."

Craig spoke before she could answer. He acknowledged the camera with a saluting wave, and said, "Craig Keller. I run the same class as Sarah." His voice resonated inside the car, a warmly professional sound, as he leaned into the microphone in front of Sarah.

The interviewer went along with it. "Well, Craig Keller, how does it feel to be beaten by your girlfriend?" He shoved his arm into the car, just past Sarah's face. She inhaled the citrusy scent of cologne as his arm hairs tickled her nose. She smiled and struggled not to sneeze. What was she supposed to do with the interviewer's arm in her face and the camera recording her every expression? If she were back in the shop and one of the guys treated her like this—like she wasn't even there—she'd speak up. She'd do more than speak up.

But what were the rules for professional conduct now? Her first impulse, to swat his arm away, wasn't appropriate. She'd be better off relying on Craig's wider experience.

Wouldn't she?

She moved under his arm, restless. Craig gave her shoulder a quick squeeze and looked directly at the camera. "She beat me fair and square. But next time—Bowling Green, Kentucky, this coming weekend—it'll be another story. I want to say, though, I think it's flattering she came in first. I taught her everything she knows."

Sarah elbowed him out of sight of the camera. Sure he'd taught her a few things, but she'd earned her victory the old-fashioned way, with hard work and hundreds of hours of solitary practice. That, and DNP, but the component wouldn't have helped if she weren't already a solid racer.

She opened her mouth to clarify, but the cameraman beat her to it. "There you have it, folks: Sarah Mattel, the quick study, and Craig Keller, the teacher surpassed—just this once, he hopes!—by his attractive student. Next up, we have—"

*Enough.*

She grabbed the microphone, slipping out from under Craig's arm. She smiled widely, as Will had advised. "You can't go without letting me thank my sponsor. I couldn't have done it without DNP Components." Smiling and smiling at the cameraman, she thought she could feel her makeup beginning to melt. Would they cut her if her makeup slid off her face? She wondered if Gordon would mind that she made up a name for his company. It sounded more professional than calling him an inventor, or co-worker. She was winging it.

The interviewer didn't cut her. He smiled with an experienced gleam in his eyes. "Of course! We can't forget the sponsors. It seems—from the decals—you certainly have a big vote of confidence. Tell us about 'DNP'."

"DNP is a hot new company based in Huntington Beach, California. They manufacture state-of-the-art nitrous systems, better and far more powerful than anything else on the market, and they have all sorts of other groundbreaking high-performance parts about to come onto the market. DNP is the reason I'm in the winner's circle today."

She tried to say more, get in a reference to her shop too, but he pulled the mic and stood just out of her reach. "Sarah Mattel and DNP! And the mentor she's surpassed, Craig Keller. Clearly these two are the ones to watch. Cut."

"Thanks for the interview," he told her in a very different tone, even as he waved back the lighting crew and wiped his forehead. "Hot out here today." He spoke his spiel at her while fishing in his pocket for a card. "We'll be airing a half-hour show of the event within the month, on FAST, channel two-oh-five. If you'd like a copy of the tape call the production company. Here's the number and the guy to talk to for that. Craig? Maybe you'll get your own interview soon."

Craig's voice had also changed, from the on-camera baritone to the more casual sound she was used to hearing. "Yep. It'll be another story next time."

Sarah took what felt like her first deep breath in hours as the camera crew dispersed. "Whew. That was intense." She turned to Craig, raising her eyebrows as she started her car in preparation to drive back to the pit area. "Taught me everything I know, huh?"

"I thought it would make for a good hook," he replied. He stared out the windshield after the departing camera crew. "The rivalry thing gives us ongoing interest. A reason for them to keep covering us." He transferred his gaze to her. "I still can't believe you've swept this race. That's huge, Sarah. Do you know how huge that is?" He stared at her as if seeing her for the very first time.

"Pretty damn huge?" She grinned at him. "Huge enough for you to go grabbin' at my limelight. But thanks for helping me. I was so nervous."

"You did fine. I'm just sorry I came across as a little overbearing. It played better in my head." He indicated the cameras, setting up at the perimeter of the car show. "They can rattle a person."

"Uh-huh." She felt a warm, gratified tingle at his honeyed tone. His profile seemed as serious—and as beautiful—as some ancient ruler on a coin as he looked straight ahead.

Then he glanced at her again, and seemed struck anew by her appearance. "But look at you." Craig held his hands out as if to display her to somebody. "You're more disturbing than any cameras. Hotter than an overheated engine." He aimed flirtatious blue eyes at her and tugged playfully at her steering wheel. "So hot you fried my circuits. Brain went offline." Craig cocked his head, looking for a reaction. When he didn't get one he launched into his best impression of a faulty circuit, jerking his body spasmodically and emitting noises that she supposed were meant to sound electrical in nature. He finished, looked at her with a laughing smile that she'd only before seen aimed at track-sluts.

"Should have used that routine on-camera. It would have made for another good hook." But Sarah was gratified. Craig *never* tried this hard with her. Was this the power of makeup and a smile, or the result of being the big winner of the race? Was it both? She glanced over, confirmed his unusual puppyish demeanor.

*Puppyish* . . . "Oh no. Ricky Racer! It's been hours. I've got to go check on him." She revved the engine, waving Will and Lee over.

Craig spoke quickly. "He's in that little dog run you made with chicken wire, right? He's fine. Give me a few seconds. At least long enough for me to ask you something. Would you like to go out, celebrate your victory? What do you say? Drinks? Dinner? *Sarah.*"

She raised her eyebrows at his tone and stopped scanning for a break in the crowd.

"A celebration dinner. I owe you that." His expression turned more serious, though his eyes still sparkled with interest. He seemed fascinated with her.

She stared at Craig. He raised his eyebrows: *well?* She couldn't deny she'd waited years for him to look at her with that particular kind of intensity. He sounded deliciously romantic, seductive, and affectionate.

It's what she'd always wanted.

But she'd left little Ricky alone for so many hours . . .

Will cleared his throat. "Uh, not to interrupt, but some other people need to use the road."

Sarah jumped, then looked behind her car. Sure enough, there was a gathering clot of cars and pedestrians. She swallowed, feeling both confused and frazzled. "Oops," she mumbled. She looked back at Craig, thinking as she spoke. "Yes, seven. No, wait. I really need to feed and walk Ricky. It's been all day and he gets separation anxiety. And then there's the award ceremony. And afterward I'm going to use the award money and check the guys and me into some much-deserved motel rooms for this last night. Where I'm going to take a cool shower." She'd had enough of the camping out. That had lost its charm by the second night of trying to find a comfortable spot in the Suburban between the tires and jackstands, with Ricky Racer occasionally deciding to play tug-of-war with her tie-downs or taking it upon himself to crawl over her face at two in the morning.

"Eight," she amended. "Will that work for you?"

"Sure. I don't have all the same commitments you do, what with the *award ceremony* and all." He inhaled deeply, exhaled on a laugh. "It's hard to get used to, isn't it? I'm dating the woman who kicked my butt." Craig gave her a small smile, but his eyes promised retribution. Then they just promised heat. He leaned toward her, clearly with the intent to kiss her. Sarah held still for the impending event, feeling as on-the-spot as she had when the cameras rolled.

Will popped his head in the window. "Oh, sorry, thought you guys were all finished. When you're done sucking face could you please *move?*"

Sarah felt her foot stab the accelerator pedal in reflex, revving her engine. "Um. I'll see you later," she said softly, pleasantly surprised at how her uncertainty and exhaustion lent her voice a certain seductiveness.

He gazed at her, and if she wasn't mistaken—no, she couldn't mistake the longing in his eyes, or his frustrated breath—her small, gentle rejection had served to stoke his desire.

The world seemed to skew sideways. It was actually happening. The dynamic was changing between them.

She tried to view it analytically, absorbing the information as useful. She was distracted, though, the neurons of her brain as fried as Craig's spazzy demonstration earlier. Craig, finally dancing attendance on her. Would she wake up from this dream, or was this the beginning of what she'd always wanted?

"Eight," Craig repeated, finally stepping out of her car and back into the intense mid-afternoon heat. Will slid into the vacated space, Lee strolling beside him on the passenger side as Sarah picked her way between the crowd toward the distant edge of grass where she'd parked her truck, trailer, and her surreptitious, possibly illegal, dog-run. She'd had to tuck it away from sight at the far side of the rows of trailers and campers, away from trees, shade, or convenient restroom facilities, but it was worth it to keep Ricky happy, and with her as she traveled.

As they wove in between the open trailers and big rigs, and past the throngs of spectators walking the pit road, Will sat silently.

"Go ahead, say it," she finally told him.

"You did fine on-camera. Gordon'll be pleased."

Sarah was momentarily startled. Why did he have to mention Gordon? "No. No, I meant about . . ." But now the news about her big date with Craig seemed silly and a little irrelevant, considering the huge race victory and the coup of the FAST interview. She'd shared the Craig saga with the work gang before, relaying her crush and the whole history, but now the timing seemed off. "Oh, never mind."

Will remained uncharacteristically silent. Lee paced the car, looking straight ahead. Sarah shifted uncomfortably in her seat, wishing for air-conditioning. And a stereo. Just when she couldn't bear the awkward, overheated silence any longer, she saw something that made her forget all about it. A small, long, brown dog lay half-in and half-out of the shade that her truck made, in the corner of the dog run closest to the track, as if he'd collapsed straining toward her. Even from a distance she could tell something was wrong. The dog lay very, very still.

"Oh no," she breathed, jamming on the gas so that a wandering spectator wearing a large, creased new manufacturer's tee in front of her had to leap out of the way. Out of the corner of her eye she noticed Will cursing and grabbing the dash to steady himself.

Her car roared up to her trailer, and she was out and running without even shutting off the engine.

A painful clench of guilt stopped her breathing as she skidded to a halt next to Ricky Racer. This was her fault. She'd been neglecting him. Food and water, and a tiny amount of cuddling she saw to it he received each day. But the racing had taken her from him for hours at a time, and after each long day she'd only fallen into exhausted slumber in the back of the truck next to the little dog at night. She'd assumed that he would be safe within his enclosed shady space, with his food and his water bowl and his blankets. Had he choked? Had he been attacked? Though she could see the individual hairs of his brown fur shining in the harsh sun, she still couldn't see his sides moving with breath. If he were dead, she would never forgive herself.

The dog's respiration was shallow but present. She gasped in relief, lifting the dog into the shade. His velvet fur was scorching hot where the sun had baked it, and matted with dried saliva.

Lee had his own water bottle out, and without hesitation he poured most of it over the dog. Sarah watched the dog's chest suddenly rise and fall so quickly that he almost seemed to be shaking. She called herself every foul name she could think of.

Ricky stirred.

"In his mouth," Sarah ordered frantically, but Lee had already pried open the dog's small mouth and positioned the bottle so that the cool water could be lapped up. He poured slowly.

Ricky turned his head the tiniest amount possible toward the stream. His thin ears had a wilted-lettuce appearance and his brown eyes were as dull as she'd ever seen them, but his pink tongue extended to catch the water.

"He'll be okay," Lee told her in his softest voice. She felt a tickle of moisture on her own face and barely managed to stifle a sob. "He really will," Lee repeated. "He's just thirsty."

Sarah grasped handfuls of grass and tried to get control of herself. She was having a very emotional day. This was unlike her. Of course, it was also unlike her to be inattentive to her dog.

"I'm *so sorry,*" she wailed to Ricky, when she could. She gathered him up into her lap, happy that he squirmed in protest. Squirming meant he was getting back to normal. She cuddled with him, inhaling his musky dog scent and not caring at all about the dried saliva.

A throat being cleared nearby made her peek up from the fur, wondering who would intrude on her moment.

"Sarah? Are you . . . can I do anything to help?"

"She's fine," Will told Craig in something close to a growl.

Sarah wiped quickly at her cheeks and raised her head to Craig. "What is it?"

Craig glanced at the wriggling dog in her lap, then back at her face. He seemed taken aback by her expression. "You didn't mention the name of your motel. I was just thinking that a motel sounded pretty good for the last night in town, and that I'd check into the same one." Craig gazed at her, clearly puzzled.

"Your dog. Is it okay?"

His forgetting Ricky's name—and gender, for that matter—suddenly irritated her. Craig should show more respect for her dog. Didn't he realize Ricky was like a little child to her? She stroked the dog into relative stillness. Craig was always calling Ricky Racer "your dog" and "it." His attitude had never bothered her before. At her apartment Ricky avoided Craig and growled at him, and Craig's minimal efforts to befriend the dog had seemed a less potent insult than Ricky's own actively expressed distaste. But Ricky was weak and defenseless now. She patted the dog protectively.

"*He* is okay, now. *Ricky Racer* just had too much sun and not enough water."

"Is there anything I can do?" Craig began, but cut himself off when he saw her glare. "Sorry. Really." He looked it, too. He grimaced as if he wanted to hit himself. "I never realized that he meant so much to you. Why don't I . . ." He gestured in the direction of his motor-home and trailer, and without waiting for any response he left.

"You never told him the motel name," Will observed with a grin. "Poor guy. It'll take him a while to track you down."

"He was contrite, wasn't he?" Sarah stared after Craig. "I really do think things are changing between us. Did I tell you we have a date tonight?" She looked in Will's direction but gazed through him, into the future. She brought herself back only with an effort. "That's fine that Craig has to hunt around for me," Sarah told Will, thinking quickly. "I might need the time. We've got to be in the award ceremony, collect the check—and Ricky is coming with us everywhere this afternoon," she added, raising an eyebrow at Will's low groan. "No arguments! You have to tuck him into your duffel bag, with some ice and a blankie. His condition is delicate. Then we have to establish a presence with the speed part vendors on Manufacturer's

Midway. And as for later . . ." Sarah smiled, a real smile in response to a challenge. "When I get to the motel, I'll need time to shower and change into girl clothes. It might take a little longer than my usual five minutes to get ready for a date with Craig."

# CHAPTER ELEVEN

Sarah answered the door wrapped in one of the motel's white bath towels, so she only opened the door a few inches. She stuck her hand out. "Give it here."

Through the space she could only see half of Will's grinning face. He held onto the small brown bag and tried to peer inside. "Nice legs. How about a little peep show?"

"How about you fork over the goods before I beat you with my hair dryer."

"You don't own a hair dryer," Will said confidently.

"True." She'd planned on styling her hair with the motel's hair dryer, hoping it wouldn't require much user expertise to blow some volume into her bone-straight tresses. She couldn't remember the last time she hadn't simply let it air-dry. But then, she was more worried about what Will had brought her. "Did you get everything I said?"

"Oh ye of little faith." Will managed to sound wounded as he passed the bag. "Check and see. And now, if you're just about done ordering us around . . ."

"I paid you and Lee half my winnings," she retorted, sifting through the bag's contents. "I get to order you around once or twice, so long as I do it nicely. It's in the rules. Where's Lee?"

"Next door at the bar. Where I'd like to be. Hint, hint."

"I think this will work," Sarah said, shaking the bag until its contents rattled against paper. "Wish me luck. I've only got an hour to get ready."

"*Only* an hour? I've seen you throw an engine together in less time." Then, in a suspicious tone, "Who are you, and what have you done with Sarah?"

She laughed and closed the door. The plain paper bag crinkled in her hand as she leaned against the motel door. She felt anonymous and sneaky holding it, as if she'd just concluded some kind of sordid drug deal rather than the innocent transaction it was.

As she contemplated what she was doing, she found herself echoing Will's thought. What had she done with the old Sarah?

The professionally made-up girl she'd seen in the motel mirror before her shower, though familiarly sweaty and helmet-bruised, *that* hadn't been her. That was some older, sexier version of her. Someone womanly.

Someone with sex appeal.

A low whine from the corner had her hurrying across the small motel room to the plastic dog crate on the other side of the bed. As she crouched before its wire front, the bag fell from her fingers and its contents spilled out.

Ricky Racer cocked his head at them. Lipstick, eyeliner, mascara, eye shadow, light beige concealer, and a travel-size tube of hair gel.

Sarah acknowledged Ricky's curiosity. "Yes, it's unusual. But it's a special night, and makeup is nothing to whine about. Hopefully. Do you have to go potty again? No, you can't possibly manage again so soon. I just took you."

Ricky seemed to grin.

"That's what I thought. You just want attention. I suppose I owe you a little more attention after today's shameful neglect, don't I? Yes I do."

Unhooking the latch on the crate door so she could reach in to rub his belly and scratch his chest, she acknowledged the debt. "I'll give you so much attention that you'll even run to

Craig for relief. So, maybe you can tell me why I'm about to risk poking my eyes out and probably end up looking like a painted Indian for him. I don't *need* makeup, or big bouncy hair, or any of that. I don't." She couldn't help the way her mind flashed to the moment when Gordon pulled away from her and left her alone. Had he been recoiling in distaste? She couldn't remember. She didn't want to remember.

A tiny yip brought her attention back to Ricky. She'd been petting too hard. "Sorry. No, it's not about Gordon. My telling Gordon those personal things was a mistake. All of that was a mistake. That last afternoon was a big mistake. I just want to dress up because Craig said I looked 'phenomenal' when I was wearing that makeup. Craig's never said I looked phenomenal before. Or that my driving is phenomenal, for that matter. And the way he looked at me after I won, it was just . . . it was everything I'd always wanted. I'll be deliriously happy when he sweeps me off my feet just like in those sappy movies."

Ricky pawed at her hand.

"Do you want another toy? Here you go," she said, handing him another beef-flavored rawhide chew. "What's wrong with me? Why am I wasting brain-juice on Gordon, I ask you. Am I one of those types that always want what they don't have? Maybe Gordon's that kind. Maybe that's why he retreated, because he found out that I'm so easy I'd let him tear my clothes off in the back of a Suburban. No challenge there. I fired myself at him like a cannonball." Sarah ground her teeth, wishing she could stop thinking about it.

"No, stop that, you can't eat the eyeliner." Sarah flicked the black eye-pencil out of the dog's reach. "What's wrong with you, anyway? There's your chew. It's even beef-basted, which probably beats eyeliner-flavor. Honestly, you're completely nuts," she told the dog and closed and refastened the crate door.

She glanced at the clock next to the motel bed. "Forty-five minutes. Why did I think I needed a whole hour? It only took the makeup lady a few minutes. Just have to do exactly what she did. Eyes, cheeks, lashes, hair . . ." Sarah looked at the cosmetics scattered on the carpet in front of the crate. "Can't be any harder than bolting together a small-block."

*Dear God.*

Sarah gazed in despair at her reflection.

She'd observed certain disasters in the shop: spills, accidents, explosions.

Nothing rivaled this.

Her eyes were as red and puffy as if she'd been crying, though she hadn't broken into tears. Yet. All she'd done was scrub the skin above and below her eyes to clear it of the extra eyeliner that she'd applied too generously.

She dropped the wet washcloth into the sink, where it lay half-in and half-out of the soapy water she'd been using to wash the rest of her face for the fourth time. The water had turned light brown.

*My poor face.*

Her mottled skin glowed pink and red, as if she'd recently suffered a bad sunburn. A bad, uneven sunburn. The powdery blusher had scrubbed off easily enough when she'd decided to redo the brushstrokes, but the oil-based concealer had streaked, forcing her to bear down hard with the rough side of the washcloths.

Her blotchy skin obviously objected to the abuse.

And her eyes . . . she'd managed to erase the excess raccoon-black of eyeliner, which turned out not to be water-resistant, but it had still taken more scrubbing. Her eyelids, bare of the intended enhancements, were swollen as if with a bad allergy. The swelling made her normally bright, clear green eyes look piggy and small.

"Oink oink," she told her reflection. A ghost of a smile appeared on the face. It made her pity the reflected smiling girl, so obviously unaware of her creeping skin condition.

Sarah looked at the clock by the bed, which she'd been doing frequently and with growing panic for the past fifteen minutes. Her panic peaked. "He's supposed to be here *now!*" Horrified, she stared back at the girl in the mirror. "No, no, no," she moaned, picking up and discarding makeup instruments. "Cool water. Soothe the skin," she instructed herself desperately, splashing cold water onto her face. "You wouldn't work on an overheated engine, and you're not going to work on *that.*" She confirmed with a peek that her skin was, indeed, unworkable. But the raw appearance seemed to be fading slightly.

Her gaze dropped to her towel-toga. "Got to get dressed." She flew to the bed, feeling her heart pounding in her chest. She hadn't been this nervous at the race, not even for the final round. Her odd panic was unseemly and ridiculous.

She made herself take a deep breath as she studied her nice black dress that she'd brought with her, scratching absently at the second white bath towel still wound around her head.

There was nothing wrong with the dress. The short gauzy length of it lay where she'd put it on top of the busy paisley pattern of the bedspread. Next to it sat her virgin special-occasion strappy black sandals.

She frowned. There was something missing. The outfit looked fine, lying there on the bed. However . . .

Her eyes went wide. She'd forgotten to pack a bra to go with the dress. She couldn't very well wear her thick, sweat-stained athletic bra underneath those spaghetti straps.

She'd have to go commando.

"The good news is that Craig won't notice my face at all," Sarah murmured to herself. She wondered if she should change

into her jeans, after all. No, they were filthy.

"Oh, man." She picked up the dress, feeling the lightness of the material.

It wouldn't conceal a goose bump.

Sarah looked doubtfully at her pile of dirty laundry in the corner, spotting the sports bra she'd worn under her T-shirt all day. Maybe she could scrunch the bra straps and wear it that way, somehow tucked beneath the narrow dress straps . . . ?

Shaking her head, she let her gaze fall on the clock face again, reviving her sense of panic.

The dress went over her head, and she worked the zipper up. She slipped the shoes on, then turned to view the finished effect.

She gasped again as her gaze fixed on her head. Specifically, on the white towel wrapped around her head. She'd forgotten to blow dry her hair!

Whipping the towel off, she stared at the matted mess of her hair. It had dried under the towel in what appeared to be a flat bird's nest.

"I have hair gel!" She rushed to the bathroom counter, so fixated on the solution that she forgot that she was wearing heels. Tripping, she cursed and managed not to fall by grasping for the counter's edge.

She pried open the cap and squirted a handful of gel into her cupped palm, which she then transferred to the top of her head, massaging in circles to work the goo in. It didn't lather up like shampoo, but disappeared into her crown. Frowning, she applied more gel, then more again until the travel-size tube was empty. It didn't seem to improve her hair. It wasn't adding the promised "bounce and body."

Lifting a lock of her hair, she felt the sticky heaviness of the coating. The hair showed no inclination to bounce.

Sarah was stumped about what to do with her hair next. The

makeup artist hadn't done anything to her hair, so she had no lead to follow.

There was no way she could show herself publicly with hair that felt—and looked—as if it had been dipped in transmission fluid.

And there was no time for another shower to clean it off. She would have to improvise.

Grabbing the hair dryer, she started brushing while aiming the hot air at the dampest and most sticky sections.

She peered in the mirror, brightening. Better. Her hair still appeared heavy and somewhat greasy, but at least it wasn't ratty and damp.

The knock on her door startled a brief yelp out of her, but she knew the dryer would mask the sound. Craig had arrived, and she wasn't ready!

She stared, frantic, at her reflection. The skin inflammation was nearly faded, but her plain face looked positively frumpy above the short, sexy dress.

The dress was far too sexy, she noticed, alarmed, as she saw the way her breasts jiggled under the fabric with her movements. It wasn't *her*.

No, it was too much of her.

Her half-naked chest didn't look as bad as she'd thought, though, without a bra. The gentle swell of cleavage pushed the thin material up and out sort of . . . sexily.

She turned off the hair dryer thoughtfully and shook out her hair. It was sleek rather than bouncy, but it worked.

Speaking of bouncy . . . jiggling visible breasts required at least some sexy lipstick to balance things out, she decided. She'd make the time for lipstick. Ignoring the next knock, she reached for the cosmetics again.

She painted her lips "Ripe Berry Red" with more accuracy than she'd managed yet, dropped the tube into the small black tool-bag that she was using as a purse, and opened the door with what she hoped was a serene smile.

"Oh my God. I mean . . . wow." Craig indicated her whole body with one wave of his hand. She admired the skillful, surreptitious way he glanced at her chest. Twice. She couldn't blame him. Her chest was hard to miss. "Sarah," he said, infusing her name with a deep appreciation.

Amusement pulled at her, distracting her from her nervousness. What she felt now, for a relief, was a gentle indulgence for this tongue-tied fellow. A man like any other, rather than the object of her long-held desire. The familiarity of the emotion made her feel more centered, sure of herself.

But his own sophisticated ensemble, from his tucked-in dress-shirt down to his softly shining leather shoes, showcased his body in a way she'd never seen before. He was, truly, an incredibly attractive man. A man who kept looking her up and down as if he couldn't believe what he was seeing. "Craig," she replied, amused, tapping her high-heeled shoe against the doorjamb.

Cleavage had so much power.

She couldn't help remembering the scantily clad Carlsdale tracksluts. She knew Craig saw right through their fawning attentions most of the time, flattering them and flirting with them just enough to be polite, but all too frequently he dated them too. It never lasted, but they had the power to interest him. They weren't jeans-and-tee kinds of girls. Many of them didn't seem to have two brain cells to rub together. They were useless eye-candy . . . but they turned Craig's head.

Like she was doing now. Only she wouldn't be like them. She wouldn't lose interest in Craig, moving on to the next big score after the second or third date. She would feel no letdown after hearing how his workday went, or discovering his real-life complexities. She already knew the real Craig. Knew him and loved him.

As she stood in her three-inch heels, with her first-place win just *one* of her day's accomplishments, she began to smile.

He looked more closely at her. His expression changed. "Hey, what happened to your face?"

Sarah considered her possible replies. "Sunburn," she finally said, closing the door behind her discreetly. "Shall we go?"

He'd pulled some strings to get them reservations at St. Louis's very best Italian restaurant, and over the fine-spun linen and romantic candlelight, they'd regaled each other with racing tales as if they were at their usual sports bar after a Carlsdale tuning session. He was attentive, entertaining, and kept his gaze from dipping again to her chest.

"To your victory," Craig said, lifting a delicate glass of wine between two fingers. She gazed at his hands, bemused. They were strong but tapered. A perfectionist's hands. Very unlike Gordon's, whose large hands and thick, clever fingers she remembered touching her.

Craig must have scrubbed and scrubbed to get the grease off and the dirt from under his nails. She knew she had.

The dark red of her own glass of Chianti glittered with flame glow as she clinked with his, then sipped. It was Craig's third toast to her track triumph, and she could tell he was still rocked by her accomplishment. Especially considering that she'd beaten even him. He seemed to be coping well enough with that, though. Aside from the way he assured her every few minutes, in their old tradition of friendly rivalry, that she would not be so lucky next time.

His admiring, flirtatious attention made her feel like she'd achieved the kind of balance that she'd always hoped for.

The waiter glided up with perfect timing to place one chocolate-drizzled cheesecake between them, and added two forks, smiling.

The moment oozed romance. She had won Craig's respect, and clearly, she had won his attention. He still looked at her as if he couldn't quite believe what he saw.

His next words proved her correct. "I just can't get over how beautiful you look. How . . . well, I'm stunned."

She felt her own smiling response at his self-deprecating chuckle. Craig at his most charming was very charming indeed. He had the knack of laughing at himself even as he worked his own angle. She'd seen his effect often enough on other women.

He continued, his eyes locked on hers. "Remember how I used to practically beg you to wear a dress? If I knew you'd look this hot, maybe I wouldn't have. There's not a guy in here who hasn't mentally undressed you."

Startled, Sarah took a furtive look around the restaurant. She was shocked to see many of the men look back at her. One even smiled and winked.

"Damn," she muttered. "You're not kidding."

Craig stared at her for a moment, then burst into laughter. "That's what I love about you. You honestly have no idea how cute you are."

She was delighted. He'd used the word "love." He saved that word for things he truly did love, like blown hemis and big turbos.

Was Craig finally falling for her?

A tingling pleasure cascaded through her, almost the same sensation as when she'd won the race. She couldn't deny the sense of accomplishment with Craig any more than she could the other. This moment had taken so long to arrive . . . and now it was here. As she'd dreamed.

When he reached out and took her hand in his, she smiled into his eyes. She felt a touch of vertigo, but attributed it to the wine she'd drunk.

"Sarah . . ." Craig chafed her fingers gently. She enjoyed the sensation, feeling it all up and down her spine. Her new power over him seemed almost to inform her that he would touch her an instant before he did. She knew the things he would say. He was hers, now, wasn't he?

How should she respond to his gentle touch? She thought she knew what she was supposed to do. She should lean toward him, uttering the sigh of relief and pleasure that had built up inside her, and look into his beautiful blue eyes with a soft, open invitation. He would kiss her, then. She'd fantasized about it before.

His touch grazed her arm as he trailed his fingers sensuously over her bare skin, climbing to her shoulder. It felt a bit ticklish, but pleasurable. She shivered.

He massaged behind her neck. He put pressure on it, pulling her toward him gently.

*Now* was when she should lean forward. The rest would follow. The moment was at hand. But if she leaned forward too much, her boobs might fall out.

She closed her eyes to concentrate, feeling his skillful fingertips at the nape of her neck. What Craig wanted was clear. What she wanted was clear. She frowned. She could almost imagine . . . Opening her eyes, she shifted slightly from his hand. His own eyes were closed, his lips slightly parted. It would be a blisteringly hot kiss. It might even be as good as *his*. But the timing was off somehow. It wasn't supposed to happen so quickly.

She wasn't ready.

"Gor—" She bit her tongue on the name.

His eyes popped open in confusion. "What?"

She hid her own eyes, panicked. "I said . . . 'gorgonzola.' " Sarah grabbed her fork and speared a piece of cheesecake. "This smells like they made it with gorgonzola cheese. Don't you think so?"

"Uh . . . I'm not sure." Craig let his hand fall from her. The sight of her cheerfully eating the cheesecake seemed to mollify him.

"Tastes better than it smells," she said, nodding as wisely as if she were a connoisseur of cheesecakes from around the world. "Have a sample."

"I was trying to," Craig said, smiling ruefully.

She giggled. He looked at her for another moment, then shrugged. He picked up his own fork and sampled the dessert. "It's good." Laying his fork down again, he took a breath, as if to say something.

Sarah got busy with her cheesecake again. "Mmmm."

Craig exhaled without speaking. He seemed confused. But he wasn't angry, she noticed, peeking up at him through her lashes. No, just confused. The cheesecake attracted his attention again.

Relieved, she chewed without tasting, swallowed. She felt bad for being a tease. But she wasn't completely a tease . . . she fully intended to consummate their new relationship. Just not right away. Not with those annoying, lingering thoughts about Gordon.

The eerie near-certainty that she knew Craig's thoughts—which wasn't so eerie, now that she thought of it; she'd known him for years—made her certain that she'd hurt his feelings a tiny bit. Or his ego. They were pretty indistinguishable with most men.

But Craig did love a challenge.

Well, so did she.

Smiling with what she hoped was just the right touch of mystery, she reached out to run one newly manicured, painted nail down his forearm and over the back of his hand. She tapped his index finger. "Are you still a playboy, Craig?"

From the way his face locked into immobility, she could tell she'd surprised him. When a moment later his throat worked, she managed to subdue victorious laughter in favor of another enigmatic smile.

"Sarah, you know those women meant nothing to me. But you . . ." he exhaled, shaking his head. The beginning of a smile tipped the corners of his mouth. "You always have." The tension between them stretched deliciously.

Their eyes met over the crumbs of cheesecake. They'd always understood each other. When the bill came, they both grabbed for it, but his reflexes proved faster. "Reaction time," he chided her as he whipped out his credit card with practiced smoothness. "It's my pleasure to pick this up. And hopefully, others?" He gazed at her with a confident smile that contained only a flicker of uncertainty. When her only reply was a small return smile, his uncertainty visibly grew, but so did the gleam of interest in his eyes.

Oh, he did *so* love a challenge.

Sarah smiled with satisfaction.

The next week would be a busy one, as they all towed out to Kentucky for the next race in the series. They'd all be thrashing to get their cars more competitive. As the second largest of the three big tri-state drag races, the event would attract dangerous rivals for the title.

Maybe it would also attract dangerous trackslut rivals for Craig. They no longer seemed quite as pathetic to her as they once did. Now that she was wearing dresses and makeup, she understood them a little better. But she also understood the source of their power, having appropriated it for herself. So long as she didn't have to do anything more girlie than wear this kind of regalia once in awhile, she would consider it an investment in reeling Craig in. She wouldn't morph any farther into a Martha Stewart. Probably. She hoped.

How she'd manage to balance being racer-by-day, Barbie-by-night she wasn't sure, but she had to try now that she had the trick of it. How astonishing that she was getting the hang of both racing *and* Barbie. Wasn't she turning out to be a woman of many talents, she thought with no little pride.

While walking to his expensive rental car, he threw an arm around her shoulders companionably. He drew her closer than was purely comradely, and whispered in her ear. "Thank you for tonight." His breath on her ear gave her shivers, as he no doubt intended.

Instead of giving him an elbow to the ribs or an impolite snort, as she would have just a week ago, Sarah added an extra sway to her walk, bumping her hip against his leg. She turned as they neared his car, leaned into him and snuggled. "No, thank *you*. Mmmm, I'm a sleepy girl," she murmured into his chest. She yawned, raising her hand to cover her mouth. *Lady-like.* The words and gestures were coming more automatically now.

She really did feel tired, though. The whole long day, from the racing, to the cameras, to the Ricky Racer emergency and the rest of it, and then the playing of these women's games, had drained her usually high level of energy. Thinking about the large, soft, king-sized bed waiting for her in the motel room, she sighed longingly, then patted Craig's chest with affection as she pushed him away.

"I tell you, I'm so glad to have a bed instead of a wad of blankets, for a change."

"I'm so glad you have a bed instead of a wad of blankets too."

She snorted, marched toward the sleek car he'd rented to spare wear-and-tear on his racecar. And, she suspected, to impress her with his upscale taste. It wasn't a sports car—more of a leather-everything land barge. Comfortable, but not very quick.

Now he would back off, she figured. Pretend either that she'd wounded him mortally, or else change the subject. Something predictable like that.

He didn't do what she expected.

"Your chariot awaits," Craig said, displaying not the slightest bit of uncertainty as he opened the shining black door, turning his most enigmatic smile on her as she folded herself into the leather. He shut the door with the same firm, authoritative air.

Sarah stared at the mahogany-paneled door, considering.

Craig drove with the assured air of one who knew his way around cars. She'd always recognized and appreciated that skill of his, possessing it herself, but just now she wished he'd drive a bit slower to give her time to think.

She was afraid she knew why he acted unpredictably.

Too soon, they arrived at the motel. Craig maintained his silence as he handed her out and walked her to her door. She began to wonder when he'd kiss her. She was surprised to find that she'd prefer to politely extricate herself from such a kiss, rather than end up on the big bed with him. It was simply too soon.

When they arrived at her room, it began. As she swiped the key card in the slot, she jumped to feel hot lips pressing on the back of her neck. She gasped in surprise and sudden shocked pleasure, and Craig made a low animal sound. He pressed his body against hers hungrily from behind, and they both stumbled forward into her room as the door opened under the weight of their two bodies.

# CHAPTER TWELVE

If it wasn't for her catching her heel on the slightly higher carpet in her room and yelping in pain as her ankle turned, she wasn't sure what would have happened. Craig's interest in her broadcast itself clearly through the material of their evening clothes, and his intent was obvious.

But at the sound of her pain, he became instantly solicitous. Concerned and protective, he supported her by the elbow and led her to the bed, the nearest place where they could sit. "Are you okay?"

"Yeah." Her cheeks burned. What an ungraceful stumble. What an awkward way to end his embrace. At least her ankle didn't seem to be damaged.

This was *not* the way she'd wanted to end their first real date.

But then again, neither was the way Craig had in mind. Did he think she was as easy as a trackslut?

He still had playtime in mind, if she could believe the gleam that returned to his eyes as soon as he saw her putting weight on her ankle.

"Can I massage it for you?" Craig's gaze was not completely innocent as he reached for her foot. "I'm told I have a healing touch."

*By a legion of thoroughly healed tracksluts,* was Sarah's first uncharitable thought. She didn't like the idea of her being counted among their number. She was different, superior. Wasn't she?

She shouldn't allow Craig to be touching her leg in such a way, moving his hand up over her knee, toying with the hemline of her dress. Though it did feel relaxing. Hypnotic. Kind of nice.

He had such experienced hands.

She marshaled her resolve and placed her own hands over his, stopping their upward movement. She wasn't a slut, and therefore he couldn't continue. Not on their first real date. Or else he'd do with her what he did with *them.*

Which would probably be extremely fun.

But afterward, he might do with her what he did with them. He might simply move on to the next conquest.

All because she was stupid enough to jump into bed with him the moment he decided to wine and dine her.

"That feels fantastic, but I'm all healed. See?" Sarah leapt up, pirouetting. Then she remembered that she was supposed to be tired. She sat down—farther from him than she'd been—and yawned once more, covering her mouth. Then she placed the back of her hand against her forehead for good measure. "I think I have a temperature," she murmured in what she hoped was an exhausted tone.

Craig looked at her levelly. "I can take a hint. No need to play the southern belle." He rose, squeezing her leg just above her knee once, almost enough to hurt, definitely enough to get her full attention. He trailed his hand off with a clever circling motion that brought a warm flush to her face despite herself. "You know what, Sarah? You're worth waiting for."

When he pulled the hotel room's door open he turned to face her once more. "Maybe I'll see you tomorrow? Almost everyone is pulling out at dawn. If I don't see you then . . ." He gave her the half-smile that had made her fall for him so long ago. "We'll hook up in Kentucky. Friday night? And please wear that dress again." Craig put his knuckles in his mouth and narrowed his eyes as if in pain. He shook his head theatrically. "Bye, Sarah."

"Bye, Craig."

Her hands felt oddly small and fragile, folded neatly in her lap. Staring at the motel's door with its red-lettered fire-escape plan, she shook her own head in an effort to clear it. Maybe she actually was coming down with a fever. Fever would explain the confusion that swirled hotly in her mind. Doubts pulled at her like a hundred fingers plucking randomly at her psyche.

"Did I really just let Craig walk out that door?" she whispered.

A tentative yip answered her. As she jumped up to do her duty by Ricky Racer, she wished for the hundredth time that the dog could speak. She could feed him, take him out to pee, and play with him until he barked for joy, but she couldn't ask for counsel about this particular situation.

When she returned back upstairs, she put him down to explore. She slipped off the dress and pulled off her heels with relief. In her underwear, she flopped onto the bed and watched Ricky sniff along the wall. As long as she was in the room to watch him and he remained quietly well-behaved, she wasn't going to keep him locked up in a cage, rules or no rules.

"Ricky, come here, I need to talk to you," she finally commanded, fending off the excitable bundle of fur when he launched himself onto the bed and began to lick long strands of her hair. "No, don't eat that. Ricky, I understand males. You are all so transparent. It's women I don't get. Why are women so confusing? Now that I'm more or less acting like one of them, I don't understand myself. Stop that. Hair gel is bad for you. Anyone would think that gel was beef gravy the way you keep gobbling it up. What's wrong with your old chew?"

Sarah cuddled the little dog on her lap, and scratched behind his ears. "Here's what I really need to know. Why is it that now, when I have Craig more or less right where I want him, I still worry that he'd just use me? And why do I keep thinking about Gordon at the weirdest times?"

The TV held no allure for her. No drama could upstage the one playing out in her own life. Twisting the edge of the comforter between two nerveless fingers, the desire to talk to someone else about it hammered at her. Should she seek out Will and Lee? No, they were likely just getting warmed up with the beer and good times, and she knew they wouldn't have a moment's tolerance for her current neurotic mood. Hell, she wouldn't either, were their situations reversed. Who needed it? But for the first time, she wished that she'd made more time to cultivate women friends. It would be a relief to confide in somebody, to get someone's honest feedback and the opinions of someone who'd understand and empathize.

*Gordon* was a good listener . . .

She was reaching for her cell phone before she could interrupt the impulse. He'd not only been a good listener, he'd offered insightful advice to her, hadn't he?

But as she dialed his programmed number, their last parting with all its unflattering implications made her tense her jaw with remembered shame. She stabbed the hang-up button just as she heard his phone begin to ring.

That was close. She'd almost made a fool of herself again.

Gordon stared at the number displayed on his phone, unbelieving. Sarah? His heart galloped in his chest. The phone vibrated against his palm, but he needed a moment to compose himself before answering.

He wasn't sure why a telephone call should be so unsettling. So he was sitting at home, thinking about her again and she called as if on cue. An odd coincidence, but hardly worth having a seizure over.

He ran a hand through his hair, took a deep breath, and then pressed the oval button in the center of the phone.

But, as he watched, the number blinked off and the phone became silent and still.

He stared at it dumbly. Why had she called him?

Why had she hung up?

She'd probably called by accident, thinking it was someone else's number. What else could it be? She wouldn't be needing his help with DNP, it being a self-adjusting component. Unless she'd messed with it in trying to improve her time.

Gordon frowned. She wouldn't be so foolish. Would she?

She *was* prone to impulsive actions . . .

Maybe she'd started to call him because she was plagued by the same battering waves of lust that assaulted him whenever he thought of their abbreviated liaison. Ever since he'd pulled the chute on their embrace that one evening, he'd been jolted every day, every few minutes by the memory of all that passion. The memory came on him with such frequency that it had developed into an annoying, constant dull ache, tempting him to take some vacation time and fly out to her.

Finish what they'd started.

But there were so many reasons against his doing that, not the least being an obligation to Red to supervise the shop and fill in producing the work that Sarah, Will and Lee would normally be producing.

Gordon rose to his feet, began to pace. He looked about his apartment in irritation. Irritable was how he felt about too many things lately. His apartment. His long hours at work followed by longer hours studying the automotive aftermarket, followed by small-hours-of-the-morning time at his computer putting together marketing plans.

But the worst of it was his nonexistent love life.

With determined practice and out of necessity due to his busy schedule, he'd long ago learned to transmute his sexual energy into hard work. There was not yet room for relationships in his plan, and therefore he had none. There was barely room even for the rare dating he needed once in awhile if only to remind himself he wasn't a complete automaton. But once he'd arrived at the place he was carving out for himself, *then* he'd relax and look around. He would have his pick of prime Southern California beauties. He would have his selection of the finest of lovelies who wanted companionship with him. As many decorative companions suitable for a stratospherically upwardly mobile man like himself as he wanted.

He could tell he was frustrated—clearly, he was frustrated—by the harem of women dancing through his head, all wearing different colored wisps of lacy lingerie. But they all wore the same face. The same body.

*Stop thinking about her.*

His ascension was taking too long, that was the real problem. So many years, and now he was nearly there. He'd be insane to think of jeopardizing that.

Gordon paced slower. He could never, in good conscience, make love to Red's daughter. She was off limits, and to remain out of his mind.

Gordon smiled grimly. Only one person was out of his mind, and that was himself. He still wanted her despite the impediments: Red, the shop, his future trophy wife . . . Craig.

Just how close *was* she to Craig? How close was she to him *right now?*

It was none of his damned business.

But according to the shop gossip, she'd chased after Craig for longer than she'd worked there. Craig was her hero, her mentor, her knight in shining armor.

Hell, she wanted him so bad she'd even asked *him* about how best to land Craig. He needed to remember that.

He'd done the sensible thing when he'd cut their embrace short.

The memory of Sarah's bare skin got his harem dancing again, and he cursed.

Gordon headed toward the bathroom, turned on the shower. Shedding his clothes, he stepped directly into the spray of water and bit back a howl at its icy-coldness.

The achievement of his dreams—the stability of wealth and power so that there was no chance he'd ever be poor again—had been a long time coming. He wasn't about to throw it all away on a passing fancy.

Sarah blew sweaty strands of hair off her face and squinted at the sun. It was already hot at the racetrack, and it was only nine-thirty in the morning.

"We still have a few hours," she told Will hopefully.

He hunched over the engine bay with the same intensity she'd grown used to seeing in him and Lee, but there was an especially tense cast to his shoulders today as he adjusted the bag of ice to cool the intake manifold.

They hadn't done well in the test 'n tune the day before, or the first qualifying round earlier that morning. Competition had poured in from all over the country to vie for the larger purse and contingency money that the Bowling Green, Kentucky, event offered. They were all fighting to stay in the game.

She was also fighting to prove she wasn't a fluke. At the first race, she'd been the dark-horse winner, going from "zero to hero," as FAST had put it in her interview. Nobody had known who she was and none of the other racers had given her any respect or even credit for being there, with the exception of Craig, until she'd won.

Here at this second race, with the first race win under her belt, everybody knew her and knew she was capable of winning.

She'd actually become something of a media darling too, as she learned to toss her blond hair and smile flirtatiously at the cameras. But as gratifying as the attention was, it had a flip side. The pressure had ratcheted up as everyone watched and waited to see if she'd just gotten lucky.

And she found herself wondering the same thing. What if she really was in over her head, and proved it with dismal passes? What if she did just get lucky?

"We're still in the running," she said, more for the sake of her own flagging spirits than for Will, but it won a tired smile from him.

It was Lee who answered, though, after consulting his watch. "An hour and a half before they call our class. Lots of time."

His soft voice was as gentle and encouraging as ever, but Will's words swept away its comfort. "I hate to say it, but we're not going to be able to get any more power out of this beast in only an hour and a half. We're probably not going to qualify for this field."

"No!" Sarah objected. Her nails clawed at the Mustang's fender, the clicking sound of them against the paint reminding her not to press too hard. She'd painted her nails. They matched the red of the DNP decals covering her car, but the gray-brown of dirt caking her cuticles and creases of her fingers sort of spoiled the feminine effect.

But it did remind her how hard she'd been thrashing to bring her car up to speed. She would be going up against Craig and the other front-runners in the Renegade class. That was, she would be if she could make her car faster. Quickly. She had to extract another couple of tenths out of her Mustang, or else she'd be just another also-ran among the hordes in the amateur classes. Not even a loser. A nobody.

"There has to be some way." Even as she said it, she thought of one possible solution. She gazed at a specific section of the engine compartment. "I know of a way."

Will wore such a serious expression that she marveled at it being on his face. "Oh, no you don't. As your crew chief, I'd be the one people blamed when your car grenaded. It's my carcass Red and Gordon would take turns kicking around, so don't you even think about touching the DNP nitrous controller. Hands *off.*"

She spoke soothingly, the way Lee did. "But it's set so low. It would be perfectly safe at a slightly higher setting."

But for once Lee didn't sound at all soothing when he spoke up. "We should call Gordon and ask." He averted his head, looking disturbed. "Maybe there's something else we can do. Tighten the lash, maybe . . ."

"Already did it," Sarah said, fighting to keep her voice low and calm. "And I am not calling Gordon. He hasn't called *me* this whole time . . ." Too late, she realized how that sounded— like she was a neglected girlfriend. She hastened to add, "He hasn't checked on our status at this event, or the last event, or asked how his component's performing, so I'm sure he doesn't care. About what we do with DNP."

"Sarah, Gordon does care." Will studied her reaction, and what he saw made him raise his eyebrows. But all he said was, "I talked with him a week ago when I called in to the shop."

Sarah pinned him with a look. Will called Gordon? She would not ask him what Gordon said. She would *not.* "Okay, so you called in. When I called Dad last week, he told me they were managing well enough without you two, at least temporarily. Why would Gordon have you check in with him?"

"Oh, I don't know that I'd call it checking in. More of a touching base. A courteous hail?" Will pondered, then threw up his arms a split second before Sarah strangled him. "Okay, okay. I called in because right before I flew out, Gordon asked me to keep an eye on things and call him when anything unusual occurred with DNP. I figured he'd like to know about the interview you gave FAST. That qualifies as unusual in a good way, since you mentioned him as a sponsor."

Sarah tried to push away a sense of betrayal. She spoke stiffly. "You could have mentioned that you were reporting on me."

"Aw, Sarah . . ." Will had the good grace to look guilty. "It wasn't like that. I only called that once, and it was more to talk with the guys than anything."

"Uh-huh." Sarah repositioned the ice bag.

Minutes passed in a silence cooler than the ice. "C'mon, Sarah," Will finally said. "Don't be that way."

Lee just looked pained.

After another minute, Sarah spoke, reluctance coloring her tone. "Well, I suppose it's water under the bridge . . . on one condition." She gazed at them both under lowered lids.

Will and Lee brightened.

"We adjust the DNP component just the tiniest bit up, and neither of you says one word to Gordon about it."

Lee opened his mouth to speak, but Will overrode him. "Deal. Just up to the six mark, though," he said, already tinkering with the gray metal unit that contained the component. He opened it. "That's just one notch up. That should be safe." Sarah peered over his shoulder, making sure that he performed the adjustments the way she'd seen Gordon do it. Lee craned around Will's other side, watching.

When it was done, Will tightened the screws on the unit. "I just wish there were a way we could test it beforehand, to get you some exact numbers."

Sarah did rapid calculations in her head. "It'll be just enough," she said confidently. She hoped it would be.

"Gordon's a good guy, you know," Will declared suddenly, making her jump guiltily. "You could do worse." He winked at Sarah and tossed the screwdriver into the toolbox.

"I could do better," Sarah retorted, deliberately thinking instead of Craig's handsome visage. And his capable, tapered fingers piloting his Mustang over the finish line. He finally wanted her, unlike Gordon. That made him head and shoulders better.

Sarah smiled at the thought of both their broad shoulders and torsos, preferably covered with some glistening oil.

"Craig and I have another date tonight," she said, as much to remind herself which torso she should focus on as to inform Will and Lee. She squirted cleaner on the windshield and polished it unnecessarily. A drop of sweat fell from her forehead and mixed with the cleaner. *Hot.* A good thing that Ricky Racer had a nice, luxurious air-conditioned motel room this weekend, she mused, or else he'd be one fried hot dog.

Tilting her head to examine the window for streaks, her ponytail slid over one shoulder, baring her neck to the sun. The skin on back of her neck tightened, reminding her that she'd forgotten to apply sun block again.

She felt greasy, which she was used to, but working in the hot sun, compounded by the smoky, exhaust-laden air that clung to her skin until it dripped off her in dirty sweat, made her feel more uncomfortable than she'd expected. The sensation made her irritable. It probably didn't help that she'd stayed out so late the night before on her second romantic dinner date with Craig. He was a charmer, all right, and it had taken all her willpower and growing skills as a bona-fide, dress-wearing temptress to fend him off. But she'd done it.

She brushed violently at strands of hair that clung to her cheeks, tickling her nose.

Craig was back in his motor-home, doubtless basking under its air conditioning. She could be there now, basking with him. He'd be happy to see her.

He'd be a little too happy to see her.

"Things heating up with lover boy?"

Sarah jumped, but Will's expression was carefully neutral. She bent to check the pressure of her slicks before answering him. "Craig's coming around. Nothing wrong with that." She tossed a wicked grin to him and Lee. "But will he still love me in the morning if I paddle his behind? On the track, that is."

"There's an image I did not need." Will gestured in the general direction of the grass where the bigger trailers and motor-homes were parked. "Why don't you go ask him how he feels about that?"

"Maybe I will." She plucked at her sodden T-shirt. "Think he'll mind the drowned garage-rat look? Do you have a comb, or a hat I can borrow? I wonder if I brought my lipstick . . . no, that's right, I didn't. Good thing, too. It would have melted all over the place."

Will was looking at her oddly. Then he shrugged, finding something riveting on the engine to gaze at. "It's none of my business," he began, staring fixedly.

Sarah intercepted Lee's quick look at Will before he found something equally intriguing to watch in the vicinity of his clipboard. "What? What is it?"

"He's a player. This . . . *thing* you've had for him, it was no big deal as long as you saw that, or at least didn't . . . But, now he's really putting the moves on you. He's . . . and you're all spruced up, what with the makeup and everything."

"I barely wear makeup," she interjected. "Today it's just the tiniest bit of Natural Gold eye shadow on my lids and a hint of lengthening Featherlash Mascara. Oh, and my nails. But the nails are special occasion."

"*That's* what I mean. You never used to care about any of that."

"Yeah, and I looked like a guy!" Sarah softened her tone. "Not that there's anything wrong with the way guys look." She smiled tentatively at Will. "Present company a smashing example?"

Will waved aside the peace offering. "Seriously. This makeover thing of yours—did you think we'd miss your carrying that purse yesterday, or that perfume you have on now?—it all started about the time Craig got serious about you. You're getting all weird because of him. You're doing it for him. I . . . *we* . . . don't want to see you get hurt, is all."

But Sarah knew her makeover phase hadn't started with Craig. Gordon's face floated, familiar and stern in her memory. He was the one who'd told her to just be herself. She was still trying to figure out who that new feminine version of her was, of course . . . but it was Gordon who'd gotten her thinking about it. Or maybe Craig had offered the catalyst, or maybe it was that far-away track official who'd mistaken her for a guy. But exploring her feminine side was something she was doing for herself.

She couldn't tell Will any of that, though. Not in so many words. It sounded weak and therapy-groupy in her own mind, much less spoken out loud for Will and Lee to mock. Or pity.

"You guys. You're sweet. Don't worry about me. Worry about Craig. Between schooling him on the track and driving him crazy on our dates, he could use the advice more than me."

She regretted her words when she saw Will blink several times. Lee just looked at the ground, but with an unhappy frown.

Will shrugged. "Okay then. That's pretty much it." He folded down the lid of the toolbox. "And that's it for here too. Why don't we all take a little break before the finals. I sure could use one," he muttered. "Lee, let's grab some roast beef sandwiches."

"Thanks, both of you," she called after them. "Really." Sarah watched them walk away, the sight of their stiff backs making her feel a little apprehensive. But they weren't the types of guys to hold a grudge, she knew. They'd unbend. They always did.

Her shirt peeled away from her skin when she plucked at it. She really was sweaty. Better cool off or else the guys would have to pour her into the cockpit. Her jeans felt like they were starting to meld to her body.

Craig's motor-home was a short walk away.

Or, there was her motel room, with nobody in it to cause her ambivalence. Nobody's hard, smooth-moving body dying to please her. Nobody's hypnotizing blue eyes gazing at her as if they'd devour her whole. Nobody's teasing touches grazing her skin, more skillful than they had any right to be.

She whistled as she piled fresh ice on her intake. She could take a quick shower in her motel. A quick *cold* shower. And walk Ricky. And make Craig wait just a little longer for her company. It would probably make him want her that much more.

She hitched a ride from another racer headed back toward the main road with its line of budget motels.

A win today, she thought as she approached the motel, would position her as the one to beat at the world finals next week. And a victory next week . . . she hardly dared to dream of it . . . a victory *on live TV* would be a coup that would erase any lingering doubts in anyone's minds.

She wondered how Craig would take it.

Thousands of people out there in TV land would know her name. Gordon would realize his selection of her for his DNP was justified.

*Gordon.* She imagined him gazing at her with admiration. Then without her telling it to, her mind switched the image: Gordon's unbridled passion, his hazel eyes darkening to midnight fire.

The thought made her weak in the knees.

"Oh no." Sarah halted in her tracks. She made herself continue walking up the stairs to her motel room, fingering the key to the old-fashioned lock. "I don't need that kind of distraction. I get enough of that from Craig. I'm *over* Gordon. Crap! Better to think of Craig. At least he's controllable," she coached herself, not caring if anyone else was sharing the hallway and would think her insane for talking to herself. She needed to hear a voice of reason.

"Sky blue eyes, cheeky grin, a body to die for," she continued, opening the door to her room. Ricky's excited barking didn't help her concentration.

"Smooth moves on and off the track, gorgeous blond hair, intelligent, *interested* . . . and did I mention a body to die for?"

Ricky grunted, hurling himself from his imprisoning crate as soon as she opened the wire door. He leapt, licking air.

"Yeah, yeah. You're happy to see me. You're happy to see everyone, except maybe Craig." Thoughtful, Sarah clipped the leash and hurried downstairs with the dog. "But then, you like Gordon. Everyone likes Gordon," she grumped, waiting for Ricky to find the perfect shrub to water. "Well, I refuse to lust for somebody who is so completely wrong for me. He made his feelings crystal clear that day. Not that I care. Big deal if he was disappointed after kissing me. So what if he took off practically running, as if I were contagious. Who gives a crap that he hasn't called me in two weeks despite my using his nitrous system and promoting it on national TV.

"I have better things to do with my time," she said, watching Ricky pee. "Not for *one more second* am I going to think about Gordon Devine."

"Gordon called."

Sarah's arm froze in mid-wave. She had to consciously order it to continue moving for the cameras that flashed in the shade of the bleachers next to the manufacturer's midway. At least she was still the reigning media darling of the event, even though she'd taken only second place at the finals. First place had gone to Craig, who she could see waving to his own set of cameras.

She'd nearly won first place. Which was still technically a pretty big deal. Not only was she a relatively unknown rookie in a newly built car, but she was a girl in the spotlight on a guy's playing field. She'd beaten most of the very best the country had to offer in grassroots drag racing, taking out class favorites Bill Sturgeon and Kurt Mallet in the eliminations. It had been immensely satisfying to serve all of them notice that there was a dominant new player in town, and her name was Sarah Mattel.

She smiled prettily at the cameras, the way she'd practiced since that interview with the TV director the week before, and tossed her long blond hair over her shoulder. Her smile didn't waver as she answered without looking at Will. "What the hell did he want?"

"You, sweetheart."

Sarah dropped her arm and wheeled on him. "What?"

Will gazed at her wickedly. "He wanted to talk to you. What did you think I meant?"

Sarah composed herself but her smile was strained. She gave the cameras one last wave, then tucked her runner-up check into her back pocket and climbed into the relative shadow of her car. As she drove slowly around the show car arena, then carefully passed through the crowds milling around the swap meet, she was conscious of Will pacing her, watching her with a knowing half-smile. Lee had fallen behind, gazing with interest at a table of performance wheels for sale.

Finally she gritted out, "What did he want to talk to me about?"

"DNP, I suppose. Or something about the shop. What else could it be?"

"I can't imagine."

"Maybe he's got a thing for you." Will gazed straight ahead.

Sarah hissed between her teeth. "Trust me, it's not that." The memory of the post-kiss, uninterested Gordon still had the power to sting.

"How do you know? Give it a chance. It'd be an upgrade from Craig."

Sarah slammed her foot down on her brakes. "What have you got against Craig? He's one of the good guys, now, you know. And he's *always* been a friend of mine, though I wanted more, and now, miraculously, he does too. Which I think is just great. *And* he's a damn good driver. He beat me today didn't he? If it wasn't for . . ."

"For Gordon," Will finished, laughing. "If it wasn't for Gordon and his DNP, you'd be trailing Craig by a lot farther than one car."

"That's it. Go away. I can't deal with you right now."

"Well, if you're going to be all pissy about it . . ."

"*Pissy?*" she exploded. But Will was already backtracking to Lee. He leaned over to say something to Lee, and Lee slowly nodded.

*Infuriating.* Sarah eased back onto the throttle, moving her car more slowly than usual away from them because she was trying not to floor it. She exercised accelerator restraint. And also exercised restraint on her pissy temper. Was she really being pissy?

Maybe a little pissy.

She'd never been called pissy before.

She'd never *been* pissy before. Unease flooded her, spoiling the euphoria from her win and all the ensuing attention. Maybe Will was right, and she'd taken the girlie thing too far. Maybe she'd subconsciously incorporated female bitchiness as a by-product of the makeup and clothes and perfume she wore. Could the lipstick and the smallest hint of eyeliner and mascara that she had on alter a person's behavior?

It was Gordon's fault. His calling and wanting to talk to her had thrown a wrench into her system, the way he always managed to do.

Which didn't mean anything except that he was unfinished business.

She smiled, relieved. The problem suggested the solution: She would call Gordon right away, before her date with Craig. Before she even showered. But after she walked the dog.

She'd apply the brakes to that unfinished business, for some much-needed peace of mind.

# CHAPTER THIRTEEN

In her delightfully air-conditioned motel room, Sarah felt nervous for no good reason. Just because she'd taken out her cell phone and reclined on two pillows, ready to call Gordon to find out what he'd wanted, that was no cause for the anxious tingles that ran up and down her arms. A business call to Gordon would be boring at best, unpleasant at worst. Probably she'd end up talking to her dad instead. A quick update on her racing status, a bit of small talk about the shop . . . it would take a couple of minutes, tops, and be as easy as coasting.

She moistened her lips with her tongue, feeling the slick waxiness of Forbidden Red Apple and the firm warmth of her mouth. She wondered if Gordon would prefer kissing her new, painted lips.

She cleared her throat. Punching the number, she took a deep breath. "You called?" she drawled when he answered.

"Yes I did. It's appropriate for me to congratulate you on your win, and thank you for promoting DNP."

Sarah waited, but he added nothing. She felt her spine straightening and her shoulders grow tight with tension. The two pillows suddenly felt uncomfortable, and she levered herself up onto one arm. "You're welcome. Is that all?"

"It would also be appropriate for me to wish you the best in the World Finals next weekend. I'm sure you'll do very well."

The irritation that had shimmered inside her when she'd first heard his cool voice eased somewhat. "Thanks. I guess."

"You guess?"

"Just congratulations, and good luck? Two weeks of nothing, then all I get is a stiff little phone call." She could have bit her tongue for letting that slip out. She was such a fool to have wanted anything else, even in her subconscious. She cursed herself and wished she could call her words back.

"Could be worse." His voice changed. It was now just as she remembered it: embers wrapped in molasses. His amusement was subtle, but she heard it.

A smile tugged at her lips despite herself. "It almost was worse."

"Sarah?"

"Mm-hm?"

"In the spirit of giving free advice—for which you once asked me—let me add one more useful item. Don't accuse a man of giving you a 'stiff little' anything. It's demoralizing."

She burst out laughing. "You have nothing to worry about."

"Ah." One syllable. In it, she could hear all kinds of things. His restraint as well as his quiet, masculine confidence, not to mention the dirty thoughts that had sprung up.

She stifled a laugh. It was his restraint that challenged her. Would he not even *acknowledge* their last meeting? She certainly wasn't going to be the one to bring it up directly. She made her tone deliberately mundane. "So how's the shop? How are your night classes?"

"I've graduated. I'm officially overqualified to be sorting these accounts payable and payroll filings. When do you get back?"

"Miss me, huh?" she teased. She lay back down on the bed. "I get back after Columbus. I'll catch things up then, promise. But isn't Dad helping out with that?"

"Red's been out a lot. Going to a lot of car shows and a few other things," he added before she could ask.

"Here I thought I was the one on vacation." Sarah stretched, grunting in satisfaction.

"I would have considered racing at that level a lot of work."

"It is, it is . . . but when you do what you love it's not really work."

"Will tells me that you've forgone the roughing-it part of the racing experience?"

Sarah blushed. "Well, today's second-place purse won't buy me a luxury motor-home, or even a big enclosed trailer, but it's more than enough to keep all of us in cheap motels and maybe buy me some frilly girl things. Next week's purse—funny how the word 'purse' means more than one thing, now—is the biggie. And I don't need to tell you how unprecedented the live TV coverage will be."

"I do wish you the best of luck," Gordon repeated, his voice warm. He was quiet for a moment. "I heard about your new style. Your . . . apparel explorations. Have you worn that black dress yet?"

Sarah smiled slowly. "Thanks in part to your useful advice, I've even blown-dry my hair and worn some makeup. I'm wearing mascara and lipstick right now."

"Going out?"

She detected an odd note to his voice. "Well. Actually . . ." A strange reluctance to tell Gordon about the dates with Craig held her tongue. Though there wasn't much to tell, yet. Just how Craig was pursuing her for a change rather than the other way around. It was news that Gordon would hear sooner or later anyhow.

His single pointed question made her feel guilty. But she didn't have anything to hide. It was *his* advice, after all, that had helped her turn Craig's head. Maybe he'd even be happy for her.

Tell him? Not tell him?

While she was trying to decide, the motel phone rang.

Startled, she gasped. She confirmed the time. "I'd better go."

"Yes. Goodbye, Sarah."

"Goodbye." She hung up, but held the phone against her ear for another few moments until the overloud jangling of the motel phone stopped.

Sarah rolled down the rental car's passenger window and leaned out, inhaling the irresistible petroleum scent of the gas station. "C'mon, tell me!" She glared at Craig threateningly, but couldn't help smiling at the way he made a zipping motion across his lips. Her smile widened with pleasure from the masculine line of his body as he leaned against the car's plain white paint, dividing his attention between her and the numbers ticking up on the gas pump.

But he wouldn't tell her their destination. "You'll like it," was all he said, with his eyes sparkling with the excitement of a kid before Christmas.

"Hope I dressed appropriately," she said, fishing for a hint. She glanced down at the clothes she'd decided on: a tight, scoop-neck T-shirt the color of a ripe tangerine and blue jeans cut low enough to show flashes of her belly, paired with her old shop shoes. Craig had told her she'd be doing some walking tonight and to wear comfortable shoes.

"You dressed exactly right for where we're going."

She made a rude sound, and rolled up the window on his laughter. Looking at her reflection in the visor mirror, she applied another layer of Moisture Gloss to her lips. Her casual attire wasn't as delicately feminine as the dresses she'd worn during her other two dates with Craig, but the bright, body-conscious shirt and low-slung jeans put her sex on display in a way that fluttering fabrics and spaghetti straps didn't.

When he'd picked her up, Craig's lustful looks while walking her to his rental car—a four-door Ford Focus this time, possibly for its distance-driving good gas mileage—made his approval obvious. When she threw an extra sway into her walk, she heard him suck in his breath. She could actually feel her self-confidence with using womanly wiles ratcheting up, and as it increased, she did more of the same: crossing her legs high on the thigh, examining her manicured nails in a way that showed them off, touching his arm to punctuate an item under discussion.

Craig clearly approved. Already in a better mood than she'd ever seen him, her feminine, appreciative responses put him over the top into such good cheer that he even spoke without bitterness about his brother David, who hadn't called Craig since a falling-out years back. "I think I'll drop by next week. Indianapolis isn't far from Columbus, is it? His wife used to cook the best chicken and dumplings in the state. Did I ever tell you that sometimes I envy Dave? He can be a prick, but he's the one with a beautiful wife and kids. Maybe I'm not cut out for that, but it does sound good sometimes." As they drove to his mystery destination he regaled her with tales of his childhood in Indianapolis, watching the Indy 500 for the first time, and deciding to become a racer. "Of course, the jobs were migrating to California. Not being burdened with wife and kids, like every other college-age Midwesterner was, I did too . . . and I'm glad, 'cause I wouldn't have met you otherwise."

Sarah smiled with satisfaction when she felt his warm hand enfold hers.

After their gas station pit stop and another hour of driving, they arrived at their destination.

"No way!" Sarah marveled at the huge tire they drove through into the parking lot of Speed World. She could hear engines roaring. "I haven't been to one of these in ages!"

"I was hoping you'd say that," Craig said, clearly delighted with her response.

They ran to the main building. Sarah grabbed at the wrench-handled doors before she could remember to let him open it for her, then shrugged, shooting him a challenging smile. They charged across the red and black carpet—its design had formula cars and checkered flags, she noticed with approval—and out the far door. The engine noise swelled. "Which would you like to lose at first?" she called over the noise. "Grand Prix? Slick Trax? Turbo Track?"

"Top Eliminator isn't your game today, is it?" Craig threw back at her, looking regretfully at the propane-powered dragsters. They were by far the loudest, and fastest.

"Right here, right now!" she howled.

Craig hung back, teased her. "I don't want to rub salt into the wound, honey. After your losing today and all. I hate to make a girl cry."

"I'm going to whup you good for that. Let's go. Unless you can't handle being beaten by a woman?"

It wasn't the same as the real drag racing earlier in the day, but the propane-fueled, 300-horsepower dragsters would give her a fun kick in the pants. Almost as fun as wiping that superior look off Craig's face. She fastened herself into the long, rumbling vehicle and stared through the plastic shield. Two black rubber grooves extended to the end of the track, straddling the roller-coaster-style median that kept the amateurs from straying off-course. Even with such a dumbed-down version of drag racing, she felt the familiar adrenaline as a fever to redeem herself. She'd come in second earlier in the day, as Craig had pointed out.

She didn't want it to happen again.

Twenty minutes and three passes later, they walked toward the building again. Sarah couldn't keep from smiling. "Buy you a drink to take the sting out?"

Craig smiled too, though there was a forced quality to it.

"You didn't just beat me, you annihilated me." He didn't look at her. Was he brooding? He was! Craig, brooding. About a game. It wasn't even real racing.

A suspicion occurred to her. "You didn't let me win, did you?" That would spoil everything.

"Hell, no," he replied with some heat. "I don't let anyone win. Ever. Least of all you. And this is just playing," Craig said, as if to himself. "It doesn't count as much as . . ."

"As the real thing. Where you're a winner and I'm a big fat loser," Sarah joked. She wished he hadn't reminded her.

"You could never be a loser."

"But at least I'm a first loser. No, that doesn't sound good either," she mused, shrugging it off. "You can decide for yourself in Columbus, when you eat my dust." It hit her, then, just how competitive Craig was. He didn't like it at all that she'd beaten him, even though it was "just a game."

"How about we play some Daytona?" Craig asked.

The popular linked racing simulator let anyone join in, but when they'd crossed Electric Alley, past all the other redemption and video games and air hockey tables, she saw they had it to themselves. She slid into the car seat, tested the brake and accelerator pedals while Craig slipped quarters into the slot. She loved the road race game, and knew Craig did too, but when she glanced at him punching the button, adjusting his car's view, she saw his most determined expression.

She punched up her own view-change, and the game began. Craig drove aggressively, diving for the apex and nudging her car into the wall at every opportunity. She laughed, nudging him back, but then he steered into her, flipping her car.

At the finish line, she came in second.

Craig's smile was beautiful to look at, and completely irritating. He extended a hand to help her up out of the seat. "Still offering that drink?"

"I think I need it more than you do," she grouched, but enjoyed the protective way he guided her back through the packed arcade. He placed his body in such a manner as to keep others from her path and didn't even look at any of the many distractions. Not a glance at the big-screen TVs with their games of baseball, or flashing neon signs or scrolling LED displays or mechanically waving flags hanging from the ceiling above the Speed World Café and Bar. He seated her with a careful grace that kept her mute. His hand lingered on her hair, then he sat, passing her a menu.

"She'll have a Hypnotized," Craig told the bartender.

"Looks yummy," Sarah agreed, craving the sweetness of its coconut rum and pineapple. But she pinned him with an accusing stare. "I'm starting to *feel* hypnotized."

"Good, it's not just me then." Craig didn't smile as he met her eyes. Her heart gave a little leap.

"It *is* you," she managed to retort in something like her normal voice. "Your . . . God, I don't even know what to call it. Your attentions," she joked. "It's like you're mistaking me for a trackslut. I should be so lucky, huh?" She sipped from her drink, glad that it was strong. She peered at Craig over the rim of her glass. He seemed deep in thought. It wasn't an uncomfortable silence though. They'd known each other far too long for that. Besides, the TVs, rock music, video games, change dispensers and constant distant rumble of engines gave them both plenty else to listen to. In fact, she could hear an old favorite song of theirs, a rock ballad.

She tilted her head back, giving her neck a pleasant stretch. Directly above them was a painted-over speaker grill, between two flags. The long line of rectangular cloths waved slowly back and forth. She spotted an Indy Racing League flag, a NASCAR® Craftsman Truck flag, and the distinctive red, yellow and black Ferrari flag toward the end. But one flag repeated after every three others, its theme repeated throughout the entire park: the black and white checkered flag.

Craig heard the rock ballad too. He pushed back his stool with a deliberate movement and offered his hand to help her up. She took it, looking at him questioningly.

"Hear it?" he asked, his soft voice seeming to enter her bloodstream and caress her from the inside out.

She nodded, mute, and wasn't surprised when he pulled her slowly toward him. Her chest pressed against his, and she could feel his body sway with hers. Her head buzzed. She closed her eyes when he kissed the top of her head.

"Sarah. You're not even in the same galaxy as the tracksluts. You never were. I was just too stupid to see you there, always there and worlds better. Right in front of me."

They turned in a slow circle, drinks forgotten. Sarah felt a velvety warm softness suffuse her entire body, seeming to envelop her from the ends of her hair down to the tips of her toes. She couldn't think. She couldn't get past her awe at his sudden confession. Nothing he could do would surprise her more than what he'd just said.

He proved her wrong, then.

He made a helpless, almost animal sound in his throat, and he was kissing her, his lips a long-awaited fulfillment. It pushed all attempts at thought out of her head, and she relaxed totally into his embrace.

He was a very good kisser.

As the song ended, she felt every inch of his body against hers as they stopped moving and just held each other. In that moment, she felt as if she were in a sensual trance. Would he wake her, or bring her back to his room, continue their embrace there? She felt almost disconnected from the thought. It sounded pleasant.

As if reading her mind, he spoke, his voice soft and knowing.

"No, we're not going to go there. Not yet. Not anytime soon. How else can I make an exception?"

Overwhelmed, she stroked down the muscles of his back, up his sides. "Mmmm, *Craig.*"

"Mm-hm?" Amused.

He meant what he said. She released him reluctantly, reached for her glass and tilted back the rest of her Hypnotized. Basking under his hot gaze, she felt a sense of achievement that sent a shudder through her body. "We'd better play a vigorous game of air hockey then."

"You like losing that much?" The competitive light was back in his eyes.

"I like to see a grown man cry. You'll do."

# CHAPTER FOURTEEN

"Don't tell me. More coffee."

Sarah could only groan assent. Another state, another hot, humid Midwestern morning of having to concentrate despite the roaring engines and shrieking burnouts. The atmosphere aggravated her headache.

She was already wiped out.

But today was Columbus, today was live TV coverage, today was the big day. Today was the largest race of the year, by far, with the biggest spectator and racer turnout. The other racers, like her, were looking to be in the limelight with their crew in pressed, clean team uniforms and their cars set on kill.

She'd dose herself with as much caffeine as necessary to pull off a win. "Black. Lots of sugar," she told Will.

The time trials had gotten off to a good start the day before, but as she made pass after consistent pass, she couldn't help noticing that she wasn't the only one running fast and steady. The competition wanted blood.

She just had to want it more than they did, she told herself. But today, the one day she should be bright-eyed and bushy-tailed, what she wanted most was some more sleep.

Going drinking with Craig and his crowd of heads-up racer buddies last night had been a bad idea. She definitely shouldn't have let them goad her into matching their shots of tequila-and-limes. What had she been trying to prove? She couldn't remember at the moment.

"You look tired," Lee said with concern. "Are you . . . do you want anything else? Some aspirin or something?"

Sarah shook her head, then grimaced at the sharp pain. "I'm getting exactly what I deserve." She crawled into the racing seat and just sat in the heat, feeling the relief of not moving.

Craig's attentions still intoxicated her, although they took her away from her racing practice and brainstorming sessions with Will and Lee a bit more than they should. She'd spent all week in his company whenever she wasn't doing the necessary test-and-tuning on her car. It seemed Craig meant what he'd said. He actually *courted* her, and continued to shock the hell out of her by not luring her into bed, though his teasing and kisses were almost enough to make her want to jump his bones. It was exhilarating, and even though they hadn't slept together yet, they still had a blast. She couldn't help wondering if becoming lovers would be the beginning of the end. Or would it just make their dates infinitely more fun?

Her hangover throbbed at the thought of such exertions, and she groaned.

"Here ya go, down the hatch." Will smiled at her pitilessly.

Shooting the hot coffee as if it were a tequila-and-lime, she slit her eyes against the scalding and reminded herself there wasn't time for pain.

"Okay. Now . . . Lee, where are we with the numbers?" She shuddered at the coffee's flavor as her taste buds recovered from the heat.

Lee watched her make faces for a moment, then shrugged, checking the clipboard he'd been carrying to all of the three races. "Erratic. We're off a little. Enough that we might not qualify for the field. It'll be close."

"Close only counts in horseshoes and hand grenades," she murmured. "And I hate to lose. Let's do whatever it takes."

"What it takes is another week of tuning and a driver without a hangover," Will said brutally.

Sarah glared at him, hoping that her reddened eyes fringed with black mascara made the determined stare more imperative. "I said no. I'm fine. I will be fine," she amended. "Lee, where's that aspirin?"

"You said you didn't want—"

"That was before you told me I've gotten erratic."

"Okay." Lee all but tiptoed away from her temper.

"Don't bully him," Will said. "He just wants to win."

"Don't we all."

"Then let's back it down and enter a class where you have a chance. Sarah, that purse lured the big dogs out of hiding. Did you know that Gil Badden is here? Runner-up is the best you could hope for in this class."

"Second place is the first loser."

"Bullshit."

Her head snapped up, but Will was already continuing. "No one doubts your skill. But have you seen those guys in action?"

"I've been concentrating on myself."

"I noticed."

Sarah's headache spiked. "What is that supposed to mean?"

"Just . . . damn, girl, just because you want to impress your boyfriend doesn't mean you need to go ultra hardcore before you're ready. As your crew chief, I'm telling you it's not a smart decision. Know your limitations."

"I don't have any more limitations than anyone else out there!" She had to remind herself that Will might blow her off as a hysterical female if she didn't get hold of her temper. "There has to be a way." She said it quietly.

Will pondered. "Nope. We're go in twenty minutes."

"There *is* a way."

"Forget it." No hint of humor, only a determination that matched her own. His face looked pinched. "I'm gone if you

211

even think about using DNP to that level. That'd be Russian Roulette. Look, I understand you want to run with the big dogs. But that's not the way."

"You don't take me seriously. This is what I do. This is what I *am*." Sarah was only half-aware of what she was saying, the throbbing in her head and the sense of betrayal in her heart combining to make her feel like one big bruise inside and out. "I have to win!"

"Here's your aspirin," Lee said with his softest voice.

She dry-swallowed the pills. "What if we called Gordon and he said it was okay?" she asked desperately.

"You can call whoever you want," Will answered, half turning away. She could see that he wanted to wash his hands of the entire thing.

"My phone," she told Lee impatiently. He fished in the backpack where he carried all the paperwork, pulling out two cell phones. He handed hers to Sarah. "Thanks," she mumbled toward him, climbing out of her car and walking away as she dialed Gordon's number.

"Gordon. It's me. I just wanted to tell you that the racing is going great. Really fantastic. You wouldn't believe how many people showed up to the World Finals—can you hear the noise?"

"I can see. I just flipped to the FAST channel here at the office."

Sarah looked around wildly, making sure there weren't any TV crews nearby. There wasn't anybody filming her. "At the office, huh?"

"I'm here with a few guys to catch up on some projects."

"That's great. Hey, got a question for you. Just out of curiosity, can the DNP component be set any higher than six? Like to eight or nine? You know, theoretically?"

She walked and held her breath at the same time, until she saw sparkling black dots swimming in her vision.

When he answered she closed her eyes. "Well, yes, theoretically. But the prototype installed on your car shouldn't be adjusted higher than five. For all the reasons I've already given you, that would be highly dangerous."

She let her breath out as silently as she could, then inhaled deeply. "I see. Okay, that answers my question. Thanks for the info, and wish me—"

"Sarah? How do the eliminations look for you?"

"I'd love to chat, but gotta go!"

"Sarah, don't do it. I can't impress upon you enough—"

"Phone's cutting out! Bye!" She swallowed the sense of guilt that threatened to force her fingers to dial his number again so she could apologize. She wanted to tell him not to worry. She wished she could just thank him for helping her to get as far as she had, and accept that she wasn't meant to go farther, not right away.

But this was her big chance. She had to be brave enough to seize it.

She counted to ten, reminding herself that the end would justify the means, and winners were the ones who wanted it badly enough. Still the panic rose in her body, tightening around her throat like Gordon's large hands turned lethal, immobilizing her with doubt.

Then she stabbed the power button on her phone and walked slowly back to her pit spot.

She addressed Will and Lee. "Guys, good news. Gordon says that DNP can be set higher than six." She paused, watching them. If they demanded evidence of his consent, she would be caught. She found herself hoping she would be.

But she wasn't. They stared at each other, then her.

"Ten minutes. Let's make the adjustments fast," she ordered, then popped her hood like an exclamation point.

★ ★ ★ ★ ★

Gordon furiously punched her number on his cell phone again, glaring at the television as if he could make the Columbus event's blue, cloudless skies turn dark and stormy. A rain-out would stop her.

He got her phone's answering service again.

And again.

His anger gave way to sick dread, then panic. She wouldn't. She *couldn't*. She simply wasn't that recklessly irresponsible.

Was she?

He checked the TV. As the race coverage transitioned to a commercial break, the announcer promised, "The finalists are in the staging lanes now, and we'll be right back for the final round after this message from our sponsor."

Gordon's panic bloomed, and he was out of his chair and yanking out the file cabinet that was supposed to contain the employment records. It contained videotapes instead. Gordon swore, flinging open drawer after drawer looking for anything remotely resembling employment records. He had to find Will or Lee's cell phone number. He had to get them on the phone. He had to stop Sarah.

Where were the damned records?

He eventually found the manila folders holding each employee's original application. There were home phone numbers for both of them. No cell numbers. Cursing Red and Sarah both for not keeping sufficient records, he called the home numbers in the hope that one of them would have mentioned his cell number on his machine.

They hadn't.

Gordon's mind raced. He *had* to reach them. He knew from the way his instinct was jittering and jiving that something very bad was about to happen.

Call the Columbus track and have them page her over the

214

loudspeaker? It would take time. She probably wouldn't even hear it over the noise, and even if she did she'd ignore it. If she were actually doing what he suspected.

He knew she was. He could see her in the picture in his mind's eyes, opening the DNP casing and adjusting the setting up, then closing it with that infuriating, smug look on her face. Completely unaware, or uncaring, that she put herself in extreme danger. Winning meant more to her than anything.

How could he reach her immediately?

Desperate, he left the office and bolted down the stairs to the back.

"Listen up, this is an emergency," he announced in his loudest voice. Everyone went silent, frozen with astonishment at the sight of Gordon with his arms held in the air in a "stop" signal and his face tightened with urgency. "I need to reach Will or Lee on his cell phone. Right now. Who has a number?"

The silence stretched and he'd already begun to cast about in his mind for other options when a voice rattled off seven digits.

"Thank you," Gordon said over his shoulder, dialing as he raced back up the stairs.

It rang. And rang.

When he was about to give up, Will's voice answered, cutting across sudden static. "Yeah?"

A roar went up in the background. It was crowd noise, not static, Gordon realized. "Will, put Sarah on the phone."

"No can do. Did you hear that cheering? She's lining up right now."

"No!" Gordon cursed tightly, glowering up at the TV. Sure enough, her yellow Mustang was positioning for launch. He asked Will the inevitable question. "Did she adjust the controller up?" He held his breath.

"Yeah." Will's suddenly suspicious tone confirmed his worst fear.

"How far?"

"Nine. Oh shit. Lee! Pull her out, signal them and get her out—oh no."

"Can't you stop her?" Gordon heard himself shouting, uncaring.

"The tree's lit. They're going."

All Gordon could do was listen and watch. The cell phone transmitted sound a bit quicker than the TV image, so he could hear what was happening a split second before he saw it on the screen. He heard the engines rev up, a sign that they were ready to launch, and the TV showed the same thing. He heard the piercing wail of both cars launching at maximum rpm, and the echoing thunder of acceleration up through the gears, and the TV images quickly followed to show what he was hearing.

Sarah was out in the lead and running smoothly.

He forgot to breathe. Maybe she would make it.

A loud pop hurt his ear, followed by the sound of screeching tires and crunching metal. In the background he heard thousands of spectators gasp.

"Will!" he shouted in a horrified reflex.

Then the images on the TV screen turned his blood to ice.

Sarah's car made it to half-track before an enormous ball of flame shot out of her hood scoop. He clutched the edge of the TV in a helpless death grip as Sarah's car, engulfed in flames, hit the wall on her side of the track, then rebounded across the track to ram the opposite wall in a horrible sliding impact. Gordon stared, panic rioting within him, agonized with the frustration of not being able to do anything except watch and listen to the chaos that was coming through the phone. The sound was somehow worse. Crew and race officials were always more calm in an accident than the average fan, but Gordon could tell from the horrified tones and the screams that this was a devastating exception. Utter mayhem came through the phone.

And Sarah was in the middle of that hellish-looking fireball out past half-track. At half-track, her car had to be going over a hundred mph. A crash at that speed could be survived, but the fire—!

He watched it unfold, and his frozen fingers let his cell phone drop to the floor. The TV announcer was going crazy, telling everybody to stay off the track, make room for the safety crew. Time stopped for Gordon as he watched the safety crew crawl across the screen with what seemed like criminal slowness. He kept his eyes on the fire. Though it was subsiding on its own, there was no movement around the car, and he knew Sarah had been knocked unconscious by the impact, just as he'd warned her she could be.

She might be burning to death while he watched.

As the safety crew finally skidded to a stop by the twisted, smoldering car, the show cut to a commercial.

He blinked at it, then dove for his phone to try Will's cell phone number again. But as he'd suspected would be the case, Will didn't pick up. He'd probably dropped his phone just as Gordon had dropped his, but on the starting line, right before sprinting down the track to help Sarah.

With no contact, and little hope of connecting with Will, Gordon swallowed the despair in his throat and began to make arrangements to close the shop, notify Sarah's father, and book them both on the very next flight to Ohio.

The TV coverage returned, but it showed nothing except the announcer's speculation about Sarah's condition as she was rushed to the hospital. The announcer included the helpful information that she'd been unconscious when pulled from the wreck and was being treated for smoke inhalation. Also that her condition was critical.

Gordon roared with frustration. He grabbed his keys and headed to the airport.

*Second thoughts are for wusses,* Sarah told herself, but couldn't silence the twanging sense of foreboding that made her nerves feel like tinfoil and caused her palms to slip with sweat on her steering wheel. She knew in her mind she shouldn't have turned up DNP again, especially to as high as nine. But this was the *World Finals.* Real racers maxed out their combinations to perform at peak ability in front of all the spectators and the live media coverage. All she'd done was what all the other racers did to remain competitive when it came down to the wire. She'd set her combination on kill.

*It'll be fine. Gordon-the-conservative wouldn't have said it would be theoretically okay to turn it up if it were even remotely dangerous.*

Still, as she inched into the staging beams, she thought about it. Should she have left it alone? What if it was too much power, and the tires blew? What if the worst happened and the engine blew?

Thoughts like those shouldn't be running through her head. She should be concentrating on nothing but staging correctly, getting a quick launch, and then going through the gears with the routine that she'd practiced so diligently and repeated successfully with each round win leading up to the semifinals.

But she was worried.

The tree flashed and she launched. The newfound power of the turned up DNP made the car far more violent off the line, and it pulled harder than she'd ever experienced. She hit second gear early, and the car continued accelerating like an Air Force fighter jet on full afterburner.

As she shifted into third gear, the eighth-mile marker flashed by, and that's when everything went wrong.

She saw the huge burst of flame an instant before she heard

the thunderous explosion directly in front of her, coming from the engine compartment. The fireball was so big and so persistent that she couldn't see where she was going. She got on the brakes at the same time she felt her car hit the right-side wall. The impact combined with the fire to disorient her, and she hadn't had time to get her bearings before the second impact came. It was more harsh. The searing pain and the sound of grinding metal faded as she blacked out.

The next thing she knew, she was wide awake and afraid as she looked out of the shattered windshield at an engulfing cloud of thick black smoke and flames licking in toward her. She was aware of a sharp pain in her ankle and ribs. As she struggled to undo her safety harness, Gordon's gruesome description of fire victims came back to haunt her:

*"Nobody really knows what that feels like, but the scientists say the skull protects your brain, so that's the last thing to die, meaning that you might feel agonizing pain the entire time you're burning to death."*

With a horrified cry, she struggled harder. She choked on the thick smoke. Spots danced before her eyes and she knew she was blacking out. The safety harness was twisted. She couldn't get free of it. Could she hear the sirens of the fire truck and ambulance?

As the car smoldered, the pain seemed to swallow her body and the smoke became suffocating. She realized that the ambulance might not get there in time to save her.

The world went away.

# CHAPTER FIFTEEN

"How's my car?"

They were her first words to Will and Lee, who'd just seated themselves in identical folding chairs next to the open door of her two-bed hospital room. Lee glowered at her. It was the first time she'd ever seen his sweet face hardened in anger.

It was nothing compared to Will's.

She spoke quickly. "They just told me that my ankle is twisted, and I have fifty-two stitches on my arm. And fourteen in my right shoulder. And a slight concussion. Other than that it's just bruises . . . and a few burns and scrapes." Her voice gradually lowered to nearly a whisper in the face of their hard looks. It was increasingly difficult to keep up her tough-guy persona. She didn't want to whine, so she didn't tell them how sore she still felt, her throat and lungs especially, or that her back felt uncomfortably tight. Her vision seemed to fade in and out strangely too, her eyes raw as if she'd been up all night instead of recently awakened by the nurse.

And underneath all the unpleasant physical sensations was an ugly mental one. She found herself assaulted by the hair-raising specter of what could have happened. She could have been handicapped. She could have been *killed*.

The realization terrified her.

Sarah squinted as her vision grayed, focusing in their direction. Will was furious.

A new kind of fear began to beat tiny wings in her chest. The guys weren't saying anything. They were her gang, her team, her friends. They were supposed to support her and be on her side against catastrophe. Why were they looking at her as if they despised her?

"Two days, Sarah. You've been asleep for two days. Your dad was here. And Gordon. And Craig, of course. We've been playing musical chairs, waiting for you to wake up."

"I'm awake," she said, even more softly than before.

"And asking about your car."

"Was anyone else hurt?" she asked, suddenly worried. She hadn't even considered the possibility.

"No. You got lucky that way."

He wasn't going to volunteer information. He looked as if he was deciding whether or not to even stay.

Words poured from her mouth. "I didn't know that would happen, on the track I mean. I didn't realize. I shouldn't have adjusted DNP. I know that now. All I remember is that I was flying along and then a big explosion went off. Knocked me out." She waited for him to elaborate. He should fill her in about the accident.

"It's all about you. As always." Will glanced at Lee, and as one man, they rose from their chairs.

"You're going?" she squeaked.

They nodded. Will patted the edge of her bed. "Take care of yourself, and get well soon." Lee avoided her eyes.

"Don't go. I need you guys."

"Not anymore. Your car is junk. Smashed to pieces. Even if we *wanted* to crew for you again," Will paused, looking at Lee to confirm. Lee shook his head. "Which we don't, there's no more racecar. Even if you got yourself a new one," he added with a sudden return of anger, "you'd have a real hard time finding yourself any kind of crew at all after the kind of stunt you pulled."

"I'm sorry," she cried. She did need them. Not just as a crew, but as her friends. Their contempt was ripping her apart inside. It was unthinkable that they weren't forgiving her.

"I'm sorry too. Look, we'll see you back in California. We have a plane to catch." And with that, they walked away without looking back. She didn't call after them. Even though her throat was full of a prickly hurt that dwarfed the misery of her other injuries, she didn't call after them.

Her car, smashed to pieces. Her two best friends—she realized belatedly that that's what they'd been—furious at her. Abandoning her.

And, she realized with a sickening inward shudder, they were completely right. What she'd done was wrong. She'd risked not only her own life, but the lives of everyone around her. She'd damaged not only her own reputation, but her crew's.

Once the story of how she'd deceived her crew got out, she would be lucky to find anyone in the racing industry to trust her.

Her racing career was over.

Her head felt swimmy and distant, and she put her hand up to try and steady it. Her hand, brushing against her cheek, came away damp. The moisture surprised her. Her injuries weren't so bad that she should cry. The guys' abandonment, and the shock of her severed career, must've hit an emotional nerve, but she couldn't recall the exact moment it had occurred. She supposed overall anguish didn't allow for such specific distinctions.

Still, she could feel dread at what her dad would be thinking of his irresponsible little girl now.

And Craig. Her mind skittered away from the thought of his contempt.

And Gordon! She groaned. With his DNP stickers plastered all over her spectacularly crashed car, he was the one she'd—

privately and publicly—spiked the deepest. What would people think of his supposedly safe speed part now?

He would despise her most of all.

As he should. They all should.

The swimmy sensation in her mind increased, and she blinked her eyes hard, trying to escape it. She might as well admit it. The accident only proved the glaringly obvious: she wasn't meant to run with the pros.

As the black dots in her vision grew and covered everything, she found herself hoping they all might somehow find it in them to forgive her. She'd lost everything but her life. Surely that had to be punishment enough?

Sarah woke to the sound of clinking plates and running water somewhere nearby, like the sounds her mom had made doing dishes after dinner when she was very, very small. Sarah was surprised to remember it. What was she, four years old? For a moment, drifting with the memories, she felt the serenity of complete peace. Smiling, she turned in her bed and snuggled in the sheets. Or tried to snuggle. Something was wrong with the sheets. They were too tight and chafed her skin terribly. She *hurt*.

So did her ankle.

She opened her eyes in alarm.

The overhead fluorescent lights illuminated the white and blue blanket and sheets that tightly covered her. She was propped up on what felt like at least three hard pillows. And the clinking-plate noise . . . Sarah's nostrils flared at a pungent scent. She looked diagonally across the room at the nurse who was rinsing out an aluminum bedpan in a small sink.

"Oh, you're awake," the nurse said with a smile. "Let me go get the doctor to check on you." She patted the steel rails of the foot of Sarah's bed as she passed, leaving damp smudges.

Sarah took stock of her body, feeling more clearheaded than

the day before when she'd first awakened to hear the doctor give her the rundown on her situation. And then there was the guys' announcement.

*Don't think about that now.*

She could see that her left ankle was still up in a splint, kept immobile by a support and pulley system. Her head throbbed from the stitches, more than her right shoulder did. Both arms, encased in bandages from just above the elbow to the wrist, worried her more. They felt painfully sensitive, as if the skin had been peeled off. She wondered if that was exactly what had happened. The doctor had called them "scrapes."

She remembered the explosion, the fire obscuring her vision, hitting a wall and then hitting another. There'd been smoke, and heat. Pain. Blackness. The ambulance ride to the hospital occurred while she was out. How long had she been out? How long ago was the accident? More than two days. Long enough ago that her ankle was splinted and her wounds bandaged, and the IV needle she dimly remembered had been taken from her arm.

One thing she remembered with ugly clarity: Will and Lee leaving and not coming back. They'd truly abandoned her. The implacable look of them was too engraved in her mind to have been imagined, as much as she wished it were a bad dream.

She'd really messed up bad this time.

Remorse and shame coursed hotly through her, leaving behind a dirty feeling of failure. Craig would be ashamed of her, maybe even embarrassed to be seen with her. And that was only part of the fiasco. She'd let Will and Lee down, she'd let Gordon down, she'd let her dad down, and she'd even let down poor little Ricky Racer. Who was taking care of him now? He was probably lonely and crying and thirsty, because of her.

Tears sprang to her eyes. She was scum. No, she was the mildewed scum *on* scum.

She pulled her sheets up as far as they could go, wishing she could disappear into them forever.

"Well, hello there." Her dad's voice boomed in the hospital room, an organic sound of life in a place of sterility and unhappiness.

"Dad! I'm so glad you're—oh." She noticed Gordon standing beside and behind him. "And Gordon. Please, come in."

Red walked toward her. "You damned idiot." His gruff words and scowl warred with a look of relief at seeing her awake. He stopped near her bed, breathing heavily through his nose while clenching and unclenching his hands. His expression softened as he looked in her eyes. "You'll be okay," he promised. "How do you feel?"

"Better. They say I'm lucky." She watched Gordon step around her dad. His arms bristled with . . . flowers?

He bent, retrieved an empty plastic vase from beneath her nightstand. The huge bunch of multicolored flowers he inserted without removing their stems' confining rubber band or filling the container with water. The vase he lowered onto the table surface with an authoritative thump that made her flinch.

Yes, he was angry.

"You *are* lucky," her dad said, and the stern, quieter tone of his seriousness made her gaze jerk back to him. "You could have been killed because of that dumb stunt." His eyes gentled. "But you lost your car, didn't you, honey? And your crew left too, I understand." He glanced at Gordon. "I guess Sarah's had enough upheaval for the time being."

"Definitely," she agreed, trying to smile. "Um. Did you get Ricky Racer out of the motel?"

Red grumbled. "Yeah, I'm taking care of the little runt. Don't you worry about him. You just concentrate on mending. And think about what you're going to do now that you can't disappear off to the track anymore. Will you please seriously reconsider college? I'd really like to see you graduate. It's times like these that it's good to concentrate on the future."

Sarah stared at her dad, marveling at his gravity about the subject of higher education. College meant so much to him. "I will," she promised. College sounded like purgatory compared to drag racing, she thought glumly. A funnel for people destined for desk-bound employment. *Worse* than purgatory.

Which was no more than she deserved.

She turned to Gordon, who leaned against the doorframe of her room, but she had trouble meeting his gaze. "I'm sorry for crashing with your decals on my car. I'll make it up to you . . ." She stopped as he shook his head.

He gave her a small smile. "No need. Just follow your father's advice, and we'll call it even. Sarah . . ." he stepped closer, his hands by his side as he looked at her with sadness. "You look like hell."

*What?* Then she stared at his face, noticing the glint in his eyes. She narrowed her own, feeling her sluggish blood begin to surge warmly in her veins. "They didn't offer me Mary Kay cosmetics with the paper gown. Deal with it."

"Ah." The single masculine syllable spoken just a few feet away rather than over the phone lines was like a brief massage to her bruised spirit. She found herself warming in other ways. She'd all but forgotten her dad was in the room.

His clearing his throat reminded her. "Well, I'll just go get a candy bar and leave you two to your . . . business discussion."

"Sarah!" Craig rushed by Red and around Gordon to bend over her bed. He kissed her on the lips. As he straightened, scanning her up and down, she saw the half-dozen round blooms clutched in his hand. The top-heavy red carnations nodded on their stems. There was something brown and fuzzy pinched between his arm and his body, as well. "You're awake. You're all right," Craig stated, his voice strained with emotion.

"You're all right," he repeated, his gaze returning to her face. He bent over her, kissed her on the forehead with gentle reverence. "I was worried about you. How're you feeling?"

Sarah was the only one to see Gordon's cold stare at Craig's back, masked quickly by business-cool.

"I'm fine."

"She's fair to middling, not fine," Red boomed, stepping farther into the room. "Back! Let her breathe."

Craig leapt back, but kept one hand possessively on the edge of her bed. "So what do you say now, tough-guy?" he murmured to her. She wondered why he was smiling like that. She supposed he was glad she hadn't sustained serious injury.

"I say those are some mighty pretty flowers." They were narrow and plain, and seemed slightly wilted to her uneducated eye, but Craig beamed at her compliment. Until his gaze fell on Gordon's massive floral arrangement. The way he couldn't prevent his eyes from darting from his handful to the vase of foliage had her biting the inside of her cheek to keep from laughing. *So competitive.*

"She's going back to school," Red declared, as if in warning. What did he expect Craig to do, drag her off to another race? Maybe he did. And maybe with good reason. Craig had always been her biggest racing influence.

Craig seemed to realize it. He understood the dynamics of her father's comment. He looked at her speculatively, then he turned with stiff dignity than seemed odd for him to address Red. "I'm as interested in Sarah's future as you are. I was hoping I'd have the chance to talk about this with you. There's something I'd like discuss, Red. Privately. About me and Sarah," he added, dropping Sarah a wink that only she saw. "Mind if we duck out?" he asked the air between Sarah and Gordon.

Sarah noticed with growing alarm that there was a small square box outlined in his front pocket.

*Oh no.*

"Sir?" Craig gestured toward the hallway as a reminder to Red, who looked his questions at Sarah. Sarah shrugged, telling him she didn't know what it was about. Though she had a suspicion. The older man shrugged, preceding Craig out into the hallway.

When they were far enough away, she spoke to Gordon. "Is *that*," Sarah nodded at the pair huddled some twenty feet away down the hallway, "what I think it is?"

"What you've always wanted," Gordon replied. His hazel eyes looked at her, but they were distant.

His voice was absolutely emotionless and it chilled her. Mixed feeling surged through her as she struggled for the right words to explain. How could she make him understand the complex relationship she had with Craig? Or that she wasn't sure she should say "yes"? "It's not—" she began, but just then Craig came back in. Her dad stopped at the doorway, a strangely resigned look on his face. He nodded at Gordon. "I guess it's time for us to move on out. Sarah? I'm so glad you're okay." He touched her foot hesitantly, then patted it with a gruffness that she knew covered his relief and affection for her. Red said nothing of Craig's conversation with him, clearly taking a non-interference approach.

*Typical.* But she was still sorry to have his solid, comforting presence leave the room.

Gordon nodded to her, and without another word followed Red out. His absence struck her forcibly too. It surprised her that she'd miss him as much as her dad. They had the same kind of strong aura, and the room seemed emptied of more than just their physical presence.

"We've had some great times lately, haven't we?" Craig's softest voice jerked her attention back to him. He stood with both feet planted exactly a shoulder's width apart, as if steadying himself. His stance also had the effect of showing off his perfectly tapered body, something he was completely unaware of, she knew. She admired it even as her apprehension grew. He grinned, mischievous. "You had to go and grenade yourself. Which isn't entirely a bad thing. Now you're my captive audience."

"Nowhere I'd rather be."

Her sarcasm was gentle, but he heard it. His didn't speak for a moment. Then, with a seriousness she'd never heard from him before, "I'm sorry you went through that. Crashing, and afterward. It must have been awful. But, you'll heal up perfectly. Sometimes these things happen for a reason."

"Which reason? Because I suck? Or because I'm a goddamned idiot?"

"Don't talk that way about yourself," he chided, a gentle smile touching her like sunshine. "You'll always be a gearhead, and so much more."

"But not a racer." The air seemed to still around her, as if her declaring it made it so.

He didn't answer. Instead, he sat on the bed and stroked her hand. "You're so beautiful."

She glanced down at the way her stringy, limp hair stuck to her sweaty paper hospital gown, and took in the countless bruises and bandages. "Yeah, I'm a hottie."

"You are to me."

Her heart couldn't seem to figure out whether to ache with joy at his declaration, or pound with anxiety. She suddenly wished he'd leave her alone for a while, so she could recover some sense of balance. He still had that little box in his shirt. Things were happening far too quickly.

But instead, Craig carefully placed the brown hairy object he'd had pinched between his arm and body onto the floor. With one finger he hooked the box—a satin-covered gray one—

out of his pocket.

He sank to one knee, and she felt her mouth drop open with shock even though she'd expected it. The box halved open on the largest diamond she'd ever seen.

At her shocked silence, Craig's smile grew. He fixed gorgeous blue eyes on hers with clear determination. He wasn't uncertain in the slightest. "Sarah. Will you marry me?"

# CHAPTER SIXTEEN

Sarah felt immobilized upon hearing the question. It was sudden, of course, but she could see that he meant it. He actually meant it. Everything she'd fantasized about for years, Craig with that look in his eyes, on bended knee, asking her to spend the rest of her life by his side.

She found that she couldn't take her eyes off the diamond, the sparkles of color deep within its facets. Craig. Husband. He'd be a good one. Didn't they say that friends made the best mates? And now their relationship dynamic had flip-flopped and he'd become the pursuer in addition to being a friend. That made things so much easier. She could just relax and enjoy his attentions. How simple to keep doing what she was doing to maintain his interest. She'd dress up for him, be both his dinner date and his buddy, race against him—no, she wouldn't race against him.

She'd never race again.

A sense of loss that seemed completely inappropriate to the moment echoed all through her. Sarah shook it off. Craig was kneeling before her. They'd always be able to talk about racing, at least. Shared interests, shared passion for . . . hobbies . . . bonded couples together.

But now that the moment was here, she wondered at the emptiness and confusion in her that seemed to have begun the moment Will and Lee departed. It was as if her reality was still skewed. She knew she should feel blazing joy about Craig finally stepping up to the plate, but joy eluded her. Hospitals were desolate places. Why had he picked a hospital? And she might be in shock and not know it. She knew she was still in mourning for her racing career.

Sarah stared down at his gorgeous unruly blond waves, at his hands grasping the ring box, and into his sky-blue eyes looking back at her so solemnly. And, of course, the enormous rock. He was so handsome, and so right for her. She felt the old attraction tug at her. But it was a muted thing. Her body had gone oddly dormant. Still healing, no doubt.

Did he really expect her to make a decision immediately, with her ankle in a brace, and her arm-skin scoured off? She didn't feel equipped to make that decision. She tore her gaze from the ridiculously large diamond. Why was he asking her *now*? Had the thrill of chasing her into a corner affected his timing? Or was he suddenly so head-over-heels for her that he couldn't bear to wait another minute?

Was he happier with her, and more comfortable with commitment, now that she couldn't race?

She honestly had no idea what the truth was.

She had to say something. "Oh, Craig." She was glad that her voice reflected how overwhelmed she felt. It would make the rest of what she said easier for him to hear.

"Craig, this is just . . . wow. Everything's happening so quickly. So many changes, and I feel terrible still. Physically. And in my head too. You know I've always had an enormous crush on you." She sighed. "I still do. So, maybe my brain is damaged now, because even though I *have* to have you in my life, I can't give you an answer right this second. I'm sorry. I'll have to think about what you've asked, give it the time and thought that kind of question deserves."

"Is it *him*?"

Craig's voice held an outraged passion that she'd never heard from him before. He was so intense that she was surprised he didn't chase Gordon down and punch him.

He half rose to his feet. She had to speak. "I just crashed with his company decals all over on my car. What do you think?" she retorted, dissembling.

Craig didn't seem completely satisfied with her answer about Gordon, but he didn't charge out the door. "Well, then . . . if it's not him, is it me?" He asked the question in a way that informed her that he hadn't before considered such being the case, and was starting to feel some doubt. His vulnerability was endearing.

She smiled gently, turning the question around on him. "You're so different lately. Our dating, I mean. I'm seeing a side of you I really, really like. That's an incredibly good thing," she added. "But why rush it? Why this, now, when we haven't even . . . ?"

Craig rose slowly to his feet, then pocketed the ring box as if it were an afterthought. He nodded. "It's too quick. No problem." He sighed, though, and as he crossed to the folding chair near her bed, his expression was thoughtful. "It's because things have been so different with us that I'm asking. To marry you." Craig clearly marveled at the words. "I can't begin to explain how confused and obsessed with you I've been lately. Then the crash made it all plain to me." He met her gaze, unflinching. "I don't want to lose you."

She couldn't help the warm, gratified rush that flowed through her at his words.

"I have something for you," he continued. Determination was back in his voice. He bent to retrieve the brown object from the floor, brushed it off. Before giving it to her he spoke. "I know I haven't been the most sensitive guy in all the world. I didn't even remember your dog's name until last week. I want to start making up for that. So. I hope you'll let me give you this."

He handed her a velvety plush stuffed dachshund. "Oh, Craig!" He'd never given her a stuffed animal before. The fuzzy gift delighted her far more than the ring. She stroked it, and her fingers encountered something flat and round. Turning it over she saw a glossy button pinned between the little dog's ears on his forehead, above his small sewn-on brown marble eyes. On the button raced a picture of Craig's Mustang with the toy dog strapped to its hood. Underneath the picture were words: "RICKY RACER rode with me at Columbus, Ohio," and Craig's scrawled signature.

She felt her throat get tight. "Oh my God, that is the sweetest thing. And you remembered his name." Her voice trembled, and tears blurred her eyes.

Craig rose, hurried to her bed where he took one of her hands in between his two. His hands were warmer than hers. "I'd hoped you'd like it." His eyes searched hers. "You okay?" He stroked her forearm and wrist, soothing her.

"Yeah. Sorry for the waterworks. It's been a rough couple of days."

"I can imagine." He drew himself up. "I'd better let you get your rest."

"Thank you," she said, grabbing his hand for a last squeeze. "For being here for me. For understanding." She felt a gratitude for his thoughtfulness that gave her words a hollow, almost desperate sound. She didn't deserve him. And yet, he offered himself along with his entire future. To her. All she had to do was say yes. One little word. Her lips almost shaped the word.

Craig looked at her. "I'm going to ask you again, you know." He backed away from her bed as if reluctant to take his eyes off her. "Think about it." He backed into his chair and she heard metal legs scraping against the floor. His flowers were pinned between one chair leg and the wall. Easing the chair forward, Craig scooped up the bouquet. He grabbed the closest liquid-filled container from the sink next to her absent roommate's bed, and dunked the stems, placing the arrangement on the counter where she could view his gift.

He approached her again quickly, kissed her on the forehead. His breath wafted over her, minty fresh and kissable. "You have my cell number. Call me when you get back home."

She nodded, biting the inside of her cheeks.

He backed out of the room, pivoted and strode away.

Sarah looked at his carnations jutting sprightly from the catheter catchbasin on the counter. The water was nearly clear. But not quite.

Breaking into a laughter that swelled to hysterical gales, she considerately muffled the noise with one of her pillows.

The last thing she felt like doing was laughing as she prepared to re-enter the shop's work area. She smoothed her denim skirt nervously, then pushed open the door from the front retail area and tried not to walk with a limp as she crossed the wide floor to where the guys were.

Everything seemed just as she'd left it. The sights, the smells, even the stereo playing rock music. The familiar sight of male bodies surrounding a small-block engine reassured her and she began to smile with relief. Maybe all would actually be as it was.

But as soon as the techs spotted her, a quiet descended until the Scorpions tune playing on the stereo wailed too loudly in the silence. Most of the guys became very busy with projects away from the small-block. Some took a coffee break, and others departed to hunt for tools that they realized they couldn't do without.

"Hey," she offered to the two remaining guys. Her face was burning already from the mass exodus.

"Hello, Sarah," Will said.

She snorted, smoothing her skirt again. "What's with the formal address?" Her heart had begun to thump with sick fear. She was afraid she knew the answer. "Hey, Lee."

Will edged partly in front of the smaller man. He scanned Sarah's clothes but his face remained inscrutable. She would have killed for one of his withering jokes, about her attire or anything else. "Is there something you need?"

She bit her cheek against the hurt that swelled inside her. "Did the clothes throw you off?" Forcing a laugh, she cast a glance around. The other guys were out of earshot. "Jeans don't fit easily over an ankle splint. Speaking of my war-wounds . . . do the others know about what happened?"

"Oh yeah. They know about it."

"And . . . ?"

"And it might work out best for everyone if you'd keep on wearing skirts and move your base of operations to the front desk."

She felt as if the floor had dropped away. A small sound escaped her.

Will exhaled nosily, clearly exasperated. "Well, what did you expect? Everyone to be one big, happy family after that?"

Lee looked as if he wanted to say something, but finally just sealed his lips and shook his head.

"Dude . . . seriously. Me, up front?" Her mind whirled. It didn't have to be a horrible thing. Maybe it wouldn't be a bad idea to give them some space. Just for a couple of weeks.

Something in her still balked. "This is *my* shop. Why should I listen to you guys?"

Lee spoke for the first time. "That's why exactly."

Sarah stared at him, but he'd looked back at the floor and refused to meet her eyes. She felt as if her face was on fire with embarrassment and dismay. "Okay. Fine."

They were still hot under the collar. She'd give it two weeks, tops, she decided, making her way back toward the front desk that would be her temporary office space. She wished it didn't feel so much like a humiliating retreat.

She'd keep some distance; let things settle.

If she knew one thing from all her time spent around car guys, it was that they never could hold a grudge for long.

# Chapter Seventeen

Sarah sat, a supplicant in the chair in front of her dad's desk. Her hands rested on the floral-print cotton material of her dress that covered her thighs nearly to her knees. She already felt constrained in the sedate, polite position that her dress forced her to assume: knees together, facing forward. If she wanted to turn and look at Gordon, she couldn't simply swivel on her rear, the way she could if she were wearing jeans. She couldn't kick out her legs out and sprawl, her position an eloquent testament to a careless state of mind.

Which was appropriate. Her mind was far from careless.

She cleared her throat nervously, and then let her breath out with relief when she heard Gordon politely leave the two men's office, giving her and her dad privacy.

Red spoke first. "Sarah. How are things up front?"

She stared at him. He didn't know? How could he not know? "Uh, not so great," she said. "I mean, the phones and invoices and filing and all is under control, and I've sold some of the display speed equipment. I'm looking forward to my ankle mending, though, because that stuff's a little bit . . . unchallenging."

There, that was the way to put it. Unchallenging. That sounded much nicer than boring as hell.

"And . . . in general? Are you still okay?"

When she caught him darting a look at her left hand, she understood. She felt her mouth stretch into a smile, the unfamiliar feel of it letting her know why her dad was concerned. She hadn't smiled a lot lately. "Oh, you mean about Craig popping the question. I haven't decided about that. He's been so wonderful, hasn't he? Dropping off Godiva chocolate last week, and sending flowers yesterday. I don't know what's wrong with me that I haven't said 'yes' yet. Must've bumped my head pretty hard, huh?"

Her dad cleared his throat. "Generally these things are decided by feelings. For example, do you love him?"

She laughed, but kept her eyes down, on her recently manicured nails. Her father meant well, but she didn't want to discuss Craig. She didn't want to taint that one remaining sense of security and success with the purgatory that the rest of her current existence had become. If anything needed changing, it was the other aspects of her life. Her relationship with Craig was doing fine. There was absolutely no need to ruin a damned good thing by rushing into a typical suburban marriage unit. "Maybe I should concentrate on business for now. Be more involved with running the shop. It'll be mine one of these days—a long time in the future, I hope," she said with real fondness, looking up at him. "Maybe it's time to take that seriously."

His response wasn't at all what she expected. "No, no, no. You should get out and enjoy yourself, like a young lady should. Maybe drive up to view different campuses, lots of them—your new Camry'll get good gas mileage—and think about what direction you want to go in your life." Her dad gave her a suspiciously wide smile, nodding as if in agreement with himself.

"I was thinking about working in the back again when my brace comes off," she said, testing the water.

"No! Now, that wouldn't work out at all." He blushed. Her dad never blushed.

"They said something to you, didn't they?" The guys still

didn't want her back there. She knew it was true even before he nodded unhappily, but the confirmation was still a blow.

"Of course, you can go ahead and work in the back anyway, honey," he said miserably, "but you know how it is. It wouldn't be the same for you. You wouldn't be happy."

About that, he was correct. Will and Lee were still polite to her, but that was a dynamic short of camaraderie. Sadly short. Same with the other guys, who knew all about her DNP fiasco.

She truly wasn't wanted. She couldn't foist herself on the guys when they'd made it so clear she wasn't welcome. How could she even strike up a conversation with them, much less fall back into her old easygoing ways, when they looked at her so suspiciously? When they didn't even want her around?

"You're right," she conceded. She rose awkwardly to her feet, favoring her ankle out of habit more than need. "I guess it's time to think about my new college major."

"I couldn't tell her. Not like that, with her ankle hurt, and the way she's been moping around. Give it time."

"I can give it all the time it needs . . . within reason. You're the one with the deadline. That big summer classic rod festival . . . in Hawaii, right? Red, don't you still want to retire and do stuff like that all the time? Why don't you tell me what, exactly, you're waiting for." Gordon felt his muscles tensing. He hoped Red wasn't changing his mind. The man was honorable, but where his daughter was concerned he hadn't always done what was best for business. "She won't like hearing it, no matter how or when you tell her."

Red exhaled slowly. "Yeah. But I've never seen her so gloomy. Not in years." His craggy face expressed everything he wasn't saying, and Gordon knew he was thinking about Sarah's mother, and the years after her death. It must have been hard for him, Gordon thought with a pang of empathy for the man he'd grown to respect so much. He was almost tempted to tell Red that the deal was off—if it distressed him so to complete it.

But just almost. A lifetime of striving kept him silent.

Red stood, resolute. "When I get back, then. Not a day later."

"Are you sure?" Gordon bit out, surprising himself. He held his breath. He still wanted the performance shop for his own. And he had in his possession the signed paperwork to enforce his claim immediately, if necessary. But he couldn't take it over like that. It would smack too much of corporate raiding, and his golden era of ownership and expansion would be shadowed by misery.

"I'm sure. It's time to move on. For both of us. She's going back to college. Eventually she'll thank me." Red said it without conviction.

Gordon blinked. "She said that? That she's going back to school?"

"Yeah." Red moved more slowly than usual to his keys and grabbed his lunchbox. "I think I'll take off early. Maybe cruise up the coast highway to that car show in Pleasanton. Got some thinking to do . . . not about the business, just thinking in general," he said in response to whatever was showing on Gordon's face. Red chuckled, patting Gordon on the back as he passed him. He hooked the keys to his '72 truck into his hand. "Hold down the fort. See you in a week."

Gordon stared at the office door long after it closed. Red never left early, especially not for a frivolous reason. It told him, as nothing else had, that Red was serious about selling the shop to him.

Which meant there was one final order of business to resolve.

If Red truly was going to inform Sarah next week, then that meant Gordon had to decide how he'd deal with the damage after the bomb was dropped on her. With any luck, her college plans would shield the worst of the blow, and she wouldn't hate him for what he'd done.

Sarah lifted a bag of office supplies from the passenger seat of her new Toyota Camry. Her leftover race winnings had gone to purchase the thoroughly boring beige, four-door, automatic-transmission grocery-getter, along with the skirts and dresses that she was getting used to wearing.

She probably could have found a decent base-model Mustang for the same price as the Camry. But then she knew she would have craved fixing it up and itched to race it. Ever since Will, Lee, and all the techs had made it crystal clear that their assistance in the back would no longer be forthcoming unless they were professionally compelled, the whole idea of wrenching with them made her ache with discomfort.

She gazed for another long moment at the dull, underpowered vehicle in front of her. She wondered how many people would realize that her driving it was an act of self-punishment of the first order. The uninspiring car would never tempt her to stray again into the realm of racing.

Which was the whole point. Driving it would help to remind her that there were many more important things in life than racing.

When she heard the unmistakable rumble of Gordon's Mustang pull into the parking space beside her to share the afternoon shade of the large oak tree dominating the western side of the shop, she tensed.

"How'd your doctor's appointment go?" he called to her, shutting his car door with a thump and hurrying toward her. "Here, let me." He took the bag from her arms, stuffing his car keys into the front pocket of his khaki slacks with his free hand.

"Thank you." Sarah couldn't keep the stiffness from her voice. The sight of him still made her heart pound and her palms sweat. But a new ambivalence had also begun to plague her, having taken root in her nervous system. Not only was he a witness to her racing negligence, he'd also rejected her as a lover after making her melt with his kisses. And if that weren't bad enough, she now *owed* him because of how she'd tainted the public perception of his DNP component. As a disappointed sponsor, he deserved her most contrite behavior. As a co-worker, he deserved her courtesy.

As a man, he deserved something cooler.

"Business meeting?" she asked him coolly, glad that her voice came out so disinterested.

"Yes." His voice was neutral, which somehow trumped her coolness. He didn't elaborate.

She made herself walk by his side, though, still favoring the ankle. The injured area showed slender and bare beneath her long skirt. It was finally free of the bulky splint. The muscles felt weakened but supported her weight without complaint as she paced him to the front door.

He opened it for her, and the familiar air-conditioned scent of metal, grease and gasoline wafted out. She closed her eyes for a moment. The scent and associations—excitement, camaraderie—were still there. If only she could make everyone forget the last month. Including herself.

The clank of metal on metal and many bass voices let her know the guys hadn't finished working for the day. She could hear their radio on the workbench playing an AC/DC song, but it was too distant to make out the words.

"Thank you," she told Gordon again, polite as she passed through the doorway.

"You're welcome." He followed her into the lobby, putting the bag down on top of the display case. Her delicate sandals clicked gently on the black & white linoleum floor as she made her way around the glass. Behind the counter, she immediately felt constrained. The receptionist/bookkeeper/retail-girl position was a bad fit for her. She chafed at the way it kept her from doing what she loved, what she was good at.

But that was the *old* her, she reminded herself firmly. The new one was still being fabricated.

She placed her purse in an unused corner of the back counter beneath a shelf, then settled onto the simple padded stool, aware that Gordon hadn't continued on through the back door into the garage and on up to his office.

"Red took off early," he told her, sliding his palms over the glass. "He left a list of some things for us to take care of over the next week."

Sarah consciously lowered her eyebrows, aware that they'd shot upward in surprise. Dad left before six? To be gone an entire week?

"Is he okay?" She slid off the stool and opened one of the wooden cabinets behind her. She handed across a bottle of glass cleaner and a paper towel, looking pointedly at the palm prints he'd made.

Gordon smiled and took the cleaner. He squirted the glass. "He's fine. A little preoccupied maybe." Sarah watched his large hand move the crumpled paper towel in slow circles, polishing. "But what about you? How's the ankle?"

"It's fine. Thanks for asking."

"Sarah . . ."

She glanced up, briefly, at his low, personal voice. His eyes looked dark and troubled. Irritated, she looked away. What right did *he* have to be troubled? She was the rejected one, exiled from the back, working the receptionist shift. Just as bad, she was driving an underpowered economy car. Worst of all, she knew every bit of the situation was her own stupid fault. There wasn't any sinking lower than that.

She plucked the cleaner from his hand and the soiled towel

from the counter. Nodding to the spotless glass, all she let herself say was, "Thanks."

The clamor of the guys crowding through the door to depart almost masked his exasperated sigh. They sounded boisterous and happy until they saw her.

"Oh . . . hey there, Sarah. How ya doing? See ya later."

"Yeah, bye Gordon."

Will and Lee and the others waved and gave tight smiles, not slowing their pace. If anything, they sped up. She waved back and kept her face neutrally friendly, as befitted a receptionist, until they'd all pushed through the front doorway.

The glass door sighed shut.

The radio had been turned off. Silence reigned unbroken except for their breathing.

"Is it six already?" she asked perkily, sliding off the stool again. "I guess I'll just unpack these supplies, then get going myself."

"Sarah." His breath hissed between his teeth.

"Yes?"

"Why didn't you say yes? To Craig," he clarified, as if she got marriage proposals all the time and might get them mixed up.

Sarah stared at him. He was asking about it *now*, weeks after the fact? She didn't have to answer him. It was none of his business. Not anymore.

If it ever was.

"I'm sorry. That was unprofessional of me to ask, and you don't have to answer," he added after her silence stretched for too many seconds. Once again he was showing only the proper, stuffy business manager that she'd first thought him. He did, however, shift uncomfortably under her stare. He put his palms against the glass counter again.

She felt her mouth twitch in amusement. "I said no because I needed to think about it."

"You did? I see."

But she could tell he didn't see. She wasn't sure if she felt relieved or disappointed about that.

"Anyway. I'm off," she said gaily. Scooping up her purse, she eased back around the counter. He could lock up.

"What about putting the supplies away?" he asked.

That was it. She slammed her purse down on the counter so hard that she heard a crack. "Gordon. I not staying late to tuck away the hand-soap and message pads and invoice blanks. All of you want me filing and cleaning." She made a scornful sound. "I am so underutilized, it's ridiculous."

"You are so *spoiled,* it's ridiculous."

*"What did you say?"*

"Spoiled. Favored and pampered and indulged. Oh, my."

Temporarily blinded by the red haze of fury that obscured her vision, she nearly missed the way his lips quirked up on one side in a crooked smile. His words bit at her cruelly, but the smile kept her from pummeling him senseless, weak ankle or no.

He didn't understand. She tried to reason with him. "How exactly is this tour of duty as shop receptionist and cleaner-lady making me spoiled? *I am a damn good technician.*"

"So good you destroyed your own car. And for the record, you were spoiled long before you put on a dress and tried out your phone voice."

Sarah had to count to ten, and then list to herself all the reasons using her metal stool to knock that calmly amused look off his face was a bad idea.

Then it dawned on her. He was needling her on purpose. A strategy. Had to be. Why else would someone like him bother? He wanted an excuse for him and her dad to fire her, to get her out of his hair. His fondest fantasy was probably that she'd quit on the spot.

Well, she wouldn't give him what he wanted.

She gathered up her dignity and hurt pride and tried to ignore her stinging disappointment.

That she still felt disappointment at his supercilious treatment of her made a sudden clear anger sing throughout her body. "Goodbye, Gordon." She picked up her purse, ignoring the ugly hairline crack under it that ran across the edge of the glass. But she couldn't resist a parting shot. "You know what? You make Craig look like damn good marriage material. He's . . ." She paused, looking at him with as much scorn as she could muster. "He's the big block to your small block."

She wheeled, pleased with her insult. Let him file office supplies all by his lonesome. Let him—

A large, rough hand spun her around, and Gordon's lips met hers as he yanked her against him. When his tongue invaded her mouth, she heard herself make a shocked, melting noise in her throat. It was just as she remembered. His kiss was just as mind-blowing, just as intoxicating to all of her senses as it had been so many weeks ago. His clever, competent tongue teased hers until she was sure her legs wouldn't support her. Then he withdrew, still holding her.

She heard the rumble in his chest against hers, and the smile in his voice. "Small block?" His hands didn't rest, but lifted her more firmly against his hard body. "I don't think so."

"I stand corrected." She barely recognized the sultry whisper as her own. It sounded so . . . ripe. And her words were untrue. She didn't think she'd be able to stand if he released his hold around her waist.

Fortunately he didn't. "What am I going to do with you? Hmm?" The pressure of his warm hand against the small of her back, and the way he half-cradled, half-caressed her body with his own informed her of what he'd like to do.

Delicious shivers of wanting raced through her body. Knowing he still desired her had the strange effect of channeling all of her ire at him into a far more potent passion. In an instant, she'd forgotten all the names he'd called her, and forgiven every bit of the disruption he'd brought into her life. With her chest pressed tightly to his, she tried to think clearly. "Tease," she accused him. "Are you going to bolt again?"

"More of a nail."

Shocked, Sarah nearly laughed. She struggled with mock outrage against his embrace, unable to keep from grinning. So the hotshot businessman had a crude streak. "You're tarnishing your white collar."

He shook his head against her struggles. "You don't mind."

"And you didn't answer my question."

"I'm not going anywhere." Abruptly, he lifted her into his arms and began walking toward the shop area. "You, on the other hand . . ."

"Where are you . . . ?"

"The back. Now."

She did laugh, then. "And what are you going to do with me there? Give me an overhaul?"

"Something like that." She felt him turn in a half-circle, as if looking for something in the large shop's darkness. With the only illumination being the little glow that leaked in from the retail store up front, and the fading twilight that seeped between the cracks of the shop's tall roll-up garage door, all she could see were shadows.

But Gordon started in a specific direction. "I've decided there's no need for me to pretend anymore," he told her, his voice rough. "You want me. I want you. High time someone around here got what they wanted without a side of guilt." His muscles shifted against her as he stopped. Letting go of her legs, he tightened his grip around her waist so that as the tip of her toes touched the floor, the front of her body curved into his.

Delighted, Sarah felt the low, narrow heels of her sandals sink slightly into something soft, and grabbed reflexively for Gordon to stabilize herself. As he held her, she exulted. He *did* want her, and was evidently leaving behind the guilty feelings that had kept him from doing this. She reveled in the warm strength of his embrace. It seemed a miracle that he'd forgiven her for DNP, too.

With his capable hands moving over the thin material of her dress, she shivered with pleasure. She allowed herself to hope, for the first time since the racing disaster, that everything would actually be okay. She and Gordon would finally go public about their attraction to each other, and the guys would come around. Screw college. She'd rather work as the head technician again. She shivered once more, a thrilling sensation magnified by Gordon's skillful ministrations. Maybe she'd even race.

"You're beautiful," Gordon said. "I knew you would be." His hands were slow and warm on her dress, and then under it.

"Guys dig the dress," she told him, trying for a flippant tone. Her voice came out all breathy again. She felt deliciously sensuous, and very feminine. As his fingers dispensed with her bra from underneath her dress, unhooking it and pulling it gently down and off her body, she had to bite back whimpers. She shifted a step back, and the back of her bare knees, where her dress material had ridden up, pressed against soft material. Twisting from his embrace, she took several deep, centering breaths of familiar gasoline-and-oil scented air to clear her head. "I don't hop into the back seat on my first date."

For she knew precisely where she was: the shop's soft center, the portable wooden table that lumped high with furniture pads used by technicians to protect painted hoods and chrome pieces from scratches. She was surrounded on three sides by thick sheets of sound-deadening Dynomat, packing material, mounds of shop rags spilling from bags, clean towels and floor mats, and seats pulled from cars. Seats just like the large and accommodating bench seat directly behind her, covered by such a soft velvet-smooth material that it felt like the lightest of caresses against her bare skin.

On the fourth side stood Gordon, minus his shirt and with one button unfastened on his pants. The diffused light seemed to lie like a mantle on his defined chest, fading into the darker area of his tapered belly and below. His voice was rougher than she'd ever heard from him before. "Hardly our first encounter, Sarah. Or even our first back seat." He eased closer to her until she had to look up at his face, and his body heat hit her along with his scent. As fingers slid underneath her panties, she cried out. She could feel his gaze on her face as he pulled her panties down and off.

She marshaled all of her strength to reply. "Yes. But . . ." *What does this mean? How will it change our relationship?* She couldn't think of a way to phrase it that didn't sound weak and whiny. She had to avoid that. Maybe she wasn't strictly a tomboy anymore, but she had standards. She tilted her head farther back to think, looking toward the high ceiling. Her eyes had adjusted enough to see the dark gray metal pipes of the sprinkler system far overhead. She wondered why they hadn't kicked on to spray down the fire he'd ignited inside her.

Gordon kissed her throat with a low growl that vibrated through her entire body, and her thoughts dissolved into one of absolution. *Guys do it like this, without guilt or worry.* Pleasure spiked through her with the feel of his firm lips and the length of him finally pressed full against hers.

The thin barrier of her dress material and his half-unbuttoned slacks whispered together. His whisper in her ear was only slightly louder. "Okay?" His warm breath tickled her ear, and she could hear his controlled breathing as he held himself back. She hauled his head to hers to kiss him hungrily on the mouth.

Taking that for the assent it was, he exhaled with a hiss that revealed his matching hunger, lifting the dress from her body. "Lie down," he commanded, unzipping his pants.

She felt daring, and deliciously kinky. They were right out in the open. It was as far from her furtive first time in a college dormitory as men were from boys.

And what a man. A stack of clean shop sheets on the edge of the seat spilled around her as she sat, staring at Gordon's form freed from clothing. Superb, shiveringly perfect, and seemingly larger naked than he'd been fully clothed.

Excitement zoomed inside her as she reclined, nude except for heels, on the velvety back seat. She felt his eyes on her. The workouts at the gym had not only made her stronger, they'd made her muscles toned and attractive, for which she was suddenly grateful. She snuggled luxuriously on the smooth softness, not missing the sharp intake of Gordon's breath as he watched her. She smiled. "Get to work."

"No." He knelt by the seat, ran a proprietary hand over her body. The controlled indifference of his touch inflamed her as no fondling could have. "I think you're forgetting who's in charge." He slipped off her shoes with sensuous, maddening slowness.

Irritation and desire swirled in the depths of her belly. How could he be so self-disciplined, she wondered with frustration. She could *see* he had needs of his own. The situation felt very one-sided, with him touching her, making her hiss out loud with desire when his warm palm contacted her nipple, yet resisting her clear invitation to join her lying down on the seat. He stroked her slowly from shoulder to hip, over her belly, and up to circle and palm her breasts again. If she didn't know better, she could mistake his even touch for the admiration of a man for a good paintjob. He betrayed his enjoyment with only the smallest, coolest smile. And also with . . .

She took matters into her own hands.

Sarah grinned at his gratifyingly audible intake of breath. It wasn't a gasp, but it was probably the equivalent for him. Feeling mischievous, she spoke without looking up at his face. "What a nice stick shift you have." She tested its girth and weight.

She looked up with suspicion. Was Gordon choking? He'd made an odd noise. His expression changed as she watched, cycling from startlement, to laughter . . . and then, when she grasped him more firmly, hot desire. She felt his hand on her head. When his fingers tightened convulsively against her scalp with her movement, she smiled with satisfaction.

*Finally.*

She felt her own desire swirl madly, and tugged him down in the direction of the bench seat. "Come here." He had to tumble down with her now, his control broken, to ravish her like a madman. He'd better.

"No."

*"No?"* She let go of him. "What do you mean, no? In case you missed it, I'm flinging myself at you. Again." She extended her arms out, crooking them back over her head to demonstrate her willing vulnerability.

"In case you missed it, I'm aware of that."

Sarah ground her teeth. "This 'overhaul' doesn't need prepwork," she hinted, barely restraining herself from grabbing him again.

" 'Any job worth doing . . .' " he quoted, throwing her words of so long ago back in her face. He intercepted her hand snaking toward him, and returned it to over her head, where he encircled both her wrists with one hand. "I prefer a patient, methodical approach."

"I *don't.*"

"Of course you don't. Immediate gratification. That's much more your style, isn't it? Self-centered Sarah." His free hand roamed over her body to her center, as if for demonstration. She saw his gaze appraising her there. His eyes narrowed with desire, but his steady, maddening strokes didn't falter. When he brought his fingers into play, she couldn't help groaning.

"Exactly. You see, the rewards are bigger with self-restraint."

"Please," she bit out between gasps. The evidence of his desire was easily seen. God, how she wanted him.

"No. You seem to be under the impression that I agree with your selfish attitude." He flicked his thumb, and she whimpered.

Then he withdrew both hands, freeing her, and just waited.

She stared at him, grasping the edge of the bench seat with one hand, and the seat-back with the other. Every muscle in her body was taut with anticipation. She was more than ready for him. What was he waiting for?

Then his words penetrated. Selfish? Maybe she was impatient, as he'd accused—she was certainly feeling impatient at the moment—but she wasn't selfish. She was very giving of her opinion. She was a good person and obeyed the law, except for speed limits, and . . . and she was kind to animals.

The image of Ricky Racer lying limp and dehydrated flashed in her mind.

Well, she was usually kind to animals. She frowned. So maybe she was a little selfish.

As recent events played out in her mind she sighed unhappily. Maybe she was a lot selfish. Which meant Gordon, damn his teasing soul, might actually have a point.

She shifted uncomfortably. He really had gotten her all revved up with nowhere to go.

Maybe she could make some amends. Pave the way to a new understanding between them. She'd show him. She would be more thoughtful, more generous.

Starting immediately.

She sat up, supporting herself with one straight arm. He was conveniently positioned. "You . . . need a lube job," and then she couldn't speak for a few moments.

"Very good," he exhaled with a laugh. His encouraging hand on the back of her head was all she needed. Working her tongue up and down, she exulted to hear him moan with pleasure. It was another first for her, and she felt pride in her performance.

When his body trembled slightly, she stopped, looking up at him. "Tell me again how selfish I am," she murmured, hearing that breathy vamp-voice again.

"Selfish, greedy, narrow-minded, lazy . . ." He looked down at her hopefully, and she laughed, nipping at him.

She squeezed gently with her hand, and was pleased at how the gesture commanded his rapt attention. She stroked gently. Then stopped. Then started again, until he cursed. "Feeling impatient? Tsk, tsk . . ."

Suddenly he lowered himself onto the bench with a low growl. "Fair enough." He shoved her thighs apart with enough force to make her gasp in surprise. "But that's enough prep work, wouldn't you say?"

"I've *been* saying . . ."

"Quiet." He kissed her, his tongue battling with hers as he penetrated her below.

"Oh . . . God," she said as the fires ignited and flared inside her, goaded by his fullness. "Don't you dare stop."

"You like ordering people around, don't you?" His voice was rough, almost angry-sounding in his passion. "Here's one man you can't. I'm going to do exactly . . . what . . . I . . . want . . . for a change." He shifted one supporting arm, driving himself deeper.

She felt his body tilt to one side as she heard him hiss with frustration. He lifted one hand to his face for examination. "Dammit. Grease on the seat springs. Got a handful of it. Hold on . . ."

"*No.*" She gave the command urgently. She didn't think she could bear it if he stopped. She spoke with desperation. "It's just grease. Grease is good. *Get me dirty.*"

"Oh, man." He paused only for a moment, looking at her with some surprise. His eyes closed once, and she saw a purely delighted smile. "You got it." As if he were detailing a car, he smeared the cool liquid over her breasts, plucking at her nipples. He shook his head, his eyes flaming with lust as he looked down at his work. Then he sensuously rubbed his own chest against hers, making her cry out at the combined sensations. He thrust deeply inside her. Their bodies warmed the grease as they slid together.

Faster and faster, she bucked up against him as he drove into her. Friction and heat and pistoning power made her gasp and shudder in nearly unbearable pleasure. Her body felt ready to burst into a million pieces. Her mind was so full of the wonder of him that she found herself making the effortless comparison to the sensation of racing—faster and faster, the world flowing meaninglessly around her. The only thing that mattered was *more,* and *more,* only this time there was someone else with her, in her body, sharing the unendurable-for-another-second g-force and bursting, with her, over the finish line.

She heard him shout, and was uncertain, for a moment, where she was.

Then he breathed into her mouth with a shuddery sigh. "That . . . was not bad."

She squeaked. "Not *bad?*" She wriggled, indignant. "Get off!"

"Exactly." He didn't move. She was glad. Her movements against him had fired her up once more.

Grinning at her, he kissed the tip of her nose with a gentleness that stilled her small struggles. "You're adorable when you're angry."

"You're okay too," she conceded grudgingly. "I suppose you'll

255

do." She thrust against him, deliberately.

"It's good to finally be appreciated." His smile was as warm as she'd ever seen it. "Even if it is just for my bodywork."

"Your stick shift is adequate."

"Your O-ring puts the wood in my shifter." Gordon's laughter broke off into a hiss of pleasure when she ground against him especially effectively. "Did I really just say that?"

"You did. Pervert."

"She-pervert. At least I didn't say 'lug nuts.' Or 'piston ring.' "

"Pit stop."

"Petcock."

When Sarah laughed, strands of her hair flopped onto her cheek. "What dirty-minded dude named a valve a 'petcock,' is what I'd like to know."

Gordon tucked the strands back behind her ear. He kissed the ear, then her mouth.

His warm breath and the lingering sensation of his fingertips made her shiver. "What were you saying about that shifter of yours?" The breathiness had returned to her voice.

"I'd rather show you."

"Then show me," she commanded, grinning. "Show me everything, big guy."

Gordon was stroking her, a soothing caress that skillfully bypassed her more sensitive erogenous zones. Despite that, she felt a tactile buzz enveloping her. Her body relaxed under his touch, even as it readied itself effortlessly for more invasive handling.

She shifted on the seat, smiling with pleasure, until she lay on her side facing him.

His eyes were lazy, mellow, with no trace of the flashing anger she remembered so vividly. She felt startled, then warmed by the naked affection in his gaze.

Being with him, next to him, fulfilled her. A lot. Her heart thumped hard, and she looked away to hide the moisture that she could feel in her own eyes. The reaction made her feel shy and vulnerable. What was wrong with her?

She tried thinking of staging strategies, customer invoicing, anything to regain her usual equanimity.

It began to work. She breathed slowly, concentrating.

"I could stay here for hours," he murmured, nuzzling her hair.

Her heart seemed to glow, her equanimity shattered. Realization hit hard. As much as she might want to sport a casual, take-it-as-it-came attitude about sex with Gordon, she knew she couldn't. She'd fallen for him.

"I could stay here all *night*," she finally replied, meaning it. Tonight and beyond. She could definitely handle sleeping with Gordon for foreseeable future nights. She tucked a leg between his, fitting herself even closer. She kissed his chest and heard him sigh with contentment.

She wondered how many hours they had left until morning. Couldn't be too many. She closed her eyes and snuggled with him. Then opened her eyes again. The guys would pile in to the back, gulping down coffee and checking the work orders. Then they'd see the two of them, curled up among the furniture pads and the packing material like a pair of crash test dummies.

As if reading her mind, he chuckled. "The techs would get an eyeful in the morning." His arms tightened around her and he squeezed her hard for a moment, clearly enjoying the feel of her body against his. "This feels too good. All night isn't enough. I'm actually tempted to give them the day off."

Give her people the day off? She bristled out of habit, until she remembered that things were different, now. She and Gordon were a team now, for one thing: the two of them against the world. He wasn't trying to sideline her authority. Relaxing, she traced a pattern—an outline of his DNP logo—on his chest. "Aren't you feeling generous," she teased.

"Where you're concerned, yes." His gaze sharpened, became intense again. "You've been one bucket of trouble after another to me since day one. Not to mention a huge distraction. Yes, distracting, like that exactly." He groaned. "Stop that," he said with an effort. "I'm trying to . . . got you!" He pinned her wrists above her head once more.

"You certainly do."

Her tone made his eyes stab a now-familiar flame, but he just shook his head and grinned. "Behave, Sarah. I'm trying to tell you I really care about you. You are so *not* what I expected," he said, but the intensity never left his eyes. "I'm not sure what to make of that. But I want you to know that tonight wasn't some one-night stand for me, and we are definitely going out properly tomorrow night. Dinner and a show. What, you don't like shows? Forget the show. Sarah? What's wrong?"

She felt the cool air against the new sweat on her skin and shivered. A sweetly aching sensation engulfed her, and she was afraid to meet his eyes. She suddenly couldn't move. The lump in her throat was the size of a hemi. She swallowed. The feeling rivaled what she felt for Craig, but it was different in scope. It was overwhelming. It had to be too good to be true. So she would be damned if she'd mess it up by getting all blubbery and emotional. "It's okay. I'm fine. Can I have my hands back?" Covering her mouth, she cleared her throat manfully.

Gordon just looked at her.

"Really, just a frog in my throat. Um. Shows are nice. I went to a Mustang Club of America car show in Long Beach just last month."

"Tell me what you're thinking," he commanded.

She tried to wiggle out from beside him, but he just rolled over on her. "No escape. Spill."

She glared up at him until he rolled back over, keeping a firm hand on the middle of her torso. "Everything's changed," she told him, frowning a little because he was. "It's . . . I couldn't have imagined this and it's . . ." *Frightening,* she wanted to say. It was scary to feel so vulnerable, but of course she couldn't tell him that. Or could she? "It's disconcerting," she said instead.

"Disconcerting. In a bad way?" She felt his hand on her stiffen like his tone.

"No." She took a deep breath. "Disconcerting in a scary way." She looked directly at him, alert for any sign of contempt that might cross his features.

To her relief, understanding and a heart-stopping smile did instead. "Oh, Sarah. I keep forgetting how young and sheltered you are."

"Sheltered?" She snorted. "Back here? Have you *heard* the guys swearing?" Remembering the guys as they used to be around her, she grinned, on familiar ground with that at least. They would come around. She'd make them come around.

"Like truck drivers. And yet, though your own collar is decidedly blue, you've been sheltered. Protected. Some might say over-protected. At any rate, it's perfectly normal to have some feelings of uncertainty, or even apprehension about a new experience. Sarah . . . did you hear me mention that I care about you? A lot?"

Happiness poured through her, and this time it was unimpeded by fear. "I care about you too. This is . . ." She laughed in sheer delight. The past weeks felt like a bad dream from which she'd just awakened in Gordon's arms. "This really is a new beginning. The guys are going to flip when they find out about us. I think I'll break it to them this morning, at the same time as I tell them I'll be working in the back again." The guys were *hers.* Enough was enough. She'd never backed away from a fight in her life and she wasn't going to start now. She pictured her announcement, imagining their shock with satisfaction. "Things are going to be a little different around here."

"Yes, they are. And—"

"Can you just see Will's face when he spots us kissing instead of fighting?"

"That'll be something. About working in the back—"

"I'm actually looking forward to doing real work again. The receptionist gig wasn't my thing. Though I look pretty good in a skirt, if I do say so myself." She smiled at him, but felt it slide from her face when he didn't even crack a grin. "But not that good," she amended. His lips were still turned down in a frown. She felt a warm flush of embarrassment. "Okay, skirts aren't my fashion strength. My ankles are too skinny, aren't they?"

"Your ankles are perfect. You're perfect. You'd be perfect at anything you tried, whether you worked in the front, or in the back . . . or somewhere else entirely. Have you considered college?"

Sarah stared at him, surprised by his earnest tone that made him sound exactly like her father—which was weird considering their current position. She shifted, feeling his skin against hers. "College. Well, yes, I've thought about it. But now—"

"Good. You've always struck me as highly intelligent and determined. I know you'll do great things. Which college?"

"Gordon. What's this about?" Where he moved his hand from her skin, she felt an icy blast of air on sweat. She tried to read his expression, but he avoided her eyes.

The small-hours quiet of the dark garage suddenly felt ominous.

"Sarah, have you considered that there's not much of a future for you as a mechanic?"

"Technician," she corrected automatically. She felt cold. This was the business-Gordon, not lover-Gordon. What had prompted the switch? "Is this about me working in the back?"

"Yes. Well, no, not exactly." His reluctance communicated itself to her via his entire body. Then he exhaled, the heavy sound of someone with bad news. "This is hard for me to say, and the timing isn't the greatest. But I'd better just come out with it. Sarah, your father has agreed to sell me the company."

Sarah heard the precise enunciation of his words, and knew that he'd told her the truth, but the reality of it denied itself. She half-smiled, one part of her mind appreciating the joke. It was a doozy of a joke. Gordon, buying her dad's shop—*her* shop. Ridiculous. And yet . . .

Gordon lay stiffly by her side, watching her with the cautious intensity of someone observing a freshly rebuilt engine being tested on the dyno for the first time.

The truth hit her like a numbing chill.

"My dad is selling my company to you. You—and my dad? And neither of you saw fit to tell me a thing."

# CHAPTER EIGHTEEN

*Betrayal.*

Her system tried to process it, but the depth of the deceit stopped her blood in her veins and immobilized every muscle in her body. Her brain circled the glaring evidence, obvious now. They'd planned this since before the races. Dad had known. He'd encouraged her toward college, she remembered numbly. Gordon had known, and he hadn't told her. He hadn't let slip the merest rumor. Not even back when they'd spoken so intimately on the phone, and now this—!

She leapt to her feet with a cry, snatching up her underwear and dressing faster than she ever had in her life.

"Sarah, it's okay. You don't understand. You're going back to college, and you'll be getting a good, a *better* job. Your technician phase here . . . it wasn't supposed to last forever. Was it? And you bought that Camry . . ." Gordon picked up her skirt and held it as if it were evidence. She grabbed it. He extended his hand toward where she stood pulling it on. She not only jerked her leg away, but sidestepped him until she was well out of reach. Gordon continued, with just a tinge of exasperation, "You never once expressed interest in the business side of things. You'll go back to college and get a good degree, you'll be happier—with an upwardly mobile job—and everything will be okay."

When his words met with her deliberate silence, she heard him move. From the corner of her eye she saw him gathering his own clothes and putting them on. She was faster than him though, and walked out as he still pulled on his pants.

"Sarah. Sarah, please!"

She realized that he would simply follow her, and in her Camry she would have quite a challenge to outrun him. So she stalked back to where he was still scooping up his shoes and shirt, and poked him in the arm. "You will leave me alone. I don't ever want to talk to you again." She met his eyes with determination, and saw his nostrils flare and his mouth open to speak.

She turned and walked away.

"Is it true?"

Sarah didn't smile at her dad, whom she hadn't seen all week. The speed shop, once her solace and haven, had felt like hostile foreign territory the whole time. Days went by, as her ankle mended completely but her heart didn't, and she had nothing on which to concentrate her thoughts except her simmering anger at her father and her fury at Gordon. Gordon tried to explain, tried to convince her to listen to him, but she found the dark side of her newfound femininity useful. Freezing him with a stare and walking away without a word was perversely satisfying. She felt frozen inside, too, though. The techs were like strangers, and still treated her differently—respectfully and professionally. They didn't even swear around her anymore. She wondered if they ever would again. She desperately missed being in the trenches.

But she determined to stick out her unrewarding receptionist job until she left it. Which would be soon.

This time she didn't come as a petitioner to her father. She stood behind his guest chair, gripping it with her hands to steady herself. She ignored Gordon, even when he immediately rose from behind his own desk and approached them.

Her dad's irritated glance at Gordon spoke volumes.

"So it is true," she breathed, tightening her grip.

"Red, it came out in conversation. I'm very sorry." Gordon moved to stand beside the desk, halfway between her and her dad.

*Conversation!* Her grip tightened further on the chair back, her painted nails splitting the covering.

Sarah kept her eyes straight ahead, looking across at her dad. She had to hear the truth from his mouth. "Are you really selling the company to him?"

"I want to retire, sweetheart," her dad began.

She exploded. "It's our company!" It was unthinkable that he should sell. He was supposed to let her have the shop if he ever retired. It was a family business. He hadn't said those exact words, maybe, but it was understood.

Well, she'd assumed it was understood. Clearly she'd been way off about that. There was an equal offense, though, in his creeping around doing deals with Gordon behind her back. His selling the company was bad enough, but to not even *tell* her? "Why didn't you say something about your plans to me?"

Red had the good grace to look down. He sighed heavily, and the breath from his broad chest blew papers around his desktop. "It always seemed like a bad time. You were so busy racing, and then traveling across the country to race, and then after the accident the techs made it pretty clear . . . and you and Craig . . . you're going to go off to school again," he said, as if any of that explained his actions. His direct gaze pleaded with her for understanding. She could see his honest confusion, and his sorrow for hurting her. She also saw all the new lines on his face. His reddish-gray hair had turned more gray than red. And his green eyes were the same sharp shade as hers, but very, very tired.

*He really does want to retire,* she realized with surprise. That

thought was almost as odd as his selling the company. He'd held it together with hard work and his bellowing voice of authority for so many years that she honestly couldn't conceive of the company without him. He *was* the company.

And now *he* was the company, she thought, turning her head to look at Gordon, who watched her father with concern.

Seeing him smooth a lock of his wavy brown hair from his forehead, she also noticed the minute signs of his own stress that she hadn't seen before. His shoulders weren't just stiff, they were rigid with tension, and his stance was that of a cornered wolf that hadn't yet determined which direction to run. Or whether to attack. She cross-referenced that image with the memory of his strong body next to hers on the upholstery and shop mats, and his easy, sensual way with her, and knew the sum of his disquiet.

So he cared about her dad. Gordon wasn't taking advantage of him, or pushing something that wasn't in his good interest. She beat back the empathy for Gordon that she felt despite herself.

How nice that he cared about *somebody.*

But . . . maybe his disquiet was due to worry about the deal falling through?

"What if I said *I* want the company?" she said boldly, addressing her dad. "That I want to run it, and you should have consulted me first because I'll never let it go without a fight?"

Her dad's troubled look intensified, but he met her eyes squarely. "I'm sorry, but it's too late." Frowning, he opened his mouth, then shut it. Then opened it again to speak. "You're going back to school. Higher education is your best option. You *said* you were, and I'm taking you at your word. I'll still happily pay for that. Anywhere you want to go."

"Out of the proceeds from selling the shop," she bit out.

"Out of my retirement account," he corrected softly. "Which

is what that represents."

Sarah couldn't think. Everything she'd known as truth just a month ago—that the shop would one day be hers, that she'd chase Craig indefinitely, and that she was finished with college as a dull exercise compared to racing—had been turned on its head. Where did that leave her? What would happen with *her?*

She glanced up at Gordon. He watched her now, rather than her dad.

His dark eyes measured her, flickering with concern. She met his gaze accusingly.

But this time instead of looking away, or appearing rightfully subdued by her icy glance, Gordon stared back. "You didn't listen to me before, but I *truly am sorry* for the way this came about. But it's time to move on."

*Time to move on.* Sarah felt her lips stretch in a humorless half-smile. That had to be the most businesslike blow-off she'd ever heard of. She nodded, backing away from them both. Move she would. Far away. As her dad had put it, higher education was her best option. "School it is." She laughed, wishing the sound wasn't so bitter. "Craig's been talking about transferring to a position in Indiana. I think he wants to be near the racing action, and his family. Maybe I'll go to Indiana State University." Anywhere to distance herself from the pile of broken parts her life had become.

Her dad scowled. "Move? You never said anything about moving out of the state. It's up to you, of course, but . . . well, it's up to you, honey."

Gordon frowned. "You're welcome to stay here, Sarah. Work here for as long as you need to."

*Sure, so long as my dress code is receptionist-appropriate. And I stay far from the techs in the garage, and out of your way.* Sarah made a cynical sound.

Craig would be at the track practicing by now, as he always

did on Friday. If she left immediately, she could catch him and let him know her decision. He'd be delighted. He'd probably whip out that little velvet gray box again.

And suddenly, living happily ever after with Craig sounded like a much-needed refuge, and not at all boring or typical, as she'd always thought marriage was destined to be. Craig's about-face, his finally coming around to caring for her, still seemed sudden, even a little surreal, but marrying him would be comforting. Craig was a known quantity. She'd wanted him forever. It was time to seal the deal. So what if he didn't inflame her senses quite the way Gordon did. At least he was her friend. She could trust him, unlike *some* people.

"Well, you did just get back in the office," she said, nodding to Dad. "I'm sure you two have lots to talk about. I'm off to see Craig."

She turned her back on them and strode to the door.

"Sarah . . ."

"Let her go. She's impossible when she's like this. Stubborn!" Red called after her.

She had just keyed open her Camry when she heard the front door burst open. "Sarah, wait!"

So Gordon hadn't taken her dad's advice? Interesting. But hardly worth sticking around for. *Betrayer.* She closed her door before he reached her, palming the auto-lock, and started up the car.

As she was exiting her space, she saw him furiously digging for his own keys. He was *following* her?

She narrowed her eyes, backing out so quickly that her head thumped against the headrest when she applied the brakes. She spared the thought that it was a good thing nobody else was in the parking lot, then floored it.

She sped from the lot, scraping the bottom of her car as she turned onto the four-lane road. No traffic impeded her escape, but she saw Gordon backing out with a squeal of tires. He swerved to avoid hitting a slower-moving sedan.

Though her foot pressed the accelerator pedal almost to the floor, the Camry felt impossibly sluggish to her Mustang-accustomed senses. She spent precious seconds kicking off her heels, then pressed the pedal the rest of the way to the floor.

The little car strained forward.

She saw Gordon in her rearview mirror, closing the distance.

Why was he following her?

Guilt, responsibility, repentance? To enlighten her about the impersonal workings of business?

Or something more intimate?

It was not enough, and it was too late. She swore, feeling impotent in the private confines of her slow-moving car. A desperate desire to be away from him and the conflicting feelings he evoked in her made her pound the steering wheel, trying to make her Camry faster.

How could she outrun him? Even now he rode her bumper. She could see him gesturing violently with his right arm: pull over.

She crooked her own right arm, and raised it finger-first.

He honked.

She felt her teeth bare in a humorless smile, the car's air-conditioning doing nothing to cool the angry heat that made her feel as if she'd combust. How dare he follow her, as if she needed or wanted his lecturing. Or anything else. He'd done enough damage.

She slowed down until he pulled around and up next to her, then suddenly turned right onto a side street. As fast as she could, she drove down the smaller road, looking for another street to turn onto, or at least a big truck to hide behind.

There was nothing.

Seconds later, Gordon's Mustang again caught up to her. He

honked two times, one right after the other. The sound was insistent.

What did he think he was going to do, follow her all day? In that case, she could probably outdo him. Her car did have better gas mileage. She laughed out loud, the sound echoing with only a small tinge of hysteria.

She didn't want to drive around all day. Her plan was to go to the race track—to Craig—and she wasn't about to do that with Gordon tailing her like some demented micromanager.

Her car skidded back onto the four-lane road, Gordon following so close that she could see the way his lips pressed thinly together. This road, she knew, continued away from the freeway that she needed. Her house also lay in the opposite direction.

That gave her the idea. He wouldn't be expecting the maneuver at all.

Using just her eyes, she scanned for cops. They would certainly frown on what she was about to do.

No cops. And no oncoming traffic.

Grinning, she tightened her right hand around the emergency brake. Her left gripped the top of the steering wheel.

*Now.*

She gave the steering wheel a jerk to the left. The moment her car swerved, she yanked up on the emergency brake.

Her car pivoted 180 degrees with gratifying abruptness. She lowered the handbrake, gave the car gas, and eased onto the pedal until the car stopped shimmying and rocking from the assault on its soft shocks. She accelerated in the opposite direction, and the moment the car felt smooth she immediately turned onto a side road, then turned again. She pulled to the curb directly in front of a large yellow Ryder truck, and crossed her fingers.

Minutes later, she uncrossed them. She'd lost him.

"Yeah, I still got it," she said with some satisfaction. The swaggering tone she heard was as pleasurable as the voice of an old friend. The relief of hearing it took her by surprise. That bold, fearless voice had been missing for weeks.

She drove down side streets, thoughtful.

If only she could have seen Gordon's face when he finally got turned around only to find that she'd vanished. She wondered if he'd be proud of her little maneuver, or if he was just pissed off. He probably was driving straight to her apartment right now, hoping to catch her there and do unspeakable things to her. She felt tendrils of desire unfurl throughout her body and she blushed, then scowled. He probably just wanted to fling more lame excuses along with a helping of holier-than-thou.

Well, she didn't have to listen to it.

She didn't.

Though he'd been right before. About her being selfish, for example. Her hands tightened on the steering wheel and her breath sped up as she remembered when they'd had *that* conversation. It wasn't fair. How utterly obscene that she still had the slightest physical desire for the man who'd betrayed her.

Desire chemically was one thing, though, and desire intellectually another. Her mind didn't want him. Her mind had more important things to occupy it. She was a strong woman, she was still a kick-ass driver, and she was certainly smart enough to know when she'd screwed up. Sleeping with Gordon was just as bad a mistake as crashing her car.

Accelerating cleared her mind, as always. Her goal clarified as she picked up speed and the landscape blurred in her peripheral vision. At least being a good racer wasn't subject to change, as so many other things were. She'd screwed up a lot, but her essential identity was still intact. Thank God.

So she'd been selfish. Stupid. Misguided. But she wasn't going to pay for it forever, sacrificing everything she was. She didn't deserve to stay stuck performing penance under the watchful eyes of those who made her heart ache. How ridiculous that any of them would think for one second she'd still work at the shop under those terms. She could choose otherwise.

A boring receptionist, she wasn't.

Smoothing strands of hair from her moist forehead, she glimpsed her perfectly manicured nails and took a small amount of pleasure in the elegant, neat look they gave her long fingers.

How odd that she'd become kick-ass at being girlie, too. Gordon would have appreciated it.

Too bad he had to go and stab her in the back.

*His loss.* She drove up the on-ramp and accelerated into the fast-moving freeway traffic, then eased over into the left lane to pass those who kept themselves to the speed limit. There was still a sorrowing loss riding along inside her, one she didn't want to examine too closely. She supposed it would dissipate in time.

She drove to Carlsdale to find Craig.

She'd out-driven him, Gordon realized with amazement as he looked for beige Camrys.

For once in his life there weren't any to be seen.

She'd actually pulled a trick out of the bag and made her car disappear.

*Impressive.*

He laughed. For her to outrun his Cobra with a Camry, that was unbelievable. That was talent, pure and simple. It was just like her.

Too bad it also indicated her desperation to get away from him.

He scowled, turning his car around. He would try her apartment, then he would try . . .

No, he wouldn't. He'd be sensible and return to the shop, or better yet, home. There he could discipline his mind away from her more easily. There weren't any compelling, lingering memories of her with him at home. He'd kept his sanctuary free of her, at least, trying to keep it as ascetic as any monk's domain in his pursuit of his business goals. If only his mind were as easily ordered.

It was probably good that she'd lost him.

She brought out every part of him that he'd suppressed in favor of ambition. She inspired a poisonous spontaneity, a distracting mental fixation, a potentially fatal-to-success bottom-line neglect.

What was it about her that stirred up a side of him that was so completely out of control? Just thinking of her, driving as fast as she could to *Craig,* made him want to strangle her.

Which, of course, wasn't the least acceptable. He needed to be poised for success, able to make tough business decisions, not mixing with the help. He needed to regain control of himself.

Deliberately, he imagined Sarah at her worst: bruised and greasy and dazed in the hospital bed after her accident. As far from his idea of a trophy wife as it was possible to get.

A feeling of tenderness moved him.

He swore, disgusted with his traitorous brain.

He floored the accelerator getting to her apartment . . . only to see that she'd chosen another refuge from him. Anything to escape his attentions.

He had to find her, corner her. He would force her to hear how the company transfer had come about. It had to be made clear to her that it was good for her dad, at least. It was just a business transaction, not something that should catapult her at Craig, who was all wrong for her anyway. He had to make her understand he hadn't meant any harm. It was *just business.*

What had happened between them was personal.

Was meaningful. Important. Necessary.

He knew for a fact it was far better than anything she could get with Craig.

But what if he couldn't find her? What if she wouldn't listen? What if she was even now speeding to wherever Craig was, falling over herself to put his ring on her finger? Craig's marriage proposal suddenly loomed large, as ominous as a smoking engine, disastrous as a failed business deal.

Dread filled him. Sarah wasn't at her apartment because she was driving to the Carlsdale drag strip. That was where Craig would be, of course. And where else would she flee but to his comforting arms?

He couldn't let her do it. She couldn't answer Craig's proposal before hearing him out.

His acceleration onto the freeway south left long black tread marks.

Sarah drove over the potholes of Carlsdale's pit area at speed, uncaring of the damage she might be doing to the Camry. Car parts could be replaced. People like Craig—her handsome, attentive, loyal husband-to-be—they were irreplaceable. Why hadn't she seen it before? Relieved that it was all becoming so clear, she scanned for his Mustang.

Movement caught her eye at the same moment she realized that the gently bouncing blue Mustang was the one she sought. Had Craig installed hydraulics? Bobbing suspensions like those favored by some Mexican car clubs wasn't Craig's usual style. She looked closer, spotting his decals. It was definitely Craig's car.

As she drove closer she realized that the bouncing was more organic in nature. Tinting on the window hid the activity within, but it was cracked open a few inches. Blond hair fluffed and bounced in the three-inch opening. Puffy, wavy, long *bleached-blond* hair.

Craig had a trackslut. Or more accurately, was having a track-slut.

Sarah stared for a moment, trying to figure out how she felt about it. Disappointed? Enraged?

Why wasn't she withered into a twisted rind of jealousy, looking at that bouncing evidence of Craig's infidelity? Maybe she was so frozen with disappointment over the shop situation that her emotional gauges had gotten stuck.

She realized that she'd parked and shut off her engine when the shadow of a tan minivan fell over her Camry from the next space over. The van's owner stepped out, hurrying around the slanted hood and directly toward her. The clean-cut blond man wore clothes appropriate to such a vehicle: preppy slacks, brown moccasin-loafers and a buttoned-up peach oxford shirt with a little logo on the chest. People didn't dress like that at Carlsdale. She stared, still uncomprehending, as Craig opened her driver-side door for her to step out.

She didn't move. She was too shocked. "Craig?" She giggled, then stopped at the look on his face. "What are you doing in that van? Why are you dressed in those clothes?"

Craig cast a look at his Mustang. Irritation and frustration crossed his features in quick succession. Then his gaze returned to Sarah, encompassing her long skirt, her kicked-off heels, her made-up face. He bent to her and held out his hand to step her out of her car. "Come with me? There's something I want to talk to you about."

She joined him, and climbed up into the minivan, marveling at its spaciousness. And its utter lack of personality. Everything was tan and spotless and refined. It had idiot lights instead of gauges. It was completely safe.

It was as bad as her Camry.

As they turned out of the parking lot, she heard the blower-boosted scream of Gordon's Cobra as he skidded in, accelerating. Gordon didn't even spare a glance at the minivan. He headed directly toward Craig's bouncing Mustang.

Sarah smiled as she realized what Gordon's first thought would be.

Craig's own engine as he steered around the other cars and exited the parking lot was so quiet she couldn't hear it. She burst out laughing as he drove.

"Share the joke?" he asked.

"I was just thinking that I can't hear the engine in my Camry either."

He drove in silence broken only by the soft classical music piping from the speakers. He could have been any young family man on his way to drink iced tea at the church potluck. A sense of the surreal gripped Sarah and she fought back another giggle. "This is really weird, Craig."

"Tell me about it. I'm hoping the end justifies the means. Hold off on the questions, I want to explain it all at once, okay?"

She nodded, feeling as if she'd slipped into some alternate dimension. Was this Craig?

After they were seated in a booth at the Olive Garden, Craig began. "You know what I'm going to ask you. I've given it a lot of thought. This getup," he said, indicating his attire and poked his thumb back over his shoulder at the minivan, "is to show you I'm capable of altering my lifestyle to a more traditional one, just as you have. I swapped cars with a buddy for the day," he explained, his eyes glowing with determination. "It's not permanent, of course. But it's to show you that I understand the new phase of your life. I support it. I want to share it. You can see that I'm serious."

He was almost too serious. They always had fun when they were together. This solemn, sober Craig was a stranger. But that could be a good thing. He was finally taking her seriously. Plus, if he wasn't afraid of being seen dressed that way, and driving a minivan, then there could be little doubt he'd truly outgrown the tracksluts.

He took her hand. "Sarah, I want to build on our friendship. Meeting with my brother and his wife last month made me realize that the best relationships are based on friendship. They're happy together. Them and the kids. And since I know I'll never meet anyone quite like you again . . . Sarah, will you marry me?"

"But how do you know I'm the one?" A part of her was amazed at her own question. The old Sarah, the one who'd carried a torch for Craig for ages and ages was screaming in her head to shut up and jump at the chance he offered. Especially now.

But something wouldn't let her.

Her world was suddenly turning on its head, and all she could feel was a rushing inevitability. "Look at us. All responsible-citizen, with our economical cars and dressy clothes. I don't even recognize us."

Craig stared at her, his eyes solemn. "I know you, Sarah. Your way of aiming for what you want and not stopping till you claim it or hurt yourself trying. Your being one of the guys, and a beauty in dresses too. And you know everything about me." He grinned, a touch of his old wickedness flickering in his blue eyes. "Well, *almost* everything. I bet you have no clue just how good I am in the sack."

She wished he hadn't said that. So much for walling away her most heated memories of Gordon.

She squeezed Craig's warm hands. "I don't know. This is such a huge deal."

"Don't put me off again." His nostrils flared with exasperation. "This is the last time I'm asking. You know I'm moving to Indiana. Come with me. I've saved quite a bit of money. We'll buy a house, and you can go to college out there."

Sarah was startled to hear him voice the same idea she'd told her father and Gordon. College in Indiana. Married to Craig. Everyone was in agreement.

Suburban life didn't sound quite as horrible as it used to.

She tried to feel it out. "It would be different, wouldn't it? Are we ready for all the things that go along with settling down? Minivans and button-up shirts. Marriage. PTA conferences. Walking the dog down a quiet tree-lined street in a neighborhood where people call the cops on loud racecars."

"We'll find a less uptight neighborhood than that," Craig promised. "And I'll personally walk little Robbie Racer. But first you have to say 'yes.' "

*Robbie* Racer?

When Craig had given her the plush dachshund at the hospital, he'd seemed so sorry that he'd forgotten her dog's name. He'd even pinned a button of his car on the dog's face with that tagline about Ricky Racer riding with him at Columbus.

Which, now that she thought about it, was kind of mean. She'd crashed hard at Columbus. But he'd immortalized his own successful pass by safety-pinning it to the spitting image of her dog's face. Ricky's poor little face.

He'd bayoneted Ricky Racer's forehead, and then gone and forgotten his name *again*.

Craig never did like her dog.

She thought for another moment, then spoke gently. "You know what, hon? I'm not too crazy about living in the Midwest. Too humid. And . . . I'm not sure the marriage thing really grabs me either. I'm not ready for that." *With you.*

Her answer made him blink. "You're not. Okay. Then I guess we have nothing else to talk about." He signaled the waitress for their check.

She flicked his hand. "Jerk. You're not ready either. You look ridiculous behind the wheel of a minivan."

"Me?" He rounded on her. "Look who's talking. You paid good money for the lamest four-cylinder on the road."

"Not for long. I'm trading it in for a base-model Mustang." She decided it as she said it, and the decision felt right.

Craig stared at her with disapproval.

"You don't think that's a good idea?"

"I thought you were finished with racing. The crash, remember? You were done with it. You were going back to school."

"Everyone *wanted* me to be done with it. What, are you afraid of the competition?"

Craig didn't reply, but his disapproving look deepened.

*So competitive.* Craig's words of so long ago about how they were alike came back to her. He was right. They'd tear one another down, battling each other in all the wrong ways.

As opposed to all the right ways.

Sarah smiled inside, but didn't let the smile touch her lips. It would be rude to smile with her next words. "Incidentally, I am going back to school. Frank Hawley's Drag Racing School."

He stared at her as if he would mould her into his ideal by will alone. Finally, he shook his head, exhaling so heavily he blew his napkin across the table. She blew it back. He smiled, a small wry grin. "Falling back into your old wicked ways, huh? Would you mind telling me, though, why you're not coming with me? We were . . . I could have sworn you were open to the idea. Is it something I said?"

Sarah gave him her most enigmatic smile. "Sort of. But it's all good."

He wasn't too hurt, she saw with relief. Her spirits rose. "And Craig? You'd better not plan on coasting along on your laurels, 'cause I'll be gunning for you next season."

"Bring it on, wannabe." His old smile warmed her. "But I've

had plenty enough of a whupping for now, if you don't mind."
She cringed with guilt, but the feeling receded when she saw his
half-smile, the one that used to make her heart skip. He was
already standing. "Now, I've got to pry those two lovebirds out
of my racecar. Before they do any permanent damage." Craig
tossed her a look of impatience, the old fire back in his eyes.
"So c'mon, already. So slow you can't get out of your own way."

The minivan accelerated back to the track with Craig behind
the wheel. Sarah marveled at how silly he looked. "I'll make you
a deal," she offered as he quickly broke the speed limit.

"What's that?"

"Next year at the races I won't tell a soul you drove a tan
minivan, if you keep quiet about my Camry."

# CHAPTER NINETEEN

Sarah showed up at work very late in the morning on Monday. All weekend she'd spent in deep thought and planning. Her tardiness, while strategic, made her even more nervous. She hoped Gordon wouldn't be too mad about her little game of car chase on Friday. Or about what he thought he'd seen in Craig's Mustang.

She hoped he didn't outright fire her. If he was buying the company she supposed it was a danger.

Her plan called for bypassing any objections her father might make, marching right up to Gordon and insisting on taking him out to lunch like two civilized business people. They needed to resolve their differences. She'd drive; she'd buy. All he had to do was come along for the ride, she'd say.

At which point she would recline the passenger seats of her new Mustang all the way back and she would jump his bones. And if that didn't sufficiently show him her intentions, she'd pull out the big guns. She'd give him flowers.

Preparation for her plan had gotten her up early. She'd worked off her nerves at the gym. Then she'd showered and spent plenty of time on her hair, makeup, and dressing. She was getting good at it, though, if she did say so herself. She wore a figure-flattering dress and strappy high heels. With her well-brushed silky hair paired with the subtly applied makeup, she knew it wasn't possible for her to look any better. It was battle-of-the-sexes grooming.

Gordon was going *down.*

She laughed softly. She'd have to find a different expression for Gordon. Or not.

Sarah stepped into the shop and immediately wondered at its quiet in the middle of the day. The air compressor was off. The radio was silent. No voices, either. Lunch break? No, too quiet for that. Someone always stayed. Gordon must've done the incredible, and sent everyone home. Even her dad.

But why?

She tried to swallow, her heart revving as if it were injected with nitrous. The gym workout hadn't sufficiently soothed her nerves. She put down a fleeting urge to retreat.

Brisk hammering broke the silence, and she knew someone still worked in the garage regardless. Was that someone Gordon? Hope filled her everywhere anxiety didn't. She reminded herself that he probably despised her at the moment, and he might just try to send *her* home too.

Well, she wouldn't let him.

But what if he just ignored her? Of course, she wouldn't let him do that either. She couldn't *blame* him for such sentiments, exactly—she'd ignored his efforts to explain and snubbed his attempts at apology, after all—but there was no way she was going to let him shut her out now that she'd finally figured out exactly what she wanted.

She tiptoed past the front counter and through the door leading to the garage.

He was there.

The whole handsome height of him stretched up, then lifted down a plastic storage container. He rooted in the box, came up with a metal clamp, which he proceeded to tighten on the engine sitting on the engine stand.

All by himself with his beautiful jeans-encased backside to her.

The mystery of the empty shop intrigued her, but she had more pressing business at hand. She slid silently past where he stood absorbed in the engine rebuild.

She would have to adjust her plan.

There was another project, a transmission swap that would serve her purpose. The old Camaro was already up on jack-stands, she saw, and the creeper lay next to the car. *Perfect.* She'd just roll on underneath and investigate. Whistling loudly, she grabbed a flashlight and a wrench and reclined back on the padded creeper. With the ease of long experience, she maneuvered herself under the car, still whistling as if she hadn't a care in the world. She felt a cool air-conditioned breeze on her bare legs. *Oh no,* she thought with a secret smile. *Has my dress hiked up? Naughty, naughty.*

She heard footsteps. She craned around to meet his gaze where he bent to peer under the Camaro.

"What are you doing?"

She grinned at him innocently. "What does it look like?"

"Messing up your dress." But his voice was suddenly thick with desire. She saw his scowl as his gaze took in her legs. Then she heard it, his telltale nervous socket-twist. She rejoiced at the sound. He wasn't impervious to her. It *would* be possible to make him come around.

She pounced on the opportunity. "You're right, maybe I should get out of these clothes."

Silence. *Twist-twist-twist.*

She lay back down on the creeper. With a few unnecessary extra wiggles, she propelled herself further under the car.

*Twist-twist-twist . . . TWIST.*

She laughed silently. Suddenly she felt a stronger gust of air, and rolling movement. She almost banged her head against the headers as he yanked the creeper back out.

He covered her body with his own.

"You're getting me all dirty," she chided him with a grin.

"I like dirty girls." He covered her lips for good measure and she couldn't talk for a long moment.

Then she whispered, remembering: "It's the middle of the shop."

"It's my shop. And you. You're mine too."

"I don't know," she said, trying to sound doubtful. "Our combination is a little volatile. There might be an explosion . . . unless . . ."

"Unless? Unless what? Sarah. I love you. I'm not letting you out of my sight again, whether you like it or not, so just tell me what the hell you want and I'll find a way to make it happen."

He could, he knew. She could even have worn jeans, she realized with dizzy happiness, and he'd still want her—the real her, competitive and stubborn and as crazy for him as he clearly was for her. She could have shown up in her baggiest T-shirt with her hair matted with motor oil and it wouldn't have made a bit of difference. It didn't matter. He loved her, and she loved him.

"What do I want? I just got it." She gloried in their shared moment. "Well," she amended minutes later, when she was able to talk, "there's one other thing you should probably know."

"What's that," he murmured.

*So confident,* she mused, the delightful tingles threatening to overwhelm her senses. He sounded so sure that he could handle any speed bump she threw at him. And he probably could. "I'm going back to school."

"That's great," he said, nipping at her bottom lip.

"*Drag racing* school."

She felt his heavy sigh against her body, and his clever fingers move up and around her throat. But they only pressed hard enough to massage.

She laughed, triumphant.

# ABOUT THE AUTHOR

**Christina Crooks** lives in Portland, Oregon. Her stories have appeared in various magazines and anthologies. Visit Christina Crooks online at www.christinacrooks.net.